NEVER COMES AGAIN

A Novel

VICTORIA MIGUEL-JOSEPH

DND Publishing | Atlanta

A gripping story of a woman's perseverance to survive under perilous and difficult circumstances.

WHEN
NEVER
COMES
AGAIN

A Novel

VICTORIA MIGUEL-JOSEPH

DND Publishing | Atlanta

WHEN NEVER COMES AGAIN
Copyright © 2011 by Victoria Miguel-Joseph

This is a work of fiction. All characters, organizations and events portrayed in this novel are either products of the author's imagination or are used fictitiously.

Manufactured in the United States of America. All rights reserved. No part of this publication may be reproduced or transmitted in any manner whatsoever without the written permission of the Author, except by a reviewer, who may quote brief passages in a review.

For information, address
DND Publishing, P.O. Box 390374 Snellville, Georgia 30039
www.dndpublishing.com

Author's Photo by DeAndrea Freeman of
Dee's Eyes Photography Studio.
Cover and Text Design by CrunchTime Graphics.

ISBN: 978-0-9831105-0-7, a trade paperback book.

For book orders, author appearance inquiries and interviews, contact DND Publishing.

Visit the official website of Victoria Miguel-Joseph at
www.victoriamigueljoseph.com.

Library of Congress Cataloging In Publication Data

Dedication

In Loving Memory of...

MICHAEL R. BENNETT

(1949 – 1982)

and

VANESSA A. CHOICE

(1957 – 1981)

Acknowledgements

First, giving all honor to God. God is number one in my life. I'm here only through His wondrous grace and mercy. He's brought me a mighty long way. Thank you, Father.

Writing has forever been my passion and this book is my rite of passage. I could not have completed this journey, which spans almost three decades, had it not been for all the people that supported me, loved me and believed in me.

Thanks to my parents for raising me with a strong hand, yet allowing me to dream. I miss them terribly and I'll love them always. May they rest in peace.

To my dear sister, my brothers and cousins, thanks for always being there. You are the best.

Many, many thanks to Camelia Cobb and Doris Caldwell, for their extensive editing contributions and invaluable feedback. When I could no longer see the forest for the trees, you helped me through.

Acknowledgements

All my love and gratitude to my wonderful husband and loving children... You continue to support me one hundred percent in every endeavor. You are the reason I work so hard and strive so high. Remember the family motto - dream big, persevere and always believe.

I am grateful to my very first readers. You know exactly who you are. *(Thanks Pollard Family Reunion 2010)*

Last but certainly not least... much love to my girls – my crew. We've been friends forever. We have created a circle of kinship that is endless and cannot be broken. You have always been there for me – through the bad, the ugly and the best of times. You have waited a very long time for this book. Wait no longer. It is done.

When Never Comes Again

Chapter One

That damn fool across the street is watching us again...

In Atlanta the dog days of summer are typically and utterly incorrigible. After a brief sun shower, the heat rises from the paved city streets like vapor shooting from a raging bull's nose. As far as I'm concerned, anyone in the South that can brave the outdoors during the months of July and August deserves a badge of courage or a gold star... at least a blue ribbon... something.

On this Saturday in early August however, a light gentle breeze is blowing. On the rear deck, the wind chimes create soothing melodies as our nation's red, white and blue proudly waves.

On the morning news, Glenn Burns, meteorologist on WSB Channel 2, predicted great weather for the entire weekend. "Cooler than it's been in weeks," Glenn claimed.

Please, Glenn, get it right today. This hot ass weather is getting on my very last nerve.

What a welcome change a temperature drop would be! Just imagining a break in the weather brings a smile to my face. Given my druthers, it would be fall all year round.

I turn away from the living room window's view to walk across to the dining room which faces the front of the house.

Peeping out the dining room window like a kid in a game of hide and seek — a chill runs down my spine causing me to shiver while the hairs on the back of my neck begin to rise.

I feel him watching. I don't see him, but I can feel him.

Quickly closing the cream colored sheers, I tell myself that whatever I'm feeling is all in my head. I straddle the air conditioning vent which is conveniently located in the floor beneath the window. The cool air blows up my shorts, puffing the short pant legs, making me look even bigger than I am.

Like that's even possible.

Steadily, I walk over to the coffee table to pick up the tall stack of mail delivered today. I plop down on the couch, feeling as if a fifty ton weight is dropping. My smile quickly disappears as I begin to examine the first letter. Electric bill. I hate to open it. I'm positive it's sky high since I've had the air on full blast the entire summer. I place it on the bottom of the stack then continue. Credit card bill, great. I open the next. Doctor bill. Next... Rich's One Day sale brochure... hmmm... nice deals. But sale or no sale, I can't afford to buy a single thing right now. To the back of the pile the brochure goes. Quickly thumbing through the remaining mail... guess what? They're all freaking bills. Good gracious, I'm batting a thousand here.

I toss the correspondence back onto the coffee table then check my watch. Man... I can't believe it's not even noon yet. It seems so much later. But then again, I did get out of bed at the crack of dawn today, something I rarely do.

Grabbing the newspaper, I swiftly scan the headlines. There seems to be nothing but bad news... the war in Lebanon, Reagan's new federalism plan and Oraflex, the arthritis drug, is being pulled from the shelves after preliminary reports link the drug to seventy-two deaths in the United States and Britain. *Whatever happened to clinical trials? Jesus.*

Gingerly, I place my tired and quite swollen feet next to the stack of tumbling mail. Taking a slow deep breath, I rest my aching back against the sofa then close my eyes and let out a small sigh. *Pam, you simply have to learn to relax.* Only half the day has passed and already my body is tired and tensed. Maybe I should take a nap? But for some unknown reason I'm extremely agitated and probably couldn't sleep even if I tried.

Somehow, I manage to quickly hoist myself to my feet. I walk over to the rear window again. I admire the swiftness and agility of a squirrel running up and down a tree limb as if it is an expert trapeze artist.

Since Glenn promises that today's temperature will not top ninety degrees, perhaps I will brave the outdoors. I should enjoy the blessings that God has so generously bestowed upon me and stop tripping and being so damn anxious. I should fire up the barbeque grill, throw on a rack of ribs and make shrimp skewers with mushrooms, onions and green peppers. A tossed salad would be nice, too. I'll top it off with some of that crumbled feta and blue cheese that I've recently come to like so much. Hmmm... yummy. Yep... that sounds so good. All I have to do these days is *think* about a certain kind of food, and man, oh man, I just got to have it. My stomach growls loudly as if to voice its agreement.

When I woke up this morning, I was feeling sort of sick. No, maybe not sick. I felt, I don't know... funny. I felt apprehensive. Yes, that's it... apprehensive. Besides the fact that my stomach is humungous due to being eight months pregnant... my stomach also felt really jittery this morning and it still feels somewhat nervous. I'm sure everything's okay though. But just to be on the safe side, I telephoned my OB/GYN, Dr. Jones earlier. He told me not to worry about a little stomach nervousness and that feeling nervous or anxious was to be expected.

"All first time mothers experience this," he said. "Just as long as there are no contractions, you shouldn't be concerned." Dr. Jones was adamant, however, about calling him if I had severe low back pain or if my water broke.

Even though this whole giving birth thing is foreign to me, I refuse to worry about my nervous stomach. I keep reminding myself that this is, after all, my first pregnancy. I only have three and half weeks to go. I'm sure that I'm just feeling anxious about the actual delivery of my little bundle of joy. Having my cervix expand to the size of a tire rim is no big deal. I can handle it. Abruptly turning away from the window, I wobble to my favorite spot in the house, the nursery.

It's quite amazing really, the ability to love someone you've never met. I love this life inside of me so much already. That's how all expectant parents feel, I'm sure. My husband Ryan and I have no idea if we're having a boy or a girl. Dr. Jones only performs ultrasounds if there are complications. And there are no problems here. I'm a healthy twenty-four-year-old woman. Therefore, Ryan and I are left guessing about the gender of our unborn child. I'm hoping for a healthy, beautiful baby girl, and of course, Ryan wants a boy. I have no idea why men think that they are more of a man if they father a son. Personally, I think it's a bunch of bull... but I'll keep that opinion to myself and leave Ryan with his chauvinistic hope. I figure I mustn't be too presumptuous and paint the nursery pink — even though most often luck is on my side. I absolutely love to gamble. But in this case, I didn't play the fifty-fifty odds... Thus, we have a pale yellow nursery.

When Never Comes Again

Standing in the doorway, I admire the bright, whimsical room. Suddenly, the baby starts to squirm and my back starts to hurt like hell. In just a few awkward steps, I make it to the white, wicker rocker which was a gift from my mother. I lower myself very slowly into the chair. Absent-mindedly, I pick up one of the parenting magazines that lie on top of the small matching end table that's placed next to the rocker. Briefly, I close my eyes and lovingly stroke my stomach, still amazed at how much I love this life inside of me. I open my eyes then thumb through the magazine but my mind wanders to the occurrences of the previous evening.

Last night, clear out of the blue, my brother Jason had proclaimed that I was having a boy. Jason is staying with me right now... which is absolutely perfect since Ryan is away working in Miami. Jason arrived just two weeks ago from Houston. Very unexpectedly, he called to say that he was sick and tired of Houston, and that he needed a change of venue. I didn't question why. I know he will tell me his reasons for leaving when he's ready to talk about it.

Without thinking twice, I had invited Jason to come to Atlanta... to keep me company, I said. Jason immediately accepted my invitation. So, here he is.

I'm really glad to have Jason here with me, especially right now. Jason and I are pretty tight, we always have been. We can talk to each other about any and everything. It never mattered that Jason is eight years older than me.

To make things even better, the youngest of the Barnett clan, Larry, is staying here as well. Larry's attending school in Marietta, enrolled at DeVry Institute. He arrived about a month ago just in time for summer classes. I feel so very blessed to have my brothers here with me. I just couldn't admit to Ryan how much I dreaded being here alone, so close to my due date. Having Jason and Larry here makes me feel safe. I know in my heart that they will look after me... and God knows I'll be forever grateful to Jason for coming here to the Atlanta. It's a win-win situation for both of us.

Turning the page in the magazine, I see an advertisement for a breast pump and wonder how the hell it works... such an odd gadget. I ignore it then continue to think about Jason.

Jason really did shock me last night when he said I was having a boy. And on top of that, he also stated that he wants me to name the baby after him. Even now it makes me chuckle to think about the lively conversation we had.

"Negro, please!" I exclaim. "You don't name babies after their uncles... you name them after their daddies!"

Yet Jason, with a stern serious expression on his handsome brown face, continues to insist.

"Seriously Pam, name him Jason," he states firmly. "Something big is gonna happen in my life real soon. I don't know what it is, but it's going to happen real soon."

After his proclamation, Jason hugs and kisses me. Yeah, we are close, but never the hugging and kissing kind of close. His actions are out of character and without knowing why, his sudden displays of affection upsets me.

"Ja... Ja... Jason." I stutter... being totally caught off guard by his persistence. "I will, Jason. If it's a boy, I will. I promise." Goose bumps appear on my arms as I say it, as well as a twinge of dread in my gut.

"Thanks Pam. It would mean the world to me." Jason replies. He's visibly relieved.

Then for the second time that night, he kisses me... a simple, sweet, brotherly peck on my cheek. The pang in my gut returns. But

When Never Comes Again

I didn't mention my feeling of dread to Jason. I simply watch him turn away and walk slowly to his room.

Closing the magazine and tossing it back onto the table, I continue to think about last night and to wonder why in the world Jason said the things he said and acted the way he did. My eyes roam the nursery as I contemplate the situation.

The bright yellow gingham bedding ensemble included the crib canopy, the bumper pads, crib skirt, diaper stacker, and even the pad cover for the white, wicker changing table. As I take in the room, I realize now that I must have purchased every accessory known to mankind. Cute little white wicker baskets with yellow gingham liners are filled to the brim with all sorts of lotions and oils. Toddler toys and various breeds of teddy bears abound in the room.

I splurged, much to Ryan's chagrin, by commissioning a local artist to paint a beautiful jungle themed mural on the walls of the nursery. There's a different animal on each wall, an elephant, a giraffe, a lion and a huge brown grizzly bear. The elephant's trunk is raised. I specifically asked for that... hoping that it's true — a raised elephant trunk symbolizes and brings good luck. The lion grazes on green grass that looks as if it's moving — perhaps the blades are swaying in the jungle breeze. The giraffe, tall and regal, munches on a large weeping willow tree. The grizzly bear reaches for a honey comb that's barely hanging onto the tree limb. Bees swarm around the bear's head — just waiting for the opportunity to sting in an effort to protect their honey. The entire mural has beautiful mountains as a backdrop as well as a blue stream that flows from wall to wall. Closing my eyes again, I can almost hear the water breaking and subsiding as it flows through the jungle around one animal's territory to the next.

Quickly rocking back and forth, I successfully propel my cumbersome body from the chair. I saunter to the crib and turn on the musical Care Bears mobile hanging above it. I observe the miniature bears go round and round as I listen to the soft lullaby. I imagine my baby lying there watching it with me. Turning away from the baby's bed, my mind promptly returns to Jason. I'm still trying to figure out what Jason's comments last night were all about. I can't understand why it's troubling me so much.

Approaching the nursery's door, I turn and take another look around the baby's room. Pleased, as usual, I close the door behind me and make my way back to the living room.

I sit back onto the couch, assuming the same position I had before I went to the nursery. As I continue to think about my life, I recognize the fact that I am happy, extremely happy actually. I have a husband that I adore and a new baby on the way. My brothers are here with me, and I have a home that I love. Home sweet home — I seem to be saying these three words a lot lately. I begin to look around... admiring how far this place has come from its humble, HUD beginnings.

Our home is a contemporary style ranch. Ryan and I found it one day when we were lost on the southwest side of the city after visiting Lawnside Non-Denominational Church. We, somehow, wandered onto Woodgreen Way trying to find our way back to I-285. When we saw the small rustic house, we instantly fell in love with it. I could envision the end-state grandeur even though it was just a bungalow and not a palace. And even though our home is relatively small... it is tastefully furnished. Ryan and I have managed to obtain some really nice pieces on our extremely modest incomes.

The full length of the living room right side wall is made of burnt red bricks which almost look brown. The entire back wall is glass and shaped like an upside down V. A single wood beam runs down the middle of it creating a perfect ninety degree angle on each side.

The vaulted ceiling with its thick beams overhead adds charm and character to the living area. The sofa and loveseat were purchased at a yard sale that I discovered on one of my many treasure hunts. The pieces cost me little to nothing. The frame of the sofa was irresistibly unique but the fabric was worn and tattered. I replaced the worn fabric with the loveliest peach floral chintz that I found at a store on Miami Circle in Buckhead. The fabric cost an arm and a leg, but the results were breathtaking. Brass and glass end tables adorned with Chinese vases and various Oriental style accessories are placed at each side of the sofa. A large peach and ivory hand woven Oriental rug — another major expense — lay in the middle of the floor beneath the glass cocktail table. A large Oriental style oil canvas with birds, flowers and Chinese writings along the side, hangs above the sofa. As I look at the picture, I realize that I have yet to find out the meaning of the oriental symbols. Yet another item to complete on my endless to-do list.

The foyer's parquet flooring matches the color of the wooden beams in the living ceiling. For contrast, the living room wall is painted a beautiful hue of gold. The wonderful thing about color is its ability to change with the light. In the mornings, the glow of the rising sun makes the walls appear almost amber. Throughout the day the color becomes richer, deeper. By evening, as the sun sets on the horizon, the walls become a light, golden brown.

Another great find... a brass-trimmed contemporary style mirror hangs on the foyer wall. To the left of the foyer is our very small dining area. So small, in fact, that I really had to be creative. I found a very low Chinese style, bamboo table and strategically placed four extra large pillows around it to use for seating. The pillows are hand embroidered, each with a different Asian design.

The house has three small bedrooms, two baths and an eat-in (I like to call it squeeze-in) kitchen. The kitchen is long and narrow with a door at the end of it that leads to a deck. The deck is high up because the back yard slopes downward. The sloping yard gives the illusion that the house is on a hilltop. The view from the glass wall in the living room is deceiving, but pretty none-the-less. Our home is at the end of an L-shaped street. There are no houses beside or behind our house, only woods... lots and lots of woods. If one has an active imagination, one could actually pretend to be on the slopes of some chic ski resort somewhere in Colorado. Problem is... the snow is missing.

There's a family, the Douglas's that resides just past the dense woods on the right side of the house. However, the only neighbors we really ever see are Al James, and sometimes his wife or children. The James family lives pretty much directly across the street from us.

Thinking about Weird Al — this is what I dubbed the idiot neighbor — gives me goose bumps. The man is such a strange character. Actually, referring to him as simply a strange character really is a huge understatement. This guy is way beyond strange.

Last Sunday, my fantastic girlfriends, Contessa, Tikki and Gerhia hosted a baby shower in my honor. On that day, Weird Al sat in the middle of his yard, Indian style mind you, and watched the comings and goings at my house as if mesmerized or in a trance. There was plenty of activity for him to see. We must have had at least forty or more guests... both men and women. And that's not even counting the caterer, balloon delivery man and a few other friends that just popped in and out.

I guess Weird Al had wanted a front row seat to witness the excitement and the middle of his yard afforded him that. For the entire Sunday afternoon that's where the knuckle head sat. He eyed us nonstop. At the time, I simply ignored him and told my guest to do the same. All I can do now is shake my head as I think of last Sunday.

WHEN NEVER COMES AGAIN

By the grace of God, once more I manage to pull myself off the couch. I walk into the kitchen to get a glass of water so that I can take the medication prescribed by Dr. Jones this morning. My stomach still feels awfully queasy. I sure hope this pill helps. I toss the pill to the back of my throat and gulp several swallows of water. Looking out of the kitchen window, I recall Weird Al's behavior just this morning.

Larry had driven me to the drug store around nine o'clock this morning to pick up my prescription. Either he or Jason chauffeurs me wherever I need to go. I'm much too big to drive myself around these days. Besides, Ryan has the "good" car with him in Florida. I was left with the old Ford Pinto my Dad gave us years ago. I wouldn't trust it as far as I can throw it. Larry drives a cute little baby blue Chevrolet Vega sport coupe that happens to be his pride and joy but my worst nightmare. It's getting harder and harder for this heavy load of mine to get in and out of that small ass car.

When Larry and I returned home from the pharmacy, I realized that once again I was overcome with the same eerie feeling I had awakened with. As we walked toward the front door, I felt eyes on me and turned to notice Weird Al watching us like a hawk from his front door.

Once inside the house, I casually mentioned to Larry and Jason that the fool across the street was watching us again.

"Hey y'all, Weird Al is standing in his front door watching us again! I felt his eyes on me when I got out of the car. I hate that shit. I wish he'd find a fucking hobby or something. Hell, we ain't cable T.V.!"

But on this beautiful, picturesque Saturday afternoon I try to overlook Weird Al's peculiar behavior. He's probably just into his house watching gig again... like last Sunday. Anyway, neither Larry nor Jason had bothered to comment when I told them he was watching us again. We simply ignore Weird Al, taking his bizarre behavior in stride. I guess we are all used to it by now anyway. Besides, the Barnett siblings grew up with crazy folk staring at us.

Chapter Two

I arrived in this world in Augusta, Georgia, born next to the last of seven children. My parents named me Pamela Vonetta Barnett. My father, Gregory Milledge Barnett, better known as Black to most, is a barber by profession. He still operates Barnett Barber Shop and probably will continue to cut hair until his hands fall off. Daddy loves what he does. In addition to the shop he owned, Daddy worked at Lenwood, the Veterans Administration on Wrightsboro Road, cutting the hair of crazy patients until his retirement some thirty years later.

When we were kids, Daddy would sometimes treat a few selected 'clients', a.k.a. crazy patients, to an outing by bringing them to our house. Daddy's clients stayed in the car most of the time. But every now and again, he would allow them to venture into our backyard under his stern supervision, of course. They were sad, harmless souls. And even though they really did seem crazy... my siblings and I were never ever afraid of them. They would wander aimlessly, sometimes gazing at the pigs in their pigpen or simply touching the leaves on a tree. Then at times, they would just stand around staring at us.

Sometimes my oldest brothers, Gabriel and Jason, would mess with them... making faces and crazy, convulsion-like body movements. But never, ever, did Daddy's clients act the fool and not once did they ever attempt to harm us.

My mother, Alicia, was, at that time... and is still, a full time housewife. Growing up, Momma had her hands full taking care of seven children. She would always fuss whenever Daddy brought his clients to the house. It didn't matter that the client s didn't do anything wrong. Momma merely didn't want them there. Momma has always been a worrywart... always thinking something awful is going to happen. Mommas always seem to be afraid of her own shadow.

But not Black. Black Barnett believed in living life. He believed in taking risks. It was the only way to get ahead in life. He swore by that. When Momma complained about the patients being at the house, Daddy only laughed. He would say, "Ahhh hush up, Alicia. Just be grateful you ain't one of 'em. Because you could be ya' know. Any of us could. Never know what tomorrow gon' bring."

That was all my father ever had to say about it and he would always say the exact same thing, again and again. But his words didn't quiet Momma. She continued to raise hell every single time the nutty clients showed up at our house.

Weird Al reminds Jason, Larry and me of the patients that Daddy brought and welcomed to our home. They were crazy as a bedbug, but harmless as a fly.

Chapter Three

The door-bell rings. I jump. *Why am I so freaking jittery and who could that be?* Then I remember. My cousin, Edward, is in town from Augusta. Earlier, Larry mentioned that he was coming over. How forgetful of me. I can't seem to think straight these days. I've got a bad case of baby brain.

Shouting, so Edward can hear me... "Come on in. Door is open."

Standing with my back to the kitchen sink and window, I can see directly into the living room and clear down the hallway. Jason, so tall and very handsome, walks out of his bedroom dressed in light green Bermuda shorts and a V-neck white tee. He smiles at me as he walks towards the door.

Edward and Jason embrace swiftly. Then, they slap hands and start talking a bunch of smack to each other. It hits home when Jason informs Edward that he's getting old.

"Man, you can't call nobody old," Edward drawls. "You the one that's... shit... what 'bout fifteen years older than me?"

Before Jason can respond to Edward's comment about his age, I yell into the hallway, "Hey there Eddie! What's happening?" I call him 'Eddie' just to piss him off. Everyone knows that he prefers to be called Edward. He hates the name 'Eddie'.

"What's up butterball?" Edward asks, smiling as he walks toward the kitchen. Standing two feet away, I lean over to hug him stretching to get my arms around him.

"I got your butterball right here!" I say as I make a fist and wave it at him. Then protectively and instinctively, I place my hands on my huge stomach. Edward places his hand on my tummy, too. The baby is active, like always.

"Frisky little butterball, at that, ain't it?" he asks, as he feels my unborn child push against my rib cage.

We both laugh.

Larry walks in, freshly showered and looking good. His tan linen pants and brown short sleeve shirt look great on his muscular young frame. He's clean shaven as always and looks older than his eighteen years. His eyes twinkle when he smiles and he's always smiling. That's one of the things I love most about my baby brother. He has a sunny disposition twenty-four seven. I pray life is kind to him always and doesn't destroy his happy-go-lucky demeanor.

Of course, all Larry wants to know is what time the food will be ready. I reply around four. That reminds me, I still have to thaw the ribs and shrimp. I take the beef ribs and shrimp out of the freezer and place them in the sink while I'm thinking about it. I begin to run water over them. The shrimp will only take a minute but the ribs may take awhile.

"On second thought, Larry, make that five o'clock," I say.

Larry and Edward consider three hours much too long to sit idle. They decide to go to the mall and check out the babes. Teenagers! I turn the faucet off, wipe my hands and go back into the living room.

"Okay, but don't mess around and eat at the mall when I'm cooking all this food!"

"Don't worry Pam, we won't. See ya later. Bye Jason!" Larry says, smiling as he walks out the door.

"Bye, Larry. Be cool, Edward. See you cats later." Jason replies.

My stomach makes a primal noise so I decide to sit down for a minute before returning to the kitchen to peel and clean the shrimp. Since I'm sitting, I pick up the phone to call Nadine, just to see what she has up today. Nadine lives just a few blocks down the street from Woodgreen Way. Nadine and I are not best friends. I mean, our relationship is nothing like the one I have with my ace-boon-coons, Gerhia, Contessa and Tikki. But Nadine is cool to hang with every now and then. Besides, it's a convenient relationship for both of us. She helps me out when I need it and I do the same for her.

I just finished dialing the last digit of her telephone number when I look up to see Weird Al standing at my front door. The door is opened, but the decorative, black, wrought iron screen is closed and locked.

What the hell does he want?

Nadine finally answers the phone, trying to sound all sexy.

"Nadine... it's Pam. Girl... hold... hold on a second. I need to answer the door."

As I attempt to raise my pregnant butt up off the sofa, Jason, who's sitting across from me on the loveseat, looks up at me in that loving way of his and says, "Don't worry about it Sis, I'll see what this fool wants."

As Jason walks across the living room to the foyer and towards the front door, I notice something long and black hanging on the side of Weird Al. Before my mind can focus any longer on the thing Weird Al has in his possession, Jason's in the foyer and almost to the iron screen door. Weird Al lifts the black thing. I still have no idea what it is. He points it at Jason.

The excruciating loud bang causes my ears to pop and my heart to stop.

I scream... dropping the telephone as Jason crumbles to the floor. I manage to get off the sofa faster than I ever have before. I run to Jason. It never occurs to me that I might be in danger or that I should be running away and not toward the assailant. Kneeling down and then lastly falling to the foyer floor, I lift and cradle my brother's head in my lap. All I see is blood... bright red blood. Blood is everywhere. Crying and screaming all at the same time, I try to see Jason's eyes, but I can't. All I see is blood. The room is darkening around me. I must be in some kind of dreadful fog. I feel like this is real yet not real, I'm here but not here.

I'm nailed to this spot, clinging to Jason's body. I hear a voice. It's a calm and soothing sound in the midst of my own violent screams and sobs. The voice speaks... *"Get out... get out..." it says. "Jason is gone."*

The words are spoken with such authority and control that I am compelled to obey. In the very same moment, I'm realizing that Weird Al is shooting at me. Slowly, but gently, I place Jason's lifeless head onto the floor then I position myself to lie on my stomach, utterly afraid and shaking. *Oh God. What shall I do? Where can I hide?*

I must be dreaming... lying in the trenches of someone's war. But the sound of another gunshot confirms that I'm not dreaming. I start to slither like a snake, which being eight months pregnant is no easy task. Yet somehow, I make my way into the kitchen. Weird Al is breaking the glass out of the panels located on the side of the door. Or maybe he's crashing in the window so that he can get to me! Oh crap, he's banging hard, what I know now is a rifle, against the iron of the screen door. He's creating so much noise that it sounds as if the gates of Hell are going to implode around me at any second. My heart is racing. I'm expecting Lucifer himself to appear before me and swallow me up into the fires of Hades.

I manage to lift my body and stand upon wobbly legs. I begin to run, as best I can in my advanced state of pregnancy, trying to move towards the back door. But the back door is locked with a dead bolt, which means I need the key to open it.

Oh God, where are the keys? Think Pam, think.

Quickly, I look around. Shit. The keys are not hanging from the hook. I reach the door, terrified. Praying for a miracle, I turn the knob. Miraculously, my prayer is granted. Somehow, right now, the door isn't locked. I continue to turn the doorknob, flinging the door open with a force that I didn't know I possessed. The door collides with the bakers' rack. All the cookbooks and every decorative whatnot that had been carefully and strategically placed comes crashing down onto the floor. I step over the mess to run out the door then down the stairs. Reaching ground level, I fall. I get up and start to run again. I fall again. My stomach hurts. I'm screaming and crying uncontrollably. I fall once more. I lie there. I don't want to run anymore. I want to rest. I want to return to my home. I want to be with my brother. I want to be with Jason. I want this day to begin again and this nightmare to be just that, a nightmare. The wind chimes are sounding. I hear them from where I lay. No longer do the chimes sound like lovely music. Now the wind chimes resonate in my ears like tones from a Frankenstein movie. I want it to stop. *God, please make them stop!* I want the earth to stop spinning. As I lie broken and confused, proclaiming all the things I want, I see someone running towards me. I can't make out whom yet.

Oh my God. God! Who is it? Is it Weird Al? Has he come around the house and through the woods after me?

My heart feels as if it's about to jump from my chest. I scream. I scream again, louder than before, as I try to grasp a rock that's barely within my reach. Stretching as far as I can, I lift the rock to defend myself. Focusing hard on the person moving towards me, I suddenly realize that it's my neighbor's teenage son and not Weird Al.

Praise God.

The young man grabs my arm and attempts to lift me off the ground. He appears to be healthy and strong, but he needs to possess he-man strength to be capable of picking my big ass up. I'm dead weight at this point, exhausted and unable to move. I'm as limp as a noodle. All I want is to go back inside the house for Jason. I want to help Jason.

Lord Jesus, please help Jason.

This teenage boy is resolved to save me. His young face reveals unwavering determination and only a hint of fright. Convincing myself not to consider any thoughts of returning to my house, I allow myself to be rescued by the brave, strong, young man. I place my arms around his neck which allows him to steady his legs and to raise my limp body from the ground.

Chapter Four

My rescuer and I make it safely through the woods and into the young man's house. Mrs. Douglas, my rescuer's mother, is waiting for us at the side door of her home. I recognize the mother because every now and then we throw a hand up at each other in passing. She immediately reaches for me and takes me in her arms.

Mrs. Douglas coos, "It's alright now. It's alright."

However, it's not all right. Not now. Not ever. I start to yell at her and at anyone else that can hear me. "He's killed my brother. He's killed my brother. He's killed my brother!"

"No. No.", Mrs. Douglas continues to coo.

It was at this moment that I wanted to kill her. She didn't know. She hadn't witnessed what I had.

I cry. "He has. He has."

Mrs. Douglas guides me deeper into her house and tries to get me to sit in a chair that's positioned in the middle of the room. Instead, I run to the corner of what looks like it's either the den or the family room. The room is dark, much darker than I can imagine a room would be in a house of mine. I thrive on sunlight and prefer lots of windows. But there is no light in this room and the only window is completely shaded by what looks like a bush in need of a serious trim.

Crouching in the corner of the dark room, protectively I hold my stomach. I begin to rock, trying to soothe myself as much as the baby. Next the tears come. The tears fall heavily down my face. Rocking and sobbing, rocking and sobbing... this is all I can do.

Mrs. Douglas decides it's best to leave me be. She turns and I hear her ask her son a question. "Are you okay?" He shakes his head then replies "yes" in a very shaky voice. Mrs. Douglas looks as if she's a bit calmer, knowing that her son is not hurt in any way. She dialed 911 as soon as she had heard the gunshots and my screams. I can hear the loud sirens. The police are approaching. Mrs. Douglas moves towards the curtains that face the front of the street. She's terrified. Her fingers tremble as she pulls back the curtains then peeks out. She's not alone in her fears. We are all petrified.

The following hours are long and agonizing. I sit in the corner, thinking my baby is dead. I know in my heart that Jason is dead, and at this moment, all I want is to die, too. The room itself might as well be tittering on axles like some magic trick. I feel dazed and bewildered. Something warm and wet is demanding my attention. Fresh blood is on my hand and I can tell that it's not the blood of my brother. Looking down... bright red blood soaks my shorts and is spreading across my hips. The blood trickles beyond the hem of my shorts and down my left thigh. I wipe my hand across the flow. Turning my hand over and over again I'm mesmerized by the spread of the red color.

I dressed this morning in white shorts and a pink and white stripped top. The shorts are now stained with grass and blood, and they are ripped by the rocks from my falls. I have on only one white sandal. The other sandal lost in the midst of fleeing from my assailant. My big toe on my left foot is stumped and throbbing. The toenail is hanging, bleeding and broken to the quick. I stand, catching a glimpse of myself in the mirror on the far wall. My narrow face is normally the color of butterscotch candy but not today. My large, dark blue, almond shaped eyes and my small nose are unrecognizable. My eyes change colors depending upon my mood, but right now they are basically swollen shut... my nose is red and bulbous from crying, yet my face as pale as sheet-rock. My overall stature is petite, despite my basketball sized stomach. The tidy French roll I styled this morning is disengaged. My jet black shoulder length hair is now wild and dirty, adding to my crazed appearance.

For the second time today, a sudden loud knock on the door causes me to nearly jump out of my skin. Mrs. Douglas walks slowly to the door and cautiously looks through the peephole. She opens the door and an officer follows her inside. She is leading the policeman towards me. Sympathetic eyes look into mine, though obviously shocked by my appearance. The officer appears genuinely concerned. Mrs. Douglas tells him that I'm the one that lives in the house next door. The officer begins to speak.

"My name is Casper, Officer Casper", he states with authority.

When he tells me that his name is Casper, the first thing that pops into my mind is Casper the friendly ghost. I wonder if Jason's a ghost... Jason, the friendly ghost.

The officer looks me in the eye and softly asks, "What's your name, Miss? Can you please tell me your name?"

I can't reply. I hear him but I can't seem to remember my name.

"Do you live next door?" The policeman wants to verify. "Are you okay?"

I try to shake my head up and down, but it feels so heavy, as if it may fall off if I continue to try to move it.

"Can you come with me?" The officer asks.

"Yes," I say, almost inaudibly.

"Mrs. Douglas states that it's your brother inside your house. Is this correct?"

"Yes."

"I'm sorry to inform you, but your brother is dead."

I say in barely a whisper, "I know."

"Can you identify the perpetrator?"

"Yes."

He extends a hand to me. I take it. He helps me to my feet and together we walk to the front door. There's another cop waiting at the door. We step outside. I can see Weird Al sitting on the steps of his porch as if nothing had happened. I see an officer walking away from him. Weird Al is sitting there, watching the police officers scurry about — looking for a suspect. He's probably feeling very smug in the fact that he knows what has happened and the police don't.

I cannot believe this ass-hole is just sitting on the steps of his porch.

Officer Casper asks again. "Can you identify the perpetrator?"

I point a finger across the street directly at Weird Al and say, "That's the motherfucker who shot my brother!"

At precisely that minute, as if he could feel my presence, Weird Al looks across the street. He sees me standing between the two police officers and I swear I can feel his gaze. Suddenly Weird Al jumps up, runs inside his house and barricades his self in. He begins to shoot out of every window of his house. He's a stark raving mad lunatic. It seems as if he'll shoot anyone in sight and he does. The officer that had just questioned Weird Al moments earlier is running away from the house but he's not running fast enough. A bullet hits him in the leg. He manages to make it to his police car.

All hell breaks loose. Policemen rush me back inside Mrs. Douglas's house. The pain in my abdomen is excruciating. Blood is seeping through my shorts and my head is reeling. The war raging outside is deafening. I try to compose myself. Think Pam. Think. I should try to get word to my family. I also need to reach Larry before he returns to the house... before he walks into the twilight zone. He's going to freak as it is when he shows up on the street, not knowing if it's his house or not. Besides, for all I know television cameras could be here filming the scene. On the other hand, the entire shooting may be reported on the radio as well.

I can't call Ryan. He's at work and he'll totally lose it. I need to call someone that can call Momma or maybe call Gabriel. Should I call Tikki? She's the strong one. Tessa and Ge would freak out for sure. No, my best bet is to call Henry. Henry is Edward's older brother. He lives only twenty minutes away in Riverdale and he can probably reach Edward. If Henry can find out where Larry and Edward are he can get to them before they hear something on the radio. Yes, that's what I'll do. I'll call Henry.

Seven, three, six... shit what is it?

Damn! I try to think of Henry's number but my mind won't focus. I try to dial again. My hands are trembling but miraculously I manage to get it right. Henry answers on the fourth ring. In a voice unlike my own, I try to find my words.

"Hello, Henry?"

"Yeah, who's this?"

"Henry." I say this time with a little more conviction.

"Pam? Is that you?"

"Yes, it's me." I start to weep before continuing. "Henry... Jason's been shot. He's... Henry, he's dead. That fool across the... hello?"

The telephone falls to the floor on the other end. I begin to yell into the phone.

"Henry? Henry?"

But, Henry is gone. He dropped the telephone in reaction to my statement. I continue to hold the phone to my ear, praying he'll pick it up on his end but Henry does not return.

I look around Mrs. Douglas's house, searching, as if, somehow, astonishingly, Henry will materialize in the room. I realize as I look around, that there are numerous people inside the house, mostly kids, but a few adults. The thing is... they're all staring at me. These folks must have come inside to take cover when Weird Al started shooting out of every window in his house. But everyone is looking at me. They all are. By now all of them know who I am. They are looking at me with expressions that seem to say "I'm so sorry," "It'll be okay" or "poor girl." But even so, no one is brave enough to approach me and actually say it to my face. No one will console me due to my frightfully savage appearance. I look like something straight out of the Congo.

There is no one else I can think of to call. I cannot bring myself to telephone my parents. I can't begin to imagine how my mother will take this horrible news. How does a woman deal with the loss of a child you have carried in your womb, nurtured and watched grow into adulthood? My father will be the tower of strength that he always is. He will grieve in solitude. I have only seen my father weep once. He didn't even cry at his own mother's funeral. The rest of my family would take it hard. Oh God. What will they think? Which is easiest, I wonder... to know about a pending death and attempt to prepare for it and just wait for it to happen? Or, is it better for death to take you totally by surprise, coming quickly and unexpectedly? I can't imagine either being any easier than the other. Death of a loved one is hard. Period. I pray my baby is alive. I'll die if I lose it, too.

I retreat to the corner of the room and hug my belly. The baby is not moving at all. It's all coiled up on the right side of my stomach, tight as a knot. The baby's scared and I'm sure it can sense my fear. The world can be a relentless and heartless place. Why is this happening? I ask this question over and over again.

Mrs. Douglas brings a large towel over. She observes the blood now trickling down my legs. I accept the towel and wrap it around my waist.

"Would you like to lie down?" She asks.

"I can't." I say.

My mind is going wild. The thoughts that enter it are as strange as the scene unfolding around me. I'm no stranger to close calls. Actually, I have always proclaimed that I must have nine lives. Considering the events that have occurred in my twenty-four years of life, I most definitely consider myself very fortunate. I've made it through some of the most precarious situations. However right now, perhaps the jig is up... and my life really is about to end.

Chapter Five

At fifteen, I ran away from home. As I reflect now, my reasons for leaving were very, very stupid... as most teenagers' reasons are when running away. I was upset with my boyfriend after overhearing a rumor that he was on a date with another girl. Of course, I didn't have the sense to ask him about it. Instead, I decided I couldn't live without him, so I ran away. Hindsight is twenty-twenty. I should have dumped the knuckle head and stepped with the next boy in line. But at fifteen everything is critical and devastating... especially anything involving a boy that you call yourself in love with.

So, being the headstrong and bold person that I was at fifteen, I actually climbed out of my bedroom window and walked to the interstate. (The interstate was only a couple thousand feet away.) It was nine o'clock at night and I'd planned to hitchhike but I had no idea where I was going. I knew that Interstate 20 went east and west. West sounded good to me at the time.

The November night was cool... the dark sky was clear. The stars shone brightly on my blue denim jacket, baby blue tank top and white elephant leg style bellbottom pants. Inside my jacket pocket, I clutched a pair of my mother's old, heavy scissors so tight that I could feel my fingers swelling.

I was on the interstate for less than two minutes when a gigantic eighteen wheeler tractor-trailer pulls over. The truck sounded like a train and it seemed to moan in agony every time the driver shifted gears. Once the truck was safely in park, the passenger side door opens and then a large hand reaches for me. All I could see is this hand. I couldn't see the drivers face, only this hand. The huge truck seemed to block out every inch of light that the stars gave off. I can't tell if the hand is Black or White. And at this point, I really don't care. I grab the hand and up into the truck I go. As I'm shutting the passenger door, the driver maneuvers the truck back onto the interstate. I stare out of the window, clutching the scissors, afraid to look the driver's way. After about five miles, I finally get the nerve to glance over at the driver. I could not believe my eyes. There was a bald, overweight, White guy sitting at the wheel, leering at me. He starts up a conversation that I have no intention of partaking in. Instead I clutched my weapon tighter. He begins to tell me that he's been on the road for twelve weeks. He says he has a wife and three kids, but he doesn't get to spend much time with them. He continues to talk while I get a crook in my neck from staring out the passenger window. I'm noticing from the corner of my eye that he keeps rolling his window up and down about every three minutes or so. The guy's chewing tobacco, which, I suppose, was better than filling the cab with cigarette smoke. He yaps on and on. I pay no mind to what he's saying until finally his words capture my attention.

"I ain't never had none from a colored girl before," he drawled.

I prayed I had misunderstood this country hick's dialog. He must've been reading my mind because he decided to repeat his news flash. I continued to pretend not to hear.

"I wouldn't take none from you or anything," he continues. "But, if you want ta' give me some, I'd try not to hurt you. I swear."

I cringed. Oh God, was this fat ass, bald head white trash about to rape me, or was this his way of hitting on me?

He kept jabbering on and on about any and everything, ignorant to the fact that I tuned him out miles ago. I continued to ignore him and I remained silent as my journey progressed. I was too afraid and way too nervous to sleep. Yet, I pretended to doze as we made our way west toward Atlanta.

The trucker made a stop off Interstate 20 at a Dairy Queen fast food restaurant.

"You gotta get in the back." He said.

I looked at him like he was crazy.

"You gotta get in the back there. It's against the law to pickup hitchhikers, so no one can see ya."

I was wary. But finally, I did as I was told and climbed into the back of the cab. There was a tiny bunk in which he slept. I immediately suspected he was only trying to get me on the little bed so that he could molest me.

Surprisingly, he didn't jump in the back on top of me. He got out of the truck and turned towards the restaurant. As he walked away, I noticed a limp. As he walked further away from the truck, I saw why he limped. He had a peg leg. A trucker with a peg leg. Hell, he had a bald head and a pegged leg — all he needed was a patch over one eye and a parrot on his shoulder.

He actually turned out to be an okay guy. He brought me a cheeseburger back, but I had no appetite. We traveled for another forty miles or so until we reached a truck stop. A sign read Forrest Park, Georgia. Captain Hook, as I choose to nickname him for obvious reasons, pulled the truck into a parallel parking space. He handled the eighteen-wheeler masterfully, despite his handicap. He turned the large horsepower engine off then turned and looked at me. It was very quiet once the truck was turned off. Too quiet for me. I looked out the window and surveyed my surroundings.

The truck stop was located on the corner of a busy intersection. There were lots of diesel gas pumps and many rows of pay telephones. There was a lady in high heels, fish-net stockings, hot pants and a knotty, nasty looking, fake fur jacket. She was talking to a guy that was trying to get into his truck. She was leaning her body into his and whispering into his ear. I guess she was what my Dad called a "lot lizard'.

It had to be about four o'clock in the morning by now so I assume that the drivers of the other trucks parked were asleep. There was a small restaurant that was well lit. A couple of late night patrons were sitting around sipping coffee.

Captain Hook decided to speak.

"I can't take you no further. You seem like a nice kid. Why don't you go on in and call your Momma and your Daddy. They probably miss you by now and they is worried sick, I'm sho'."

He reached into his back pocket and extracted a well-worn brown wallet. He pulled a bill from it.

"Here, take this. Go on, take it. Now go on in there and call your folks and get cha' som'um to eat. Take it."

I had hesitated a tad longer than I should have. He was about to put the twenty dollar bill back in his pocket when I reached for it.

"Thank you."

Those were the only words I spoke to Captain Hook. I climbed out of the truck and never looked back as I walked toward the diner. I still clutched the scissors in my pocket and now the twenty dollar bill, too.

As I entered the diner, all eyes focused on me. I'm sure everyone wondered where the little black girl materialized from. I stared right back at them. I sat in a booth. Immediately, the waitress came to the booth and asked if I wanted anything. I ordered a coke.

"That's all?" she drawled.

"Yeah, that's all." I replied sheepishly.

The waitress at the truck stop looked an awful lot like the one that played in the television sitcom, Mel's Diner, named Vera. Like Vera, this waitress was tall and lanky, with a beehive hairdo. Her hair was also the same dirty blond color. She chewed gum as if there would be no tomorrow, popping it about every half second.

The look-alike Vera returned with my coke and plopped it down in front of me. She looked warily at me, and asked, "You alright, Sugar?"

That's all it took. I burst out crying. Vera put her arms around my shoulders and asked, "What's wrong, Sugar? What's wrong?"

I tried to get myself together. My nose was running and Vera plucked a napkin out of the dispenser and handed it to me. I loudly blew my nose and balled the napkin into my hands.

"I'm okay. I ran away from home and now I think that maybe it was the wrong thing to do."

"Ah, sugar, you just walk yourself right there over to that there telephone and call your momma. I bet she's waiting to hear from you."

"I guess," I said.

"Go on," Vera prodded.

She got up from the booth to let me out. I moved slowly, contemplating making the call. She shooed me, with a gesture of her hands. I picked up the receiver and dialed zero.

"Collect call from Pamela." I said into the phone.

My mother picked up on the first ring. She accepted the collect telephone call and I could hear the relief in her voice.

"Pamela. Pamela where are you? Are you alright? Where are you?" she asked again.

I hesitated.

"Pamela Barnett," she said, "You better tell me where you are!"

I groaned and somehow found the words to tell her that I was about three hours away from home. I had hitchhiked my way to Atlanta.

Daddy got on the phone then. He was firm yet calm. *Typical Daddy.*

"Pamela, I need to know exactly where you are so that I can come get you and bring you home."

"I... I'm not exactly sure."

"Well then, put someone on the phone that can give me directions."

"Okay, Daddy." I gesture for the waitress. I hold my hand over the mouthpiece of the phone and asked if she would be kind enough to give my father directions to the diner.

"Sure, Sugar." She said, with her southern drawl. She takes the phone out of my hand and begins speaking to my Daddy. When she finished, she gave the phone back to me.

I slowly take the phone. "Hello?" I say timidly.

"Pamela, stay just where you are until I get there. Do you understand? Do you understand me?" Daddy says, speaking louder than before.

"Yes Daddy, I understand." I replaced the telephone on the hook and begin to cry, again.

I don't remember if the tears had come because I was relieved or because I was scared to death of what Daddy was going to do when he got to me.

Vera walked back over to me and put her arm around my shoulder. She led me to the booth and said that everything was going to be alright. She brought me a plate full of food to the booth and placed it in front of me.

"Eat, child." She commanded.

So I ate.

Daddy arrived around eight o'clock in the morning. Jason of course was with him. Jason grabbed me and hugged me tightly. He had kissed my forehead, looked into my eyes and asked if I was alright. I nodded yes.

Then Daddy, never being one to show emotion or affection, had staunchly said "Let's go."

I slept all the way home.

I knew even then that I would never understand the pain that I had caused my mother. Maybe one day, I had thought... if I ever became a parent myself, I would comprehend the agony that I put her through.

When we got home, Momma had taken me into her arms and hugged me fiercely. She was so happy to see me. She said that the Lord had answered her prayers and that she was so grateful to have me home where I belonged.

I hugged her back and started to babble on and on about how sorry I was.

"Its gon' be alright now, baby" Momma said softly in my ear. "Let's just put this all behind us and move on. Come now child, let me take a good look at ya."

Then she led me by the hand to my bedroom.

Once Momma was confident that I was truly okay, she helped me undress then I took a long hot bath. As I lay in the bathtub, I thought about how bold and stupid I had been, hitchhiking all the way to Atlanta... with a trucker, no less. I knew I was lucky and blessed to have made it home unharmed.

Upon exiting the bathroom, my daddy was waiting for me.

"After you get dressed Pamela, I want to see you in my room."

Somehow, I had managed to nod yes, but I was scared as shit. I knew I was going to get it. I could tell Daddy was upset by the way he had called me 'Pamela'. Daddy only called me that when he was pissed.

I dressed slowly, procrastinating as long as I could. I knew that I couldn't put it off any longer without making a bad situation worse, so I walked across the hall and tapped on Daddy's door.

"Come in." His voice boomed.

I walked into my parent's bedroom. Daddy was perched on the edge of the bed, like a hawk ready to swoop down upon its prey. But he surprised me. He patted the spot next to him. I sat down.

"Pamela," he had begun. "What you did was stupid and very dangerous. You could have been raped or murdered or both. We could be picking up your body parts from the side of I-20 right now. And then to learn, that all of this was done because of some little nappy-headed boy! Girl, if you ever do anything crazy like this again, I will kill you myself. Let me tell you this. There are many, many fish in the sea. Do not ever throw your life away over a fish. If the one you caught stinks, toss it back into the ocean, cause there's a million others just waiting to nibble the bait."

Daddy looked at me so intensely that I could have sworn that he was looking straight into my core. He hugged me then and started to weep.

"If anything had happened to you child, I don't know what I would have done. You're my baby girl, my heart and I love you."

I started to cry, too. We held each other tightly. That became a defining moment in my life... one that I would cling to forever.

To this day, I've never seen my father cry again and never again has he told me that he loved me. Yet the bond had been established and our friendship forged forever.

That experience changed everything between me and my Dad. From that night on, I made the effort to have a relationship with my father. Whether it was stopping by the barber shop just to say hello or picking up the phone every now and then to ask how he was doing.

Some of my siblings probably called it 'sucking up', but I didn't care what they thought. I knew for sure that my Daddy really loved me. And that's all that I ever needed and wanted to know.

Thinking back on that time when Daddy and Jason came to my rescue... I realize that Jason has always been willing, ready and able to take care of me. I can't help but ask now... *"Who will come to my rescue this day? Who will be there for me now?"*
Jolting myself back to reality, I retreat into my shell. I feel so very alone. I rub my belly, still trying to get some movement. It doesn't work. The baby is coiled into a very tight knot.

VICTORIA MIGUEL-JOSEPH

Chapter Six

As the hours grow long, the cops continue to guard Mrs. Douglas's house. The standoff between Weird Al and the police has already lasted several hours. It seems the madman has enough ammunition to start World War III. During the gloomy, horrible hours, I contemplate this crazy man's actions... *Why would he do something like this?*

The house is filled with police officers, there to protect and serve. The officers inside are conversing on their walkie-talkies with the policemen outside. In a scratchy in-and-out tone, the message comes over the radio... "Perpetrator is on the loose. I repeat. Perp is on the loose. Move in. All units move in now!" Abruptly, two of the officers sprint out the door. The others move to cover the windows.

Instinctively, I get up... moving to the window as fast as I can. A SWAT truck comes to a screeching halt across the street in front of Weird Al's house. The SWAT team rushes out of the truck in double file, head gear on, weapons in hand. It's like a scene out of NYPD Blue. I still can't believe this situation is real. The cops disappear into the woods along side of Weird Al's house. I hear gunfire... lots of gunfire. Had it not been August, I would think that it's the fourth of July. Through the window I look up in the sky expecting to see fireworks. But the gun fire seems louder than any fireworks I have ever heard. There's lots of shouting, although I can't make out what the cops are saying. The officers inside the house now have on ear pieces, guns or rifles in hand.

Now I hear blasting sirens. Two ambulances come to a quick stop but the paramedics never get out. As I continue to watch, I wonder what is happening. The officers inside the house remove their ear pieces and instruct everyone to stay put. They try to calm the children and tell the adults that it's almost over.

What's almost over? My life?

One thing's for sure, my ordeal most certainly is not almost over. This is the beginning of the end for me.

All of a sudden there's activity from the ambulance and I see SWAT members returning from the woods. Then I see Weird Al. Two cops are literally carrying him. The ambulance attendant wheels the stretcher to the curb and the cops place Weird Al upon it. I know he's not dead. If he were dead, they would have covered his body from head to toe with a sheet or placed him in a body bag before returning to the streets. And why would he need an ambulance if he was dead? The paramedics lift the stretcher and roll Weird Al into the emergency vehicle. The ambulance takes off at lightning speed... leaving a bewildered, yet excited crowd behind.

The wounded police officer gets assistance from the paramedics in the second ambulance and off he goes. Soon yet another ambulance pulls up, siren wailing, lights flashing. By this time, it takes some maneuvering to make its way through the crowd of rubberneckers that have lined the streets.

It all reminds me of a scene from one of my favorite movies,

"The Wizard of Oz". After Dorothy's house falls on the Wicked Witch of the East, the Good Witch tells all the Munchkins in Munchkin Land that it's safe to come out now. Officer Casper is reassuring everyone that's it's all over. He claims it's safe to leave Mrs. Douglas's house.

SWAT has completed their job and now they're leaving the scene the same way they came. Police officers are doing their best to control the area. They're instructing the crowd to stand aside, to stay back and to allow the ambulance stretcher through. An officer walks into Mrs. Douglas's house. The ambulance that just arrived is actually for me. Officer Casper escorts me towards the vehicle.

I look around, frightened and cautious. There are so many people. Everybody and their momma must have showed up to see what is going on. People seem to be flowing out of, instead of into, their houses. There's a massive crowd gathered behind police lines. The bright yellow crime scene tape with its thick black writing is recognizable from seeing it so many times on television.

My eyes spot Henry amongst the crowd. A police officer is physically holding him back behind the yellow tape. Henry looks up from his struggle and sees me too. But the officer isn't letting him through. He's pleading with the officer but to no avail. Our eyes connect as the paramedic lowers the stretcher and helps me onto it.

"Henry. Henry." I say, loud as I can.

But no one hears. Up goes the stretcher and into the ambulance I go. Then, for the second time that day, I witness a sight that will stand out in my mind until the day I die. My baby brother is wallowing and thrashing about in the middle of the street.

Larry's crying and screaming, repeating over and over again the same phrase. "Oh God, no. God, no. God no." he wails.

Larry's absolutely inconsolable. Once again, the feeling of helplessness consumes me. All I can do is look at him. I try to form the words so as to call his name but no sound comes out. Just as the paramedics are about to close the ambulance doors, Larry finally looks up. He sees me inside the ambulance. He jumps up and starts to run towards me. I reach out to him as best as can. My arm extended as far as it can go.

Larry reaches out for me too. And just as he comes only inches from the vehicle... the doors are slammed shut and the ambulance takes off with sirens blasting.

"Larry. Larry." I call his name. The words are barely audible. The driver is saying something to dispatch. His words are garbled. I can't understand what he's saying. The other paramedic goes about his duties of placing a mask over my mouth and nose. He connects an I.V. tube to my arm then shoots some concoction into my vein. I feel myself sinking into a black hole. I sink farther and farther as I hold my stomach, continuing to cry silently.

Here I am again... all alone except for the unborn child inside me. But even more so, I pray that my baby is still alive.

Please, Lord... please, let my baby be alright.

I have no idea why my life has been turned upside down and inside out. But there is one thing I do know for sure... My life will never be the same again.

Chapter Seven

The ambulance speeds down Cascade Avenue and through the streets of Atlanta. I lie inside the speeding vehicle wondering if my unborn child will make it... wondering if I'm going to make it. I try to open my eyes but I can't. My lids feel like weights.

Am I asleep? Has this all been a horrible dream? Nope. It happened. I saw it. It's real. Weird Al shot Jason. Jason is dead. Casper said so. Where are we going?

It seems like we've been traveling a long, long time.

How will Larry find me? Will Henry find me?

I wish I could just stop thinking. But I can't.

Why is this happening to me? Why? Why? Why?

I ask myself the same question, why, for what seems like the millionth time. I take a deep breath, trying to calm myself. Deep in my soul I know this is the question I must learn not to ask. Momma always said that there are some things in life that have to be accepted and never questioned. I pray that I come to accept this.

When I finally manage to open my eyes, I'm no longer in the ambulance. I'm in a cold sterile place lying on top of an operating table. The bloodied white shorts are gone and I'm wearing a drab hospital gown that's open in the back. I can feel the draft blowing on my backside. I turn over — trying to close the gown behind me but the IV is getting tangled. For a moment, I believe I'm having a nightmare. I pray I'm having a nightmare. But reality strikes when a very short man with an extremely large moustache and hair that's much too long, enters the room through swinging double doors. He's wearing a white lab coat, has a stethoscope hanging around his neck, and he's smiling at me.

What the fuck is so amusing? Why is he smiling?

"Hi there, young lady," he begins. "I'm Doctor Nolan. How are you feeling?"

I don't respond. My mouth is dry.

"You are going to be just fine and the baby is fine, too."

Hearing the mention of my baby, I manage to form a few words. "My baby is okay? Are you sure?"

"Yes, you are both okay, but I'm keeping you here overnight for observation. It's only a precautionary measure... to keep an eye on the baby, to make sure you're both stable. Your body appears to be in a state of shock. You have been through quite an ordeal."

"But, the baby's okay?" I repeat.

"Believe me, the baby is fine. The heartbeat is steady and strong."

"Where am I?"

"Crawford Long Hospital."

Before I could ask my next question, Larry and Henry rush through the double doors. The doors swing back and forth zealously. I can feel a charge of air from their movement. Larry grabs me and holds on to me for dear life. We remain this way for what seemed like a very long time. When Larry finally turns me loose, he asks if I'm all right.

"I guess so." I say. "The doctor says the baby is okay."

"Is he positive?" asks Larry.

"That's what he told me."

Larry sits on the edge of the bed then hugs me again. My arms are wrapped around him tight, my face buried in his neck. I finally lift my head, but still holding onto Larry. Henry is standing near the door speaking with the doctor. I can't help but notice that Henry is fidgeting. This makes me wonder if the doctor's keeping something from me. Once Henry and the doctor finish their conversation, they both walk over to me. Dr. Nolan says he's going to have the nurse make the admission arrangements. He nods his head at Larry and Henry, and then leaves the room.

"How you feeling, cous?" Henry asks. Then he shakes his head side to side. "Sorry that's a stupid question."

"It's okay Henry. I knew what you meant. But why did you drop the phone like you did when I called you? I didn't know what to do. I didn't know who else to call. I had no way to reach Larry and I couldn't bring myself to call Momma. Why'd you drop the phone?" I start to cry again.

"Pam, I was stunned. I drove right over to your place. But they wouldn't let me past police lines."

"Yeah, I saw you when they were putting me on the stretcher."

"I tried to explain to them that I was your cousin and that you had called me. But they still wouldn't let me through. Sorry. I tried to get to you."

"I know. You're here now."

Henry continues. "I called Ryan, Pam. He should be on his way right now. He said he would ride the jump seat on the plane if he had to. He couldn't..."

Larry interrupts Henry. "What happened, Pam?" His face begins to collapse as tears roll down his face.

"I don't know. I don't know. That crazy fool across the street came over as soon as you and Edward left. He shot Jason as Jason walked to answer the door. He shot right through the screen door! Jason never had a chance."

Reality hits me again and I become overwhelmed with emotion. "Oh God Jason. Jason... Jason."

The fetal monitor starts to beep very fast and the blue light above the room's door begins to flash. The nurse walks hurriedly into the room. She informs Larry and Henry that they have to go now. She says she's about to give me a shot to keep me calm and to help me rest.

"Y'all can come back a little later on." The nurse says sweetly.

Larry kisses me on the forehead, smoothes my hair and says they'll be back soon and to try and get some rest. I close my eyes as the nurse thumps the syringe until it squirts fluid then sticks it into the IV connection taped to my hand.

I have so many questions that I want to ask Henry. Did he call my parents? How did Ryan take the news? Where is Ryan? My questions will have to wait as I begin to drift out of consciousness.

Chapter Eight

Feeling extremely groggy, I open my eyes and look around. The hospital staff has moved me to a private room. The soft blue color on the walls is supposed to be soothing, I assume. However, nothing can soothe me right now. I try to move but my arms and legs hurt. My muscles are sore and I have a headache. My mouth is dry. The room is cold. I pull the covers up over my shoulders. I caress my belly.

Where's Ryan? Has his flight arrived from Florida yet? Ryan, the love of my life, I need you with me so badly.

Ryan has been working in Miami for several weeks now. He was given the option to be either furloughed or to accept a better (and permanent) position as a computer programmer in Miami. We decided having a job in Miami was a lot better than no job at all. With the baby coming and me on maternity leave from Southeast Air, really there was no choice. The decision was a 'no brainer'. Besides we love the benefits that come with working for the airlines.

We both love to travel.

I had actually come to terms with Ryan being in Miami. I didn't want to go to Florida. The baby's nursery was all set up and I didn't want to change doctors. Dr. Jones had been my OB/GYN for over five years. Ryan would come home on his days off and until now, everything had worked out fine.

It wasn't as if I was pregnant and living alone. My brothers live with me. They were there for me. Jason and Larry, my dear brothers...

Larry had graduated this past June from Eastside High School. He'd always wanted to go to school in Atlanta. So when Ryan left, I invited him to stay with me. Larry had been accepted to a couple of schools. But he chose DeVry University and so far he was enjoying his stint at DeVry. Not yet nineteen, Larry is optimistic about life. The world is his oyster. He stands about five feet eleven, has beautiful brown skin and a smile that melts your heart. The ratio of men to women in Atlanta is about one to eleven, so Atlanta has definite perks with the promise of an active social life for Larry.

Jason, on the other hand, hadn't been happy with his life in Houston. When I first told him that Ryan was moving to Florida, he immediately began to worry about me. He would have volunteered to come to Atlanta to keep me company in Ryan's absence in a flash. He knew when he called to say he was sick of Texas, that he had a place with me. Jason and I had always been the closest of the seven children. He was a Scorpio and so am I. Our birthdays were only two days apart. And even though Jason was eight years older than me, we had a strong connection. We always had great fun together. Jason was loving and kind. He was a very handsome man. He was tall and always dressed sharp. He wore his hair permed, his signature throw back look. I often teased Jason, saying that he was a wanna-be pimp. All the ladies wanted to get with Jason. He was fun, generous and handsome. What was there not to love?

Jason had women in several cities. He never severed ties or burned bridges. He really could have gone anywhere, but he chose to live with me. Jason Barnett, the ladies man, God's gift to women. I teased him constantly about being a 'dog'. He would always answer by quoting the lyrics from the song *"Atomic Dog"* by George Clinton. I can hear him now.

"I have to chase the cat" he'd sing. "Nothing but the dog in me."

Jason had been married once but had long since been divorced. He has beautiful little twin daughters with his former wife and an older son from an earlier relationship. They were all still just young children, children now without a father.

Jason had been in Atlanta less than three weeks. He had come here to protect me in the absence of my spouse, just as he had protected me all my life. The one thing a person thinks could never come has come. The thing most people fear most... death. Yes, the unconceivable has happened. Jason has protected me at the cost of his life.

"God, how did this happen? Why did this happen?"

I need someone to please tell me this isn't true. But no one is around to respond to my plea. I close my eyes and begin to pray, begging God to please turn back the hands of time.

VICTORIA MIGUEL-JOSEPH

Chapter Nine

The creaky sound of the door being pushed open nearly causes me to jump out of my skin. I'm still a nervous wreck. Ryan rushes into the room, looking worried and in a state of disbelief. Ryan must have really rushed to get here because his normally well manicured appearance is shockingly disheveled. His curly brown hair looks as if it has not been combed at all today and his shirt and pants are wrinkled. Ryan's six foot five, two-hundred and ten pound frame appears awkward as he makes his way to my side.

"Pam! Oh God, Pam!" He hugs me close and places a hand on my stomach.

"The baby's okay." I say.

"You sure?"

"Yeah, Honey, I'm sure."

"And you?"

"I'm better now that you're here."

"Pam, I can't believe this! What happened? What in the world made Al do something like this?"

"That's the million dollar question, isn't it?"

Ryan's still shaking his head in disbelief.

"I mean, he just came over and shot Jason? Did Jason piss him off somehow? Did Larry? Did you?"

"No. No... Not that I know of."

"Why would he do this? Why in the world would he do something like this?" Ryan rubs his head.

"Ryan, I don't know why Weird Al would do this. All I know is that I was sitting on the couch talking to Nadine on the phone. I had just called her. Larry and Edward had pulled out of the driveway less than five minutes before he came over but Al had been watching us all day. He just came to the door and shot Jason as he approached the front door. He tried to kill me! I ran to Jason but all I saw was blood. I ran out of the house not knowing if Al was behind me or not. I just knew the back door was going to be locked but it wasn't. I fell down and Mrs. Douglas's son helped me into his house. Mrs. Douglas called the police. Do you know the bastard was sitting on the steps of his porch like he had no clue what was going on? I mean, he was just sitting there until he saw me come outside with the cops. When he saw me, he ran into the house and barricaded himself in and then he started shooting. I swear Ryan, it was awful. This fool must have had enough fire power to kill everybody in the neighborhood. He shot a police officer for God's sake! I couldn't think. I didn't know what to do. I thought the baby was dead."

Stopping for a moment to catch my breath and to blow my nose, I continue.

"During all this, the baby was balled up into a hard knot and didn't move. I just knew I had lost it."

There's a light tap on the door and Larry, Edward and Henry walk in. They all embrace and then I ask Henry the question I had to know the answer to.

"Henry, did you call Momma?"

"No, I called Gabriel. Gabriel said he would drive up to Aunt Alicia's. He couldn't believe what I was telling him. I also saw Nadine. I forgot to tell you that. At the house... I mean at the police scene, on the street. She had tried to get through but the cops had everything blocked off. She was worried sick about you. But I told her that you were not shot."

"I'll call her when I can. Have you spoken to anyone?"

"I called my mother. She said that she was headed to Aunt Alicia's, too. Knowing mother she might beat Gabriel there. Mother also said she would call the other brothers and sisters."

"Oh God. I hope Momma's okay. How do you react when you're told your child is dead?"

I shift myself in the hospital bed. For the first time since everything happened, I feel the baby move. I take Ryan's hand and place it on my stomach.

"See. I told you the doctor said the baby is all right."

Before Ryan can respond there's another tap on the door. Two men walk into the room. One is tall and skinny, the other one short and fat. The skinny one begins to speak.

"Hello. My name is Detective Graham and this is Detective Ross. We're with the Atlanta PD. Mrs. Hogan, I presume?"

"Yes."

"I'm hoping I can ask you a few questions."

"Yes."

"You live at and own the property at 1450 Woodgreen Way?"

"Yes."

"Jason Barnett is your brother, correct?" Detective Graham continues his questioning without missing a beat.

"Yes."

"Do you have any idea why Al James would want to harm your brother? Or you?"

"No."

"We spoke to his wife and children. She couldn't offer any answers either. Just so happens, none of his family was at home at the time of the crime. The officers at the scene didn't know if he had them hostage in the house or not during the shootout. But just so happens, his wife and kids were at Six Flags. Good thing, too. From the way that Mrs. James talks, he probably would have killed them, also. The woman is obviously scared to death of her husband and she claims he not only abuses her but the children, too. Al James has several priors. Assault. Domestic violence. Unlawful possession of a firearm. Just to name a few."

Now the fat detective starts to talk in a much slower drawl than the boney one.

"We are terribly sorry... about your brother, Ma'am. Things like this... things like this... ought not to happen... but they do. Makes no sense at all. But we found... found some interesting stuff at the James's house. Letters. Letters written to Mayor Jackson. Threatening-like letters... letters telling the Mayor how to run the city! How to run the city of all things! And pictures. Color photographs of you. Of you and your brothers to be more accurate. Just pictures of your comings and goings. Yep. Strange. Very strange!"

The fat officer speaks in fragments. It seems as if he has to catch his breath between sentences. I don't have the patience now. Detective Ross continues.

"Ma'am, did Mr. James... did Mr. James ever make any advances toward you? What I... I mean, do you know if he was infatuated with you?" He doesn't wait for an answer.

"We see this type of thing... thing all the time. A man fantasizes about a woman. Then he sees another man come... into the picture... and he just goes bonkers. Could be Mr. James thought... thought your brother was your boyfriend."

What the hell are they talking about? Could that be what was on the crazy sick bastard's mind? Did Weird Al have a thing for me? Why would he take pictures of us?

I begin to think about all the odd stuff that had happened over the past couple weeks. Things that didn't make any sense at all... until maybe now. The dead squirrel that showed up on the front porch two days ago... The car brakes giving out last week when they were fine just the day before... Jason could have been hurt then. He had no way to stop the car. It proceeded to go down the embankment at the end of the road and almost hit a tree.

No, this can't be. Could these things have been the handy work of Weird Al? Could he have tampered with the car brakes? Was the dead squirrel on the porch some sort of sick warning? Oh my God. What if he had went on a rampage the day of my baby shower? The Sunday when he sat in his front lawn watching us? Holy shit. This guy is a total maniac.

"Mrs. Hogan?" It's Detective Graham again with his skinny ass. He shakes me out of my reverie by speaking my name loudly again. "Mrs. Hogan?"

"Yes."

"Mrs. Hogan, how can we contact you if we need to?"

"Contact me?"

"Yes, contact you?"

I had never pondered this before? How will they contact me? It certainly will not be at 1450 Woodgreen Way. I will never sleep another night in that house. Currently my address is Crawford Long Hospital. Where do I go from here?

Detective Graham seems to be getting impatient. He's shifting his weight from one leg to the other and because he's so skinny, his bones are sticking out through his shirt. It looks as if he's going to break a hip every time he makes this move.

He clears his throat loudly. "Mrs. Hogan?"

"Yes."

He looks at me like he's saying to himself... 'oh crap... here we go... we're back to one word answers again'.

Ryan steps in and announces that he's my husband. I hadn't realized that introductions had not been made.

"You can reach us in Augusta," Ryan says. He gives my parents' telephone number and tells the detectives that we will be staying there for awhile.

Detective Graham writes the information down on the note pad he's looked at on and off since he first walked through the door. He also jots something down briefly and passes it to Ryan.

"You can reach us at that number, anytime. Alright?" He abruptly flips the note pad shut and shakes Ryan's hand. Both detectives thank us for our time and promises they'll be in touch. Then they tip their hats and leave.

Larry is the first to break the silence that envelops the room.

"Can you believe this? Why would he take pictures of us? The sick bastard! And writing letters to Mayor Jackson!"

"Damn, I knew he was weird but never in my wildest imagination did I think he was a schizophrenic." claims Ryan.

Everyone is flabbergasted. How could all of this be happening across the street and we not know about any of it? If Weird Al had such an extensive criminal record, why wasn't he behind bars? How could he own a rifle?

I finally manage to say something.

"Do you think he meant to kill me and not Jason?" I ask. "I mean... think about it. Jason had only been here two weeks. Weird Al didn't even know him. Could Al have had a crush on me? Did he think Jason was my man? Did he think he was defending my honor in some fucked up way?" My head falls in shame and disgust.

Larry shakes his head from side to side. "This is some wild and crazy shit. Un-fucking-believable shit."

Suddenly I get a very sharp pain in my stomach. So sharp it makes me scream out!

"What is it Pam?" asks Ryan.

It hurts so bad I can barely speak.

I groan. "The baby."

The fetal monitor makes the beeping sounds again. Only this time the beeps are much faster than before.

Ryan runs out of the room and returns with the nurse in a flash.

"Okay, out!" commands the nurse. "Everybody out except the husband."

The nurse begins to take my vitals and checks the fetal monitor. Ryan's standing in the corner, panicking and afraid.

The nurse looks at Ryan reassuringly and says, "False alarm. Looks like mother and baby are fine. The pain is not from contractions. I think its stress. When she's stressed, the baby's stressed. Your wife can do without any more visitors tonight and definitely no more excitement. I'm about to give her something to relax her and to make sure this baby stays put for now. The doctor will be back in the morning." She gives Ryan a stern look this time before continuing. "Sir, I suggest you get some rest also. And if you don't mind me saying so... you look like you could use some. If you plan to stay here with your wife, that chair reclines. I'll bring you some sheets and a blanket. There's an extra pillow in that closet over there."

The nurse administers my shot and asks if I need anything. I say no. She smiles warmly, leaves the room and returns promptly with the sheets and blanket as promised. Ryan thanks her. She dims the lights and exits.

Ryan tells me he'll be right back. He wants to tell Larry, Henry and Edward that I'm okay and that he's staying at the hospital with me tonight.

"I'll tell them goodbye for you," Ryan says. "And that they should go on home. They'll be back tomorrow. "

Before I can argue with him, Ryan sweetly raises my hand to his lips, kisses it and exits the room.

I start to cry. The tears come in rivers. My heart feels like it's breaking into a million pieces. This cannot be happening. This cannot be happening.

Ryan returns and is disturbed to see me crying.

"Pam, oh baby. Come on now."

He climbs into the small bed and lies next to me. He holds me tight while rubbing my belly. He doesn't speak, he allows me to grieve. I cry for a long time, lying in Ryan's arms. Eventually, I fall into a dreadful and troublesome sleep.

Chapter Ten

Ryan opens the blinds of the hospital room allowing the glaring morning sunshine to pour in.

"Pam? Pam, wake up baby. How do you feel?" He asks.

"I'm okay. What time is it?" I stretch and feel a slight twinge in my stomach.

"It's about ten forty-five. You were sedated last night and you needed the rest, so I didn't bother to wake you up. The nurse has been in already. She said all your stats are good and the baby's vitals are fine. They're releasing you this morning."

Releasing me? Releasing me to where? Where will we go?

"I'm not going back to Woodgreen Way, Ryan. I'm never going back there. Never. Never again."

"Calm down, Pam. Please don't get upset. It's not good for you or the baby. We're leaving today for Augusta. Your Momma and Dad are on the way here now."

"They are?"

"Yes, they are. And they should be here soon. We'll stay with your folks and figure out what's next later. But we do have to go down to police headquarters to speak with the detectives before heading to Augusta."

"That can't wait?" I ask, praying that it can.

"No it can't. Detective Graham called the hospital early this morning. They are really moving fast on this case. Al James is unconscious. So of course they can't get any answers from him. The detectives found new evidence and want to share it with us. "

"Fine. If that's what I got to do, that's what I got to do."

"I ran out this morning and got you some clothes and toiletries. Come on... let me help you get dressed."

The next few hours are hazy. It's almost as if I'm outside of myself and I'm looking at a movie in which I play a victim. I'm going through the motions in this fog and the fog seems to be getting thicker and thicker. It's funny how a person can remember some things with crystal clear clarity and other things you can't remember at all. My memory of Jason's death is as clear as a bell, yet this very morning is a hodgepodge of faceless hospital staff combined with empty emotions.

The paperwork for my dismissal is finally complete at two-thirty. My parents arrive just minutes later.

Momma is the first to enter the room, arms extended and opened wide. Daddy follows.

"Pam, baby."

"Momma." I catch my breath as I try to say her name. "Momma," I try again. Momma, I'm so sorry."

"Shush child. How are you and my grandbaby? You got to be strong now child. You hear? You got to be strong."

Daddy wraps his arms around the two of us, remaining silent the entire time. I can see the pain in his eyes. I know he's hurting. Momma looks as if she's aged ten years since I seen her last. She's being strong for me. I can only imagine how she's feeling. My heart hurts so so bad. It is the most intense pain, it hurts so much that it's actually hard to breathe. My air supply seems to be cut off. I don't think I'll ever recover. I sob and shake as my parents strive to soothe me. We embrace for a long while. Finally, I feel as though I have the strength to let go of them.

"I'll try to be strong Momma." I kiss her on the lips. I kiss Daddy softly on his cheek.

Speaking for the first time, Daddy simply states "We'll get through this."

I'm glad to be getting out of the hospital but nervous about going to the police station. Ryan directs Daddy down Peachtree Street towards Techwood Drive. It is a short trip from Crawford Long to the address Ryan has.

"Ryan, you sure you got the address right?" Daddy asks, obviously a bit doubtful.

This is no regular police station. It looks like an old tore up warehouse. It's huge and nothing says police station.

"Yes sir, this is the address Detective Graham gave me. He wrote it down himself then handed me the paper."

We pull up and park on the street right outside of the mysterious building. There are no windows other than the double glass entry doors which have old newspapers covering them.

Daddy presses the door-bell. A buzzer sounds and the door clicks, then opens. We enter cautiously. As we walk up to the one and only desk we see, a desk Sergeant looks up and smiles.

"Good afternoon folks. May I help you?"

"Yes. I'm Ryan Hogan. This is my wife Pam and her parents, Mr. and Mrs. Barnett. We are here to see Detectives Graham and Ross. They're expecting us."

Immediately, an officer escorts us to Detective Graham's desk.

The frightfully thin man stands to meet Momma and Daddy. Detective Ross walks toward us eating a bag of chips and drinking a Coke.

Fat ass.

Detective Ross places both the chips and the Coke down on the desk, wipes his hands on his pants then shakes Daddy's and Ryan's hand. Momma's looking at Detective Ross like he's some kind of fool. She nods her head at him.

Politely, Detective Ross pulls up a chair and asks if I want to sit down. I suppose I'm receiving this gesture because of my pregnancy, since no one else is extended the same courtesy.

Just as before, Detective Graham speaks first and Detective Ross observes. He flips through his little black note pad.

"Let's see here. We appreciate y'all folks coming down here. I know y'all anxious to get going. Uhh. Let's see. Mr. Hogan? You and your wife still planning to be in Augusta... and can still be reached at 706-883-9256?"

"Yes. That's correct." answers Ryan.

"Okay then." The detective licks his lips and continues.

"So the reason we asked you to stop by is that we found some more evidence that we thought you'd be interested to see."

In an oddly high pitch, I ask, "What is it?"

"Well, we found some more photographs. Only these are intimate photos..." He clears his throat. "...of you and your husband. There are even a couple of you alone, one of you in the shower and one with you in pajamas while doing the laundry."

I gasp.

Oh my God. Does this mean that Weird Al had access to my home? He had come into my home?

I take a big swallow. I feel as if my tongue is stuck in my throat. Somehow I manage to get the words out.

"Detective, this man came into my home and violated my

privacy? Was he a peeping Tom?"

Detective Ross steps in now.

"It certainly looks that way, Mrs. Hogan. Did you have a key hidden outside? Or did you ever hear anyone, or anything?"

I'm trying really hard to focus and to think before answering.

"Well, there have always been times when I thought I heard something. You know, like bumps in the night or that feeling that someone's watching you? There was this one time when I turned quickly in the shower, feeling as if someone was there. I got out the shower and walked through the house because that feeling that someone was watching me was so strong. But I never mentioned it to anyone. I just assumed it was all in my head."

"As far as we can tell, Mr. James didn't enter the house after he murdered your brother. But currently, we're still dusting for prints."

"May I see the photographs?"

Ryan looks at me sympathetically. "Pam, are you sure you want to see them?"

"Yes. I'm sure."

Detective Graham opens a large vanilla envelope and pulls out some Polaroid snapshots encased in plastic. He passes them to me.

I remove the plastic and there for all the world to see... is Ryan and me making love on our waterbed. The picture is clear as rain. The picture of me in the shower is dark and not as clear. But it is definitely my backside in the picture. Embarrassed, I pass the photos back to Detective Graham without viewing all of them.

"Where did you find these?" I want to know.

"They were under the mattress in Mr. James's bedroom."

I can't take anymore of this. I'm beginning to feel as if I'm suffocating. "Are we finished?" I ask. "I don't feel very well."

"Yes." The detectives answered in unison.

Ryan helps me up from the chair. Momma takes me by the arm

and walks me out of this depressing place. Daddy remains behind, speaking with the detectives. He has a worried expression on his face, yet he attempts to smile at me as I look back.

Daddy finally comes back to the car. We can now get moving. Ryan gives Daddy directions and before we know it we're on our way home.

At last, we're leaving this cruel and wicked city, headed east as the sun sets in the west. We're on our way home... on our way to Augusta. I'm exhausted. The baby seems to be getting heavier by the minute.

Daddy's driving Aunt Rose's car, a brand new Cadillac Deville. He left his beloved Chevy truck at home. And even still in the Caddy, it's a tight fit with all of us traveling. I'm sitting in the back seat between Larry and Ryan, leaning over towards the front seat so I that can be closer to Momma and Daddy. I feel really out of it. I dread what happens next. I dread my life at this point.

I want to ask Momma and Daddy if they went to the coroner to see Jason's body before arriving at the hospital. But I can't bring myself to say the words. I have so many questions. Where is Jason's body now? Are they doing an autopsy? Is his body in Augusta already? Or is he on his way back to Augusta now, just as we are?

As if to answer my question, a long black hearse whizzes by traveling at least eighty miles per hour.

Is that Jason's ride home?

Home. Augusta, Georgia is home, my real home. Jason will be buried in a small town just outside of Augusta. Never thought I'd be going back to Augusta under these circumstances. Never.

People from all over the world know of Augusta, Georgia. Some know of Augusta, Georgia because of the golf course at Augusta National. The world's most prestigious golf tournament, the Masters, is played at Augusta National. The Masters brings thousands of tourists to our fair city each year. Others know about Augusta because of James Brown, Godfather of Soul. 'Augusta G-A', James Brown fans and native Augustans would always say.

But for me at the moment, Augusta is neither golf haven nor soul town. Instead, Augusta is a place of refuge. It's the place I call home.

Victoria Miguel-Joseph

Chapter Eleven

Growing up in Augusta, my siblings and I lived a relatively good life. We were by no means rich, but we certainly weren't dirt poor either. Daddy had only a sixth grade education. Yet he's the smartest man I know. Daddy always invested in real estate... purchasing a small lot of land or a small house here and there. Daddy was very shrewd. Matter of fact, some folks called him downright stingy. Amongst those that referred to my Daddy as such, was his loving wife and my Momma. But being shrewd was one of the characteristics that I admire most about my Dad. You have to wake up pretty early in the morning to pull something over on Daddy. He was cool as they come. As Daddy always says, "I can tell you what time it is without looking at my watch." Now that's pretty damn cool.

In the early years of my parent's marriage, they lived in a small shack on my paternal grandmother's property in Evans, Georgia.

The elder children, Gabriel, Jason and Lois, were delivered by mid-wives in that very shack. By the time I was born, the family was living in a slightly bigger five room shot-gun house located on a street ironically named Lucky Street. The name certainly didn't reflect the reality. There was absolutely nothing lucky about it. Seven children and two adults occupied the house by the time Larry was born. All the boys shared a room. There were two sets of bunk beds tightly positioned in the small room. Lois and I shared a room. Larry slept with Momma and Daddy. A small kitchen and living room completed the space.

One memory that will always stand out in my mind occurred when I was only seven years old. It was a freak accident that happened on Halloween. Yep. All Hallows Eve.

My brother Ethan and I were playing cards in the tiny living room. Larry was only a year old at the time and he was in the room with us playing with a small red truck. Momma stood in the kitchen doing dishes when she looked out the small window above the sink to see a drunk driver plow through the porch next door and straight into the side of our house. Momma later told the police that she tried to scream when she saw the car coming but no sound came out of her mouth. The vehicle hit the house with such force that it caused Ethan and me to be lifted from our seats and thrown to the floor. The old-fashioned electric floor heater in the room fell on top of Larry. Ethan was disoriented and lying beneath the rubble of sheetrock and furniture. I had been pitched to the other side of the room. I managed to get up and that's when I saw Larry pinned underneath the heater. My adrenaline kicked in and went into overdrive. I ran across the room faster than I'd ever run before. I raised the heater from on top of my baby brother. In the end, we were all okay. The only serious injury sustained was a second degree burn on Larry's right hand, a scar that's visible to this very day.

The white cops had a good ole' time that night making jokes, saying things like our family was tricked instead of treated that Halloween. Ha, ha, ha. The Barnett's were not laughing. We were mad as hell. Needless to say, my brothers and I didn't go trick or treating that night. We had had enough scary shit for one day.

The year was 1966, and times were tense during that era. The civil rights movement was in high gear. Again, I was just a kid, yet I remember watching the news and seeing Dr. Martin Luther King, Jr. I remember thinking that this good looking Negro man has a powerful voice. I got chills just hearing him speak. At that time, I understood what the civil rights movement was about and I was also smart enough to know that things were changing.

We moved away from Lucky Street a couple years after the Halloween episode. Gabriel and Jason had graduated from high school, joining the Air Force and Navy, respectively. Gabriel was stationed in Okinawa, Japan. Jason was based somewhere in southern California... San Diego, I think. My sister, Lois, was a senior at T.W. Josey High School and was determined to remain there. Lois had no plans of changing schools her senior year. Ethan did change schools and entered John M. Tutt. At the time, Karl and I went to Tutt, too, since the school was grades one through twelve.

Daddy had said that city life in Augusta was changing for the worst and he didn't want his children growing up in that sort of surrounding. The area we moved to was called Martinez. It was very rural and very White. 'Country' is what Lois called it. Lois hated Martinez. She rebelled at every opportunity. Lois was always a hell raiser. She's seven years older than me and we're as different as night and day. Lois spent as little time as possible in Martinez. She said... and I quote "Martinez is as country as an outdoor shit house" unquote. Lois and I were not really close growing up. I was the annoying little sister that constantly got in her way. But regardless to that fact, I knew Lois would be there for me if I needed her.

I liked our new home in Martinez. As a matter of fact, I not only liked our house because it was bigger than the tiny house on

Lucky Street... I really liked Martinez. It was quiet, much unlike life on Lucky Street. I enjoyed being surrounded by all the trees and I loved the little creek that ran alongside our property. Sometimes I would sit on the bank of that creek for hours, thinking and dreaming. I imagined that one day I'd be rich and famous. I would have a big house and a fancy car. I'd have two beautiful kids and a cat and a dog. I imagined that my husband would be a good-looking powerful man like Dr. King. I would picture the life ahead of me as I pitched pebbles into the water, watching the ripples they made. I called the creek 'my spot'. And... I didn't appreciate anyone intruding on my time there.

There was this boy that lived around the corner from our house. He starting picking on me and giving me a hard time the first day he laid eyes on me. Basically, he was a ruffian and a trouble maker. His name was Jesse Thomas. Jesse was no good and he looked the part. Jesse couldn't have been no more than five-feet two inches tall and probably weighed around one hundred sixty pounds. He must have been around fourteen years old. He didn't go to school so I really didn't know how old he was. But Jesse had one distinguishing feature that set him apart from most boys his age. He had a deep a scar on his face that ran from his left eye across his nose and all the way down to his cheek to the right side of his chin. No one knew how Jesse got the scar, although there were many speculations. Some said his Momma did it. The story goes that one night Jesse tried to kill his Momma in her sleep. He tried to strangle her with a rope but supposedly Jesse's mom slept with a butcher knife under her pillow. So as Jesse tightened the rope around her neck, his mom grabbed the knife and slashed his face. They say that's why his Momma's not around and why Jesse lives with his Grandma. Others claim Jesse went up against a gang of five boys and that earned him the scar on his face. All I know is that I constantly felt uneasy whenever he was around me. I never liked the way he licked his lips whenever he looked at me. When I was ten, Jesse showed up at my favorite spot. I was sitting there day dreaming, swinging my legs, and watching the minnows in the stream when someone sneaked up behind me and grabbed me around my neck pulling me to my feet. He had me in a wrestling-like head lock position, only vertical. I tried to wriggle free, wanting to see the face of the person that grabbed me. I could feel his breath on my neck. It made my flesh crawl. But when I see a hand sliding down inside my pants, trying to pull my panties down... I immediately realized two things... one... the punk was going to rape me and two... it had to be Jesse Thomas. I screamed as loud as I could then I took a huge bite out of his arm. He yelped and let go of me. I kicked him in the shin with all my power throwing myself off balance. I almost fell into the creek but I didn't and I took off running. He was nursing his wounds while I was running towards my house.

I never told anyone what had happened that day because I was afraid they might accuse me of provoking Jesse somehow. I was a tough kid and even though I was small in size, I had the heart of a lion. Jesse Thomas never bothered me again. Every time I saw him after that, Jesse looked the other way.

Daddy had been right about Augusta becoming rough. In May 1970, six black men died in a single night on the streets of Augusta. It all started because a sixteen year old black youth was allegedly tortured in jail and died there. Soon after his death, burning and looting took place. On television, it was reported that white motorists were pulled from their cars by black men and beaten. Before we knew it, Augusta was the scene of the worst racial violence in years. The rioting lasted all night, finally ending the next day before dawn. At the end of the riot, six black men had been shot in the back by police and died.

Integration took place that same year. I was entering the seventh grade. I made the one and only failing grade I ever received in school during the first six weeks. Adjusting to being educated in the 'White World' of integration was not easy. However, once I learned the rules of the game, I never forgot them and I always executed my every action based on them. I could play the game to get ahead just as well as anyone else. Very early on, I learned when to speak up and when to keep my mouth shut.

Throughout elementary and even high school, I had a hard time making friends. Most girls in my neighborhood and the ones at school, too, assumed I had an attitude. I would overhear them whisper things like "she thinks she's cute." Hell, I knew I was cute. Besides the fact that everyone said so, I felt that I was beautiful inside which automatically makes you beautiful outside.

But the haters implied that I thought I was cute because of my skin color and my eyes. I didn't ask for blue eyes or to be light skinned... I can thank my granddaddy for that.

Being a light skinned Black person in the sixties and early seventies was not easy. Other Blacks called light-skinned Blacks 'red' or 'high yellow'. There were many dark-skinned Blacks that hated light skinned Blacks. It was hard for all Blacks during this time. Back then, if you were dark skinned, White people didn't want to give you the time of day. Yet, some seem to tolerate light skinned Blacks. And then there were some Black people that thought they were better than other Blacks. Oh yeah, some Black folk actual thought that if they were light skinned, they were better.

Blacks have forever suffered from that old house nigger, field nigger syndrome – a syndrome that was, of course, manufactured solely by the White man – yet immortalized by the Black man. It's a concept that I could never relate to. My Momma is light skinned and my Daddy's skin is black as chimney soot, thus the nickname 'Black'.

I love both my parents to death and never missed an opportunity to let anyone know this. We were brought up to respect people for who they are, not because of their skin color.

Black Barnett has been in business for as long as I can remember. Daddy operates a Barbershop in an area where a lot of my school mates live. The area, called the 'Hill' is really named Sand Hill. But you know how we do... everything and everyone gets a nickname. Every young man and their father on the hill, knows my dad.

That whole 'she's light and think she's better than me theory', that some of the school kids tried to brand me with, just didn't hold up... no matter how hard they tried to make it stick.

One thing I've come to know in life is that people can be jealous for no reason at all. Or they can act petty because they have nothing better to do. I came to this realization at an early age. A lot of the girls in school hated my guts. I had to learn at a very young age to do what's in my heart and to follow my first instinct. I had to be a leader and not a follower. I went for the gusto even if others didn't understand why. There were times when I was ridiculed or teased for my actions. Yet, I always tried to follow my passion and my dreams. Most of my peers simply thought I was crazy or that I was just trying to be like the White folk, acting better than I really was. I was talked about for being a cheerleader and being popular, for having white friends, for being smart and for even being the teacher's pet.

I had only one really close friend in school and that was Bebe. Bebe and I were about as different as two people could be. I was outgoing and very involved in school activities. Bebe was shy, quiet as a church mouse.

Bebe's skin was the color of milk chocolate. She was shapely and full-figured. She was beautiful. Bebe had no idea the affect she had on boys. She always remained quiet and kept basically to herself except for the time we spent together.

In my junior year of high school, Daddy bought me this fly car. It was a 1970 Ford Torino, red with white racing stripes. It wasn't the typical girl car. Then again, I wasn't a typical girl.

Each morning, I would pick Bebe up at her house on Magnolia Lane. We would ride to school together, laughing and talking about school and sharing our hopes and our dreams. We were cool like that.

Bebe was a great listener and the person that knew me the best. But even Bebe didn't know all my true feelings and secrets. Bebe would have been shocked and appalled. She may have even shunned our friendship. I think that's what scared me the most, losing Bebe's friendship. As strong as I pretended to be... I was afraid to confide my true feelings to those I love. I lived a life burdened with secrets never told.

No one could have understood. There were times when I hated the way I looked. My looks seemed to always bring me problems — problems that I didn't understand but problems that I could easily blame on my appearance. What else could it have been? I certainly didn't ask to be treated differently. Why did Jesse try to attack me? What could have caused a teacher to seduce me in the laboratory closet or make a relative make inappropriate advances? Why did an older neighbor whisper unsuitable words in my ear when no one was looking? Why did my first date try to rape me? I was a magnet for inappropriate sexual behavior and I hated myself for it.

As a young adult, I blamed my looks for a lot of things that happened to me. I couldn't confide in anyone about the things happening in my life. Definitely not my parents. My sister and I were not close growing up. I couldn't even confide in Bebe. Even now as a grown woman, thinking about certain events cause me deep pain and uncontrollable shame.

My fondest memories of childhood are going to Broad Street in downtown Augusta. Everyone did their shopping downtown on

Broad Street. There were no malls in Augusta when I was growing up. I didn't even know what a mall was back then. Broad Street was the heart of Augusta. Broad Street was always bustling with activity. It was that hustle and bustle that excited me.

Daddy would pile us into his light green deuce and a quarter and drive us into town. He'd treat all seven of us to twenty-five cent hot dogs at Bowers and penny candy at H.L. Greens. I loved those Bowers hot dogs. I lived for those trips with Daddy, which came far and few between. Spending time with us was not Daddy's priority. Working and being able to support his family was.

The other true pleasure I experienced growing up was going 'up the road'. That's what my family called traveling to Columbia County.

Columbia County is about twenty five miles outside of Augusta. Momma and Daddy were born in Columbia County, Evans, GA. My maternal Grandmother, Momma Corletta, God-fearing, church-going woman that she was, raised her thirteen children in a no nonsense type fashion in Columbia County. My grandfather, Daddy Caine, was fifteen years older than Momma Corletta. He had passed away by the time I was five. But all my life, I heard tales about my granddaddy. Tales about how he'd pass himself off for White in order to buy goods and to be able to own land. There were tales like the one which claimed he had twenty-eight children. From what my Momma says, it's actually true that no one knew exactly how many children Daddy Caine had really fathered. Daddy Caine had been quite the ladies man back in his day.

'Up the road' was really fun and where I always wanted to be`. There were dirt roads, baseball fields and country stores. Uncle Ross, Momma's oldest brother, owned a store with a baseball diamond behind it. Country folks from all around Columbia, Richmond and Lincoln County came to the baseball games. Inside the store were big jars of pigs' feet, beef jerky and fat dill pickles. A juke box played

Stevie Wonder, Smokey Robinson and all the Motown sounds from the sixties. A pool table was in the middle of the store. The men played billiards for money, while others threw dice in a corner or pitched pennies. When I was little I loved to dance and everyone 'up the road' loved to see me dance. People would pay me quarters to dance for them. I can see myself in pigtails, dancing around the pool table, laughing until my stomach hurt and buying myself Jolly Rancher candies with my newly earned money.

Everybody in the country enjoyed life. Everybody was carefree and happy. Everyone knew everyone else. Everyone was kind. Everyone was friendly. I felt safe and happy 'up the road'. As kids, my family traveled to the country together. We had played there together and we had laughed there together. I have a million happy memories, all from 'up the road'.

Enough reminiscing.

Taking a deep breath, I feel my heart ache as I wish I could turn back the hands of time.

Looking out the car window, a sign reads 'Greensboro'. We still have about an hour to go before reaching Augusta.

I lean back and rub my stomach, thinking again about Jason. Jason is going to be buried 'up the road' at Mt. Canaan Baptist Church. Just like me, he had loved being there. Soon, he will never have to leave. Jason would remain 'up the road' forever.

Chapter Twelve

I wake up in my father's bed disoriented and confused. Another day has passed... I suppose. For a moment, I'm thinking everything is normal. I'm simply at my parent's house visiting. But then again, I am in my father's bed and not the guest room. Why is that?

I hear voices... lots of different voices in another part of the house. I can clearly make out one voice in particular. I hear my Aunt Mary speaking in her distinctive high pitch voice that sounds almost like she's singing instead of talking. I hear her saying "...that child has been through too much, way too much."

She's talking about me. That much I'm sure of. Yes. Too much. I agree. I've been through too much. An old saying suddenly pops into my head...'that which does not kill us makes us stronger'. At the moment I have serious doubts about this. No offense, God.

I get up out of the bed and make my way into the living room. Yep, the gang's all here... Momma, five of her eight sisters, my sister Lois, all of my remaining brothers and about seven or eight first cousins. I walk into the living room and everyone goes silent. You can hear a mouse pissin' on cotton.

"Hi," I say in barely a whisper.

"Hey baby." Momma says. "How you feelin'?"

"I'm okay, Ma. How are you holding up?"

"Don't worry about me sugar. Momma's doing just fine. Can I get you something to eat?"

"No, Momma. I don't want anything to eat."

Everybody's still looking at me like they're expecting me to freak out or pass out or do something strange. They're all handling me with kid gloves. They act like I might break even if someone spoke too loudly. I suppose Momma told all of them that she think I shouldn't attend Jason's funeral service. I guess they're all conspiring against me, siding with Momma. They're trying to get me to stay home and trying to figure out who's going to have to babysit and stay home with me. Momma thinks I'll go into labor or something if I go to the funeral. But it really doesn't matter what she thinks or what everyone else has to say. I'm going. I don't give a shit. Come hell or high water, I am going to my brother's funeral!

I suppose I am behaving badly. I refuse to eat. I don't have an appetite. But I will drink. Drink liquor that is. I fully realize that drinking at this stage of my pregnancy is not good, but it's the only thing that numbs the pain.

I walk towards the settee (that's what Momma always called the sofa) and everyone in the room starts in on me with all their 'baby stay strong' and 'it'll be all right sugar'. Everyone is telling me that I have to eat for the baby's sake. And that I certainly don't need any liquor. You got to take care of yourself and the baby they keep saying. But do I care? Hell no. Fuck the baby! Fuck all y'all! Fuck everything! They have no idea what I'm feeling. I'm just trying to survive... just trying to numb the pain.

When Never Comes Again

It's crazy how fast things can happen... how fast things can change. Without asking permission, things happen that change our lives forever. Things happen when we are least prepared and when we are most prepared. The very thing I was so concerned about losing two days before, I no longer cared if it lived or died. I want to die. It's not fair that I'm alive and Jason is dead. I know it's because of me that Jason is dead. He was in my house. He died at the hand of my crazy neighbor. And all I want now is to join him.

The phone rings. A distraction, thank goodness! Now maybe everybody will shut the hell up and leave me the fuck alone! Just stop staring at me, please! Gabriel picks up the phone.

"Hello. Yes. No. This is Gabriel Barnett, brother of the victim." Gabriel fidgets with the phone cord, twirling it until it becomes tighter and tighter around his index finger.

"No," he continues. "Yes. Yes. Thank you for letting us know." He hangs up the phone and tries to whisper unsuccessfully. I overhear Gabriel telling Momma that Weird Al has died. Momma's shoulders fall and Gabriel puts an arm around them. I'm not sure how I feel about this news. At first I feel nothing. I'm numb. But then in the same breath, I realize that I'm mad! I'm mean, pissed and fire-breathing mad! The son-of-a-bitch ought to be dead I say in my head. He and his entire goddamn family should be dead! I'll never ever forgive them for ruining my life... my family's life! How can I?

Momma speaks in a low voice. Suddenly I'm transported back to the moment. The thoughts in my head vanish. Momma's telling Gabriel that she's thankful we won't have to go to trial and that she's relieved it's over. Gabriel simply nods his head in agreement. His eyes are tearing up.

Gabriel and Jason were like two peas in a pod. Only a year apart in age, the two had been close all their entire lives. They ran the streets together, went to school together and even joined the Armed

Forces at the same time. I know that Gabriel is going to be lost without Jason. Hell, we are all going to be lost without Jason.

Momma sits down on the couch. She lowers head and puts her face in her hands. She begins to cry. I cannot stand to see Momma cry. My knees get weak and immediately tears are rolling down my face, too. I wobble in my pregnant way over to Momma and kneel down beside her. I take her hands away from her face then I put my arms around her soft flabby body. I kiss her cheek then hug her as close as my large belly allows me. My heart is breaking for her. I've been so wrapped up in my own feelings that I never thought about poor Momma. Momma is definitely not in the best of health herself. She has hypertension and diabetes. Plus she's having an extremely bad hair day! I release her and smooth her unruly hair.

"Momma, your hair is wreaking!" I say smiling at the same time.

She smiles right back at me through her own tears. "I know child. But you can't talk cause yours ain't no better. Your hair is... how'd you put it? Wreakin? Well yours is wreakin, too!"

I run my hand across the top of my head. She's right! I probably look like Don King's lost twin or something right about now.

"Yeah, you got that right. My hair is a mess!"

I try to get to my feet then rub my head... attempting to smooth this wild ass hair of mine.

"Momma, I'll get Lois to do something with my hair. Don't worry. Is she going to do yours today?"

"Nah... Baby... Mary's gonna pull the hot comb through mine. And speaking of that, we better get started if we going to make it to the funeral parlor on time."

Back to reality. Damn!

"Mary!" Momma yells. "You ready to get started on this head of mine?"

And with that she's back to her strong self again, taking care of things that need taking care of. The Rock of Gibraltar, that's Momma.

Jason's body would be ready for viewing by the family this afternoon. Later tonight the wake is being held. Funny that it's called a 'wake' when the main attraction is far from being awake. Momma agreed that I could attend the viewing and then the wake. But I assume she still thinks she's barring me from the funeral.

"But I've got news for her and everyone else," I say out loud and only to myself as I wobble down the hall looking for Lois.

Lois washed, rolled, and styled my hair. She decided that I should wear it down and straight, with just a little curl on the ends. This was a quickie hairdo. Neither Lois nor I had the patience for much more than a simple hairdo. As Lois finished fussing with the one stray curl, she asked me if I still had my mind set on attending the funeral.

"I sure do," I say defiantly. "I'm not going to miss saying goodbye to my brother."

"You could say goodbye tonight at the wake."

"Well, I don't want to say goodbye at the wake! I want to go to the funeral like everybody else!"

"Everybody else hasn't been through the trauma you've been through Pam." Lois says as her nose turns red and I know she's about to get upset.

Lois continues.

"Sis, we just don't want you to have to go through no more than you have to. You've been through enough. And what's up with all this nonsense with you drinking alcohol and shit? Pam, I know you're upset, but drinking is not going to bring Jason back.

It's only going to hurt the baby and possibly hurt you, too. You know Jason wouldn't want that. You know how excited he was about this baby."

"I know."

"So will you stop drinking and at least try to eat some food?"

I mumble. "I guess so."

"Now that you're talking like you got a little sense... and because you seem determined to go to the funeral... have you considered what you might wear? It's not like you packed and brought anything with you when you came home to Augusta."

"Nope. Don't have a clue. All I have is basically the clothes on my back. I slept in Momma's nightgown."

"Feel like a trip to the mall? We got plenty of time before we have to leave for the funeral home. I need to pick up some pantyhose. We could run into Rich's. Rich's has a maternity department. So how about it? You need to get out of this house anyhow. You haven't left since you got here."

"Alright, cool. Let me slip on something. I'll find something of Momma's to put on and I'll be ready to go in about twenty minutes." I walk over to Lois... kiss her cheek and say, "Thanks Sis... I love you."

"I love you, too. But don't be getting all mushy and shit on me." Lois laughs. "You know I can't stand that kinda shit."

"Yeah, I know. Forgive me," I say, as I smile and wobble to Momma's bedroom to find something too little for me to change into.

The Augusta Mall is packed today and it's only Wednesday. Lois finds a parking space close to the entrance that reads "For Expectant Mothers Only."

"How fortunate for us you're pregnant," she snickers, as she swings her blue '81 Chevrolet Jimmy into the parking space like a professional race car driver.

We enter Rich's department store. It feels nice and cool. It's only ninety degrees today. We make our way to the hosiery department and Lois becomes engrossed in selecting just the right pair of pantyhose. I browse around at the belts knowing there's not a single outfit in my closet that requires a belt. I pick one up anyway and admire the design. I'm still looking at the belt when I hear my name, my maiden name.

"Pamela? Pam Barnett?"

I look up and standing in front of me is Barbosia Atkins. We had attended elementary and most of high school together. We were never friends. We were simply acquaintances. I never cared much for Barbosia. She had a big mouth. She always had something to say but the words that came out of her mouth never meant much of anything. I think she just liked to hear herself talk.

"Hi Barbosia," I say, as my eyes travel from her head then to her feet. She hasn't changed much since high school... still slim and tall with beautiful pecan brown skin, big brown eyes and shiny short black hair that was always cut in the most recent style. Barbosia has the prettiest, deepest dimples I've ever seen.

She is a beautiful girl, but her personality made her seem much less attractive.

"Oh my God!" Barbosia exclaims. "I thought that was you!" Her eyes travel to my stomach and she continues to speak loudly.

"Whoa, girl! You are very pregnant! When's your baby due? Soon, I'd say from the size of your belly. I had heard you got married. You were what... about eighteen or so when you married? My goodness girl that's so young! Why'd you get married so young? Everyone thought you must have been pregnant then. Where's your husband? I'd love to meet him. Heard he's a New Yorker. Is he here with you?" She only slows down to catch her breath.

I roll my eyes then I stare at her unbelievingly. Some things never change. Barbosia has managed to pepper me with a half dozen questions in about five seconds! Still a big mouth! Talking loud and saying nothing. I feel a twinge in my back and begin to rub it.

"No, my husband is not here with me."

Before I could say anything else, Lois appears by my side and takes over.

"Pam, we need to get going. We have places to be, people to see," she says quickly as she winks at me.

I know that Lois realizes that I don't want to talk to this person. She probably rushed over as soon as she heard Barbosia firing away with all her questions and judgments. Augusta's a small town and just about everybody knows everyone else. I'm sure Lois recognizes Barbosia Atkins. As a matter of fact, I think Lois may have graduated with one of Barbosia's older sisters.

"Yep, you're right," I respond hurriedly, too, letting Lois know that I've caught on.

"Got to run Barbosia. You take care."

"Toot-a-loo," sings Lois as she wiggles a few fingers in Barbosia's face and pulls me away by the arm at the same time. Barbosia is left with her mouth hanging open. If she even said goodbye, I didn't hear it. Besides, do I care?

Before I know it, Lois and I are on the escalator headed to the maternity department. Lois looks at me then bursts out laughing.

"I knew you were cornered." Lois is still cracking up. She's holding her stomach, she's laughing so hard. "Thought I'd better lend you a hand. Man, that girl is a piece of work! 'Everybody thought you were pregnant then'" Lois mimics. "Damn she got a lot of nerve!"

"You know who she is, right?" I ask.

"Oh yeah, I know who she is. She's one of them Atkins girls," Lois says purposely.

I smile.

Lois puts her nose up in the air.

"She one of those 'think they high and mighty girls that also talks way too much.' She went to school with you."

"Oh yeah. You got it. And she was a pain in the ass then, too. Didn't you graduate from Josey with one of her sisters?"

"Yep. Auriel Atkins. She was okay. We were never friends or anything but she was cool. She did talk a lot too though... must run in the family! Talk, talk, talk... talk, talk! I think she lives in Dallas or somewhere in Texas now."

Lois is definitely in the power shopping mode. I can barely keep up with her. When we reach the bottom of the escalator, she turns the corner like she's on wheels. I hang on to both sides as I carefully and slowly step off.

"Okay," Lois says frowning as she looks back over her shoulder at me.

I can read her mind. She's saying bring your slow ass on.

Lois continues.

"Enough about the Atkins sisters. We are on a mission, remember? Here's maternity. Let's find my very pregnant sister something cute to wear and then we need to buy you some shoes... cause your little ass feet sho-nuff can't fit into mine."

VICTORIA MIGUEL-JOSEPH

Chapter Thirteen

Nervously, I sit outside the viewing parlor of the funeral home. I look like a young, fat kid wearing my new sleeveless dress made of blue and white seersucker fabric. The length of the dress comes to about four inches above my knees, which totally adds to the childlike character. What in the world were Lois and I thinking, buying this little immature looking maternity outfit?

My brand new Liz Claiborne navy slip-on shoes are comfortable but cute. These were the only pair I could find that looked half-way okay with the dress. My hair is tied back with a navy and white ribbon. Lois did a great job curling my hair earlier but the heat of the day caused me to pull it up off my neck.

Jacob's Funeral Home has long been an icon in this neighborhood. Daddy must have some sort of connection with the Jacob's family because everyone that's ever died on his side of the family, the body has been handled by Jacob's. Aaron Jacob, the owner, attended school with Gabriel and Jason. His parents had long since passed on and he now operated the funeral home with the assistance of several employees. The business appears to be thriving. Death is a great investment. It's guaranteed.

The funeral home is a quaint place, even charming, if a funeral home can be described that way. In the foyer there are big beautiful live tropical plants strategically placed all over. A Zen-like water fountain gurgles softly. Reproductions of eighteenth century Queen Anne furnishings offer a light, comfortable and graceful appearance throughout. The waiting area which is directly outside the viewing parlor has beautiful floor-to-ceiling windows which allow a perfect view to the garden area. This time of year the garden is in full bloom with gorgeous red and white tiger lilies, pink, white and red begonias and red and yellow tea roses. The shrubbery and lawn are the greenest of greens and meticulously manicured. Just looking at this place, I could swear it's a Spa where people come to renew, revive and rejuvenate. Not a place where the dead are brought to be embalmed then dressed up and put on public display.

I've sat here for a least an hour, staring out the window and nervously awaiting my moment to go in and see Jason's body. Many have come to pay their respect and I've graciously accepted the condolences of what seems like a zillion family and friends. Whether entering or leaving, every visitor made their way over to me to speak. Some of the words spoken were comforting and others just outright stupid. But it's the thought that counts so everyone says.

Now that it seems as if everyone in Augusta has viewed Jason's body, it's my turn. I guardedly make my way to the casket. Oomph! The baby kicks me in the rib as if to urge me on. I reach the casket and my heart skips a beat. Jason looks peaceful. People always say that, but he really does. He looks peaceful and happy. There's a content smile on his face. He looks free. My heart skips another beat. Only this time, I feel like someone's twisting it. I try to compose myself. I try to tell myself that Jason's okay. That he's in a better place. But then the reality of it all comes down on me like a sledge hammer. The fact remains... Jason is dead. I will never hear his laughter again. We will never hang out together again.

Before I can help myself, I throw my arms around the casket and lay my cheek upon Jason's cold hard face, sobbing uncontrollably and apologizing again and again.

"Jason, I am so sorry! I'm so sorry, Jason! Jason, I'm sorry! You're here because of me. It's all my fault, Jason. It should have been me, Jason. It was supposed to be me!"

Wanting to climb inside the casket, I try to lift my leg but my stomach gets in the way. I can't seem to lift my leg more than a couple of feet off the floor. I just want to lie next to Jason. I want to join him. I need to join him.

It actually takes Gabriel, Ethan and Karl to pull me away from Jason's casket and to get me out of the parlor. Larry and Lois try to calm Momma as she weeps softly in Lois's arms. My grief is more than she can handle. Daddy holds on to his stern demeanor but he's obviously shaken as he takes off his glasses and wipes his eyes.

I continue to scream 'I'm sorry' all the way to the car. I just want to die. I just want to be with Jason. But my death is not imminent and the life inside of me will not let me forget this. So for now anyway, I just pray that this baby will stop punching me in my ribs.

VICTORIA MIGUEL-JOSEPH

Chapter Fourteen

Momma and Daddy are sitting on the front pew in the church. It's half of a pew really, with a large column next to it that appears to be holding up the entire ceiling. I'm sitting in the pew behind them. For the first time in my life I see the two of them holding hands. I can see Momma's face twitch as it sometimes does when she's nervous. Daddy's still as stone. The choir is loudly singing *"His Eye is on the Sparrow."* I hear muffled sobs all around me. My head is pounding and I can hear my heart beat, despite the choir. Hindsight is twenty-twenty because Momma was right. I shouldn't have come today.

After the burial, everybody congregates at the family house. There's lots of food and drink. Funerals always end up like a party once the repast is over. Everyone gathers to talk about the dead and to drink like there really is something to celebrate.

As I walk around aimlessly listening as people tell stories about 'good old' Jason, finally, I just can't tolerate it. I start to drink. My pal Hennessey and I begin to get very cozy as old friends tend to do. I start to drink like there's no tomorrow... which in my opinion, there isn't. Everyone around truly thinks I've lost my ever-loving mind. My family is on my heels, trying to take the glass and my old pal Hennessey away. Finally, Gabriel has had enough. Before I know it he snatches the bottle of Hennessey out of my hands then slaps the glass. I watch the glass hit the cement floor of the carport and the liquor splash out of it. All I can manage to say is "Why didn't the glass break?"

Gabrielle gives me the evil eye then starts yelling at me.

"If you don't stop hurting the life inside of you, I will snatch that baby right out of you myself!"

I look at him and slur "Just try it... I'd like to see it!"

Gabriel knows how stubborn and hardheaded I can be. He didn't have the patience for me at this moment. He grabs me by the arm and begins to pull me into the house. Next he proceeds to announce to the world...

"Pam says goodnight folks!"

In my highly intoxicated state, I thought perhaps, I had learned to fly when Gabriel suddenly picks me up and cradles me in his arms with a precision movement that was so fast yet so smooth.

Suddenly understanding that I'm not Superwoman and that Gabriel ain't playing, I demand to know what the hell he's doing.

"What cha' think you doing, boy? Gabriel, put me down!" I say emphatically.

He ignores me totally as he opens the bathroom door. The shower is running. What the hell! Gabriel snatches the shower curtains back. I know this boy is not about to do what I think he's about to do! Oh crap!

Gabriel sits me in the tub knowing I can't get my big tipsy butt out of it. The water is freezing! Fully clothed and yelling curse words at the top of my lungs, I scream vehemently.

"You asshole! Who the fuck do you think you are! Shit! Lois just did my hair!"

WHEN NEVER COMES AGAIN

Gabriel only turns to sneer at me as he slams the door behind him.
I crouch in the tub sobbing as the cold water begins to kill my buzz.

Victoria Miguel-Joseph

Chapter Fifteen

The next morning, I awake with one seriously hellacious headache. As I turn over I see custom drapes and colorful walls. Instantly, I know I'm at Karl's house.

Karl and Mia have custom draperies in every room in the house. Mia has a personal decorator, Mr. Willabee, which she talked Karl into because "she just had to have him." Mr. Willabee is an old ass man that dresses like an old ass man and even worst smells like an old ass man. On top of that he has a decorating style that is well... to put it politely, an acquired taste. I have no clue how Mia came across this guy... undoubtedly from one of her no-taste, no-class, and think-they-fancy friends.

I roll out of bed and stare at my reflection in the dresser mirror. *Damn, I look rough.* I head for the adjoining bath. I push the door open and see more custom drapes and a wall color that makes me want to puke. I turn on the faucet. As I lean over to splash water on my face, I smell coffee. Thank God Karl and Mia allow themselves coffee. The pair is very health conscious. They eat well, exercise daily and basically they have no vices. But, then again, they do have that damn decorator! Ha! I giggle to myself then immediately grimace in pain.

"Ouch!" This pain has me crying out loud. Shit my head hurts. How did I get here anyway? I wonder as I massage my temples. I'm sure I'll find out soon enough. I bet Karl can't wait to get on my case. That's a welcome thought. Oh well, he can take a fuckin' number and get in line.

I finish up in the bathroom then glance at the clock on the night table. It's almost ten-thirty. I thought it was at least afternoon. Miraculously, my suit case is here too. I bend over to grab my pants and a pain in my back hits hard. Whoa! What's up with my back? The pain goes away just as quickly as it came. I get dressed and leave the bedroom. I'm ready for that coffee. As I approach the staircase I hear voices. The first step I take down the stairs causes another pain to shoot down my lower back. I grab the hand rail and take a deep breath. I hold my breath and place both hands on my belly.

"Okay little girl," I say out loud to the baby. "I know you're pissed at me for drinking yesterday and not feeding you properly. I'll make it up to you today. I promise."

I continue down the stairs making it to the bottom without pain, seemingly having been forgiven by the baby. Karl and Mia are sitting at the kitchen table. Karl is reading or pretending to read the paper, his prematurely bald head peeping over the top of the paper.

Karl is very dark-skinned and very tall. He's a bit overweight in his mid-section due to all the beer he drinks while watching UGA football. He's only a few years older than me but he lives the life of a much older man. He works hard, plays poker every weekend. He's trying to live the American dream... that and keep his young, beautiful wife happy.

"Well, well." Karl starts in on me. "Look what the cat dragged in."

"Good morning. Ooh wee... my back."

"You okay?" Karl asks, genuinely, it appears.

"I think so," I say, my voice shaking. "My back hurts and I feel like I need to do number two."

"Okay. TMI," snaps Mia.

I gather myself, trying to get through the next wave of pain. *Don't snap back, Pam. Try to be nice.*

"And good morning to you too, Miss Mia. I'm fine thank you. You?"

"Morning," she says back snidely. "Want some coffee?"

Oh, now she's being nice?

"Yes please." My voice is dripping with sweetness.

Karl can't hold it any longer.

"What the hell was wrong with you yesterday, Pam? Drinking like that? I bet you don't remember Lois changing your wet clothes or even coming here last night, do you?"

"No, Sherlock, I don't. Remember that is. Hell, I'm depressed. I'm hurting. We all deal with shit in different ways."

Another pain shoots through my back then down my leg. I lean onto the countertop and gasp. Something is happening. The pain is awful.

"Karl, can you please get me the telephone? I want to call Momma. I think I may be in labor."

Oh God, what if I am in labor? The baby's not due for four weeks. What if I did hurt my unborn child by drinking so much?

Karl had already dialed the number and it was ringing when I put the receiver to my ear. Momma answered on the first ring.

"Momma, you there?" I can barely get the words out. "Momma, I feel constipated or something and my back feel like it's going to break in two."

"Oh baby, you in labor. You in labor. Tell Karl or Mia to take you to University. Damn, I mean dog-gone-it. We never did make that appointment with the OB-GYN that Mary told us about. Anyway, I believe she did speak to him about you. I'll call Mary. Don't panic. Take deep breaths, Pamela... and count. Put Karl back on the phone. Hurry child. Let me speak to Karl!"

Momma's the one in a panic. She rarely curses. I guess this must be the real deal. What the hell did she mean when she said count? Count what?

Another pain hits. I buckle over expecting the worst. But it's not too bad... rather like bad menstrual cramps. I motion for Karl and he realizes I'm trying to hand him the phone.

"Hey Momma," Karl says nervously.

"Karl," Momma speaks in a very deliberate tone. "Pam is in labor. I'm about to call Mary to find out the name of the doctor she wanted Pam to see. In the meantime, start to time her contractions. Tell Mia to get Pam's bag together. I'll call you back after I talk to Mary."

Karl places the receiver in the cradle and begins to bark orders. He is tripping big time. Every time I have a contraction this nutty, tall, black ass fool falls to the floor like he's the one having the baby! I just want to slap him! Momma, please call me back in a hurry. My prayers are quickly answered. The phone rings.

Karl stands up holding his stomach like he truly can feel my pain. He picks up the phone receiver.

"Ma?"

"Hey. Mary called Dr. Chinn and he says once the contractions are ten minutes apart, head for the hospital. Karl? Karl! Do you hear me? Are you alright?"

"I'm fine. I got it. She's not far from that. I'll call you when we are on the way. Don't worry Momma. I'll take care of Pam. I will."

Half hour later, Karl rushes me to the hospital. The nurse at University confirms the baby is coming. I wish Ryan was here with me. I wish he was here to hold my hand. But Ryan just left Augusta yesterday because he had to get back to work. I was such a bitch to him yesterday. He's the only bread earner in this family and I should have understood that he needs to work. Now I want my husband.

As the medical staff wheels me into the delivery room, I'm alone. Momma has not made it yet and I certainly didn't ask Karl or Mia to come into the delivery room.

Lying on the table with my legs in stirrups, I stare at the mirror on the ceiling, pushing, screaming and watching as my baby emerges from my womb. He's silent as he enters the world. I suppose I was making enough noise for both of us. And even before the doctor announces that it's a boy... I know it. Tears stream down my face. All I can think about right now is Jason. I can see his face looking lovingly into my eyes, and I can hear him saying to me the words I'll never forget. *"You are having a boy, Pam and that I want you to name him after me."* I had not believed Jason's prophecy.

The nurse cleans the baby, weighs him and takes his vitals. She places this new life into my arms. I stare into his beautiful hazel eyes and gently caress his little cheeks with my index finger. The baby's head is full of curly hair that feels like silk. He's so beautiful, the most beautiful baby I've ever seen. At this very moment, I realize that I have all the reason I need to live. I smile at my son. I feel a level of gratitude, love and hope that, just days before, was impossible for me to feel. I never thought my heart could feel this much love.

The entire labor and birth had happened in just a few hours, start to finish. I figure God must have decided that I had been through enough in the past few days without having to sustain hours and hours of labor. *Thank you God!*

My mind drifts from Jason then to Ryan as I stare at my son. Did anyone call Ryan? Surely, someone must have.

I'm so tired. My eyelids are heavy... but I want to be awake when Momma gets here. I have to ask if Ryan knows the baby has arrived. The nurse takes my son from my arms but promises to bring him back once I'm settled in my room. I yawn. I'm beat. I feel as if I just delivered a Mack truck and not a six pound three ounce baby. I'll close my eyes for just a minute... just a little while.

I drift into a deep and sound sleep.

A telephone rings... arousing me from a peaceful and much needed sleep. I look around confused at first... then realize I'm in the hospital. I touch my stomach. It's real. I've had the baby. I locate a clock up on the bare egg shell colored wall. It is nine o'clock at night. I stretch to reach the phone and grimace in pain. I'm sore and it feels as if I've just pulled my vaginal stitches. My coochie aches. I pick up the phone, knowing already that it's my husband.

"Hello." My voice sounds raspy.

"Hello, hello. Pam. Pam is that you?"

"Who's this?"

"Dawg. This Dawg. Help me. Help me, Pam."

Dawg?

Dawg's an old buddy of Jason's. I vaguely remember seeing him at the house yesterday after the funeral service. How in the world does Dawg even know that I'm in the hospital? Never-the-less, Dawg is on the other end of the line.

Before I could reply to his plea, Dawg continues.

"Pam, Pam I been shot!" he shrieks. "I'm down here in the Bottom. Help me! Please?"

What the fuck? Of all the preposterous things... why the hell is he calling me? It's not like I can help him. I'm in the hospital. He's in east Augusta, in an area called the 'Bottom', and rightfully so.

"Dawg, why are you calling me?" I ask incredulously as I lean on one arm attempting to shift my sore body. "How the hell can I help you, goddamn it? I just had a baby... I'm in the freaking hospital!"

"Help me." He continues to plead.

I'm completely flabbergasted as well as frustrated... and pissed. How am I supposed to help this idiot? What does he expect me to do? *Stupid a-hole.* I have to do something. I certainly do not want him calling again and again. I'll never get any rest.

"Dawg, I'll get you some help. Okay? I will. But please don't call me again!" I slam the phone down for emphasis, but pick it right up again to call Daddy. Momma answers half asleep.

"Pam you okay baby? We came by the hospital earlier but you were knocked out! My grandson is so-o-o-o cute! He's simply adorable! Lois called Ryan. He said he'd get a flight out as soon as he can. He was thrilled to hear he has a son!"

"Yes the baby is beautiful, isn't he? I'm glad y'all got a hold of Ryan. Everything's okay Momma. I just need to talk to Daddy for a minute. Is he awake?"

"Yeah sugar. Okay. See you tomorrow. Here's your Daddy."

She hands Daddy the phone without further ado.

"Hey, Pam. What's going on baby? You alright?" he asks as he swings his long legs out of bed. He proceeds to put on his slippers then walks to the kitchen. Opening the fridge, he lifts the water pitcher and softly places it on the counter. Next he opens the cabinet, selects a plastic cup, rather than a glass, and pours the water.

The sound of the water being poured into the cup makes me feel like I have to pee.

Once Daddy gulps the water, he asks again, "Pam, you okay?"

I quickly assure him nothing's wrong. I go on to inform him of the phone call from Dawg. Daddy is furious.

"Dawg's an alcoholic, Pam. And a druggie. He hasn't been shot. He's delusional." Taking another swig, he chokes on the water. Daddy coughs for what seems like forever before continuing. "Don't think twice about what he's saying." Daddy is trying to get his voice back, clearing his voice a couple more times. "I'll take care of him. Go back to sleep baby. You just get some rest."

Dawg's call upset me. How dare he call me in my hospital room with some absurd bullshit? Why would he make up a story like that? The last thing I feel like doing is dealing with another sick wacko. I realize that we're all upset over Jason's death, but that's no reason to involve me in his ridiculous hallucinations. I'll never forgive Dawg for calling me tonight. I know one thing... I ain't even trying to find out what happened – if anything really happened at all. Frankly, I don't give a shit. It's just one more strange and reprehensible episode in my life. *Damn him.* I continue to silently throw curse words around in my head as I finally feel myself falling back to sleep.

I'm wide awake as Ryan enters the room. He appears frazzled and jumpy.

"Hey baby! I got here as soon as I could but I can only stay tonight. I gotta be back at work Monday morning. I'm working a double shift. You know we need the money. Where's my son? I want to see my boy."

Why is he speaking so fast?

"I'm fine Ryan, thank you. And, oh yeah, I love you too."

"Sorry baby." He leans over and lightly pecks my cheek. "I'm a little out of it. I worked late again last night. I was totally shocked when Lois called to say that the baby had arrived. Little man couldn't wait huh?"

What the hell is wrong with this man? As soon as he arrives he tells me he can only stay one day. He's acting very odd. I can't put my finger on it but he looks like a deer caught in headlights. I want to tell him my latest episode last night... but decide not to. Ryan's much too edgy already.

"Nope, I guess he couldn't wait. I was only in labor a few hours. And the pain wasn't even that bad. He didn't even cry when he was born. He's gorgeous. As I held him, all I could think about was Jason."

"Come on Pam. You've got to put the whole thing behind you. Jason's gone and there's nothing no one can do to change that. I know you're hurting, but you have me and the baby to think about now."

"Don't you think I know that?" I ask. I feel my blood pressure begin to rise. "If there was a switch I could turn off inside my head... inside my heart... that would stop the pain I feel and the things I see, don't you think I would?"

I blow my nose loudly then continue to vent.

"It's the life I just gave birth to that's keeping me strong, that gives me something to live for. Before the baby came, I didn't give a shit about anything! You have no idea what it's like to watch your brother be shot down in cold blood and to have to run for your life. To lose someone you love in the way Jason's life was taken... you just have no fuckin' idea!"

Ryan wraps his arms around me but I pull away.

"I'm sorry, Pam. You're right. I don't know what that feels like. But I do know that we have to move on with our lives. We can't..."

The nurse taps on the door interrupting Ryan as she proceeds into the room.

"Hello, hello!" she says, in her cheery-song-like tone. She's holding our baby, touching his nose with her index finger and making small baby sounds. She turns her face from his to ours, realizing that she has interrupted a very tense and intimate conversation. Yet, she plays it off and she doesn't skip a beat.

"You must be the proud Papa!" she announces jubilantly. "Your handsome son looks just like his Daddy!" For the first time since his arrival, Ryan appears genuinely happy. The nurse gently places the baby into Ryan's arms. Holding the baby seems good for Ryan. He immediately appears less agitated. A calm aura surrounds him.

Smiling widely at our son, Ryan whispers, "Oh my God, Pam. He's perfect. The perfect baby. We did good."

The sight of Ryan and the baby together warms my heart. I never knew I could feel so much love. If only the past could be changed and Jason was alive to see his nephew. I shake my head trying to release the pain. I will not dwell on things I cannot change. I will not. Think happy thoughts Pam. Only happy thoughts I tell myself again and again.

"Ryan? We have to name him. I have a name in mind. I want to honor Jason's wishes. You can pick the middle name if you want. Okay?"

We agree to name our baby Jason Ronald Hogan. Ronald after Ryan's father.

"Ryan, let's call him Jay. Is that okay?" I ask. Saying the name Jason all the time right now is just too difficult for me. Besides I like the sound of Jay and the way the name rolls off my tongue with ease.

Ryan tries the nickname out. He coos.

"Hey there Jay. Jay, my little man."

Jay seems to like the name, too. Ryan places the baby in my arms and we sit together on the bed as a family for the very first time.

I hear noise outside the door. The entire Barnett clan shows up at the hospital. Ryan's glad to have them all around. It's almost as if he's more comfortable when he isn't totally alone with me.

"Hey baby! How's my daughter doing this morning? Give me my grandbaby!" Momma leans over and kisses the top of my head... like she's done since I was a little girl.

"Hey Pam. How you doing Ryan?" Daddy reaches for Ryan's hand and pulls him in for a congratulatory hug.

"Hey... good job Sis." Lois exclaims and she takes Jay from Momma and plants a kiss on his rosy cheek.

Even Gabrielle is no longer pissed at me. He hugs and kisses me on the check then whispers an apology for putting me in the shower. Ethan and Karl are looking over Lois's shoulder making very uncharacteristic baby sounds at Jay. The room door opens again, Larry enters bearing gifts. He's carrying a gigantic teddy bear with a blue ribbon around its neck and a beautiful floral arrangement.

"We named the baby." I announce proudly.

"Family... meet Jason Ronald Hogan. We're going to call him Jay." My voice cracks as I speak. Momma squeezes my hand. Silence fills the room.

Daddy looks at me with watery eyes.

"That's a fine name, Pam. A fine name." He says proudly.

Everyone in the room is focused on the baby. There are smiles and tears of joy. Goo-goo, ga-ga sounds abound and hearts, for the moment, are light. It's as if I can read their minds. Jason Ronald Hogan is alive and healthy and that's all that matters. It's all that matters in the world.

VICTORIA MIGUEL-JOSEPH

Chapter Sixteen

The days that follow are extremely hard. It seems as if I never speak with Ryan. His phone calls are sporadic. Two weeks have passed since Jay was born and I can count the times we've talked on one hand. I miss Ryan terribly. I have no idea what's going on with him, but I've never been one to let sleeping dogs lie. We have business that needs to be handled. I guess I'm the one to handle it.

I decide it's time to go to Atlanta. The house can't continue to sit as if we're returning to live in it. And even though Ryan claims to have hired a Realtor... he hasn't bothered to inform me of any details. Of course, Momma and Daddy do not want me going to Atlanta. Both offered to come with me. But I have to go. And I have to go alone.

"You shouldn't be taking that baby to Atlanta! He's too young! You ain't hardly well yourself," Momma states firmly.

"Momma, it's okay. We'll be fine. Jay is two weeks old and I feel all right physically. We'll be okay." I say it while trying to believe it.

"Ryan claims the house is on the market. You know this. I told you this. Everything in the house has to be packed. I'll need to put them in storage until I figure out what to do next. Momma, no one but me can decide what to keep or what to throw away. You never know how fast the house will sell. It's got to be done. I've put it off as long as I can. At least Ryan hired an agent but the rest is left to me."

I can tell Momma's relenting, at least a little, as she shakes her head from side to side. I take a softer tone.

"Momma, I'll be back tonight, probably by ten." No one had spent a night in the house since the shooting. And I certainly didn't plan to.

So much for Momma relenting... she continues to fuss while I dress. She insists I drive Karl's car. She knew I wouldn't drive Daddy's truck. I didn't want to put Karl and Mia out of their way, but Karl insisted, too. He wouldn't hear otherwise.

I get Jay settled into Karl's 1979 Toyota Corolla. Momma sadly kisses me and then says good-bye to Jay.

"Call me as soon as you get there, you hear?" Her voice sounds worried.

"I will, Momma. Please try not to worry." And with that we are off.

I think about my life as I drive, stopping once along the way to take Jay out of his car seat because he's fussing so much. Maybe Jay doesn't want to go back to Atlanta or to that house either.

I would have never thought that my life could have changed so drastically. Last year this time, I didn't even know I would get pregnant let alone imagine anything else that has happened. You just never know what twists and turns life will bring.

Once Jay and I arrive at 1450 Woodgreen Way, it takes everything in me to muster up the courage to walk back into that house. I sit in the driveway for the longest time, expecting Weird Al to be lurking in his doorway across the street or to walk out of his house. Somehow I gather together enough guts to get out the car. I grab Jay's carrier. We walk towards the front door. I suppose the realtor Ryan hired had the panels on the side of the front door replaced. But the same wrought iron screen door was still in place. I notice the lockbox hanging from the handle. At least Ryan had taken the initiative to engage a realtor. The lock-box is proof that he had actually hired an agent to sell this place. It seems that's about all Ryan had done lately.

I unlock the screen door, holding it open with my shoulder. Next I unlock the door. I wonder if anyone has viewed the place. Since Ryan's not sharing any information, I have no idea if there are any prospects... serious or otherwise. As far as I know, no one other than Ryan, the agent or maybe the police, had been inside since Jason's murder.

As I enter the foyer, I observe that the blood is no longer on the floor, except for where it seeped into the carpet. It looks as if someone had tried to clean that up too. However they weren't very successful. I scrutinize my surroundings. The parquet floor was bloodless and in good shape. The carpet really needs to be replaced. I can smell blood. Until now I never realized blood had an odor. I mean, I've heard or read that animals could, of course, smell blood... and creatures like vampires or others with supernatural powers.

I walk intrepidly across the floor... surprised at my bravery. I expect to see a body outline or something like that drawn on the floor, like in the movies. But there's no outline.

I place Jay's carrier down in the foyer, in almost the exact spot that I'd last seen my brother alive. Before I can stop myself, my valor crumbles and I begin to cry gut wrenching sobs that rack my entire body. What in the world made me think that I could do this? Jay begins to cry, too. I lift him out of the carrier and hold him close to me. I turn and look at our reflection in the mirror in the foyer. There is dried blood and what appear to be flecks of skin or bone matter on the mirror. I stand frozen in my spot. I slowly raise my hand to touch the foreign substance on the mirror. I am instantly taken back to the horrible day. Jason had been shot at very close range, in the neck, with a high-powered rifle. The bullet exited through the back of his head. The coroner said that Jason never knew what hit him. That he died a painless death. That's just something to say in an attempt to make the survivors feel better. How would doctors really know if a death is painless or not?

I see two bullet holes in the glass wall. The police had stated that Weird Al shot his rifle at least four times before returning to his house... only once at Jason and possibly three times at me. I wonder where the fourth bullet hit. Everyone says that I was lucky and that it just wasn't my time to die. Well, I'm dying now.

I walk over towards the front door thinking that I need to remember to tell Ryan to get the glass wall repaired and to get the inside of this place cleaned up properly. If the agent he hired replaced the glass pane on the side of the entrance door, why didn't she or he get the rest of this stuff taken care of? Maybe, it just hasn't happened yet. I'll remind Ryan anyway.

Now that Jay and I both are calmer and he's no longer crying, I need to do what I came here for.

Eventually, I make good progress. Jay's sound asleep in the baby carrier. Every time I move from one room to another I bring him with me. The baby bed is still in the nursery, but I can't allow myself to let him out of my sight. There are so many items to pack. Lots of stuff will be sold. As I move from room to room, memories flood my head. Who would have thought that I would be doing what I'm doing right now and under these circumstances?

I take Jay with me into the nursery. The bright yellow walls and the beautiful mural simply make me sad. The nursery items are all brand new... never used. How heartbreaking. The nursery that was once my favorite spot in the house, I can't bear to look at anymore. *No. Stop it Pam! Don't dwell on things you can't change!* I shake my head as if doing so would exonerate the memories and purge the pain.

All the boxes I brought in when I arrived are now full. I place the final piece of tape across the top of the very last box. I look around the bedroom. There's not a lot left that I can do here. Ryan's going to have to do the heavy lifting or get someone else to do it. I wipe my hands on the end of my big denim shirt. My blue jeans are filthy. I did bring a change of clothes with me just in case I needed them. Guess it's a good thing that I did.

I grab Jay and head for the kitchen. I check my watch as I walk down the hall. It's been four hours since I arrived! A trickle of sweat runs down the side of my face as I open the fridge, scanning for something to drink. I open the vegetable compartment and reach for the Coke nestled behind spoiled celery hearts. I think of the stuff that I have to take care of and begin to file them away in my mental Rolodex. One... have the utilities turned off. Two, remind Ryan about the needed repairs. Three... Ding dong! It's the doorbell. I freeze. Who could that be? I didn't tell anyone other than my family in Augusta that I was coming. Perhaps it's a potential buyer or the real estate agent. I move timidly to the door. I peek around the kitchen door and through the Chinese screen that outlines the dining area. Through the window I see that it's Mrs. Douglas.

I place the Coke on the kitchen counter and lift Jay from his carrier. I walk gradually to the door.

"Hello."

"Hello Pam. It's Nancy Douglas from next door. I saw the car pull in earlier. I just want to know how you and your family are doing. Plus I am hoping to see the baby."

Carefully, I unlock and open the door. Mrs. Douglas is smiling widely.

"How are you Pam?"

"I'm fine, thank you, Mrs. Douglas. Come in."

She comes into the house for the very first time.

"I don't know how to even begin to express my gratitude to you and your son." My voice is cracking.

Mrs. Douglas holds up her hand while shaking her head from left to right.

"There is no cause to thank us, Pam. I thank the Lord that you and this precious baby are all right. May I see him? Hold him?"

"Yes. Of course, please excuse my manners. Mrs. Douglas, meet my son, Jason Ronald Hogan... the light of my life. Jay..." I whisper in his ear. "...meet Mrs. Douglas."

"He's beautiful, Pam. Absolutely beautiful. Hi there, Jason Ronald Hogan." Mrs. Douglas whispers as well.

Then a look of concern crosses Mrs. Douglas's face. Slowly and carefully she begins to speak.

"Pam, I don't know how to tell you this, except to come right out and say it. Mrs. James would like to talk to you. She came to me last week and asked if I would relay her message. She is very upset over what her husband did. She thought perhaps you wouldn't agree to see her, so she gave me this letter to give you."

"She's right. I don't want to talk to her. Moreover, you can take that letter back to her. What can she possibly say to me? How dare she even think about showing her face to me?"

I'm angry now. No, I'm pissed! Nothing she can say or do will bring Jason back.

"I blame her," I shout. "I blame her damn kids. I blame each and every one of them. I don't want to hear a word she has to say. While she and her children were having a grand fucking time at Six Flags Over Georgia, her crazy-ass husband was on a goddamn rampage! No. No. I do not want to talk to her. Not now. Not ever!"

"Calm down, Pam. Don't get yourself upset."

"No, Mrs. Douglas, I'm not upset, I'm mad. You tell her she's going to have to live with what her husband did, just like I'm going to have to live with it."

"Well Pam, I'll leave you to your work now." Mrs. Douglas has no idea how to handle my outbursts of emotion. "Take care of yourself, Pam. And take care of your beautiful son."

Calming down a bit, I reply, "I will. Thanks again, Mrs. Douglas, for your help and for your son's help. I don't think I would be here had it not been for you and your son. I am eternally grateful for your kindness and compassion."

"Anyone would have done the same thing," she says as she turns toward the door then leaves.

As I watched her go and close the door behind her, I wonder if I will ever see her again. In my heart I know that I will not. I blame Weird Al's family for his incredulous actions. Right now, it's easier to blame someone... anyone really... because I need to share the guilt that I feel. I feel so responsible and guilty that Jason is dead that I transfer blame anywhere else I can. I will never forgive Weird Al and his family. Never. And I pray I never have to lay eyes on any of them ever. In my mind I know that I have the wrong attitude, but right now I just don't give a fuck.

After Mrs. Douglas's departure, I do my best to cool down. I keep saying that I'm not upset. But it's impossible to convince myself. I am upset, visibly upset. All of a sudden I remember the stash that Ryan and I keep. It's been hidden forever... long before Jay was conceived. Hopefully, the cops didn't search the house for any reason and find it.

Hastily, I grab the baby carrier and head for the bedroom closet. I lift the loose plank from the floor board. Voila! There it is. I lift the small plastic bag revealing the dope Ryan and I kept hidden. Inside are a thin rolled joint and a small amount of cocaine wrapped in foil. I open the foil, stick my finger into the white substance then tap my finger on the tip of my tongue. The familiar medicinal taste brings back memories of some wild but fun times; days gone by when I didn't have a worry in the world.

Feeling around under the floor, I'm determined to locate what I'm searching for. Then my fingers touch it. I pull out the marijuana pipe that Ryan and I had used so many times before. After inspecting it, I place it next to the plastic bag on the floor then continue to feel around under the floor board. At last, I find the lighter. I get up, brush my knees off. After placing the foil and the joint into my pant pocket, I take the glass pipe, wrap it in an old towel and stomp it. The sound of breaking glass startles Jay, who had begun to fall asleep.

"Shhh, it's okay, baby," I croon as I sit the carrier in front of the huge bedroom window, which almost measures from wall to wall.

Opening the bedroom door that leads outside to what is now a dead flower garden, I walk around the side of the house quickly to throw the towel and its broken contents into the trash can located on the side of the house. I take a seat on the crooked and broken bench directly outside the bedroom door so that I have a clear view of Jay. I dig into my pocket and take out the contents. I look around me. There's nothing but woods. There's no one in site. I use the tip of my nail to scrape the cocaine from the foil. There's only a taste. Good thing, too. I finish what's left then fire up the joint. I inhale slowly and deeply, and then choke on the smoke as I blow it out. I feel better already. I sit until I realize I'm near the very spot where I fell when trying to escape my assailant.

When Never Comes Again

Get your ass up and get back to work, Pam. Focus on the task at hand. You really don't need this stuff to get through.... Or do you?

I vigorously clean the refrigerator just to get my stress level under control. Keeping busy always helps to keep my mind off the pain I constantly feel in my heart. Eventually, I get all the things I want and need packed and loaded into the car. The rest will have to go to storage. I change my filthy clothing then feed Jay before leaving.

As I walk back and forth trying to get Jay to burp, I see someone walking up the street. The closer he gets to the house the more agitated I become. Finally, the young man reaches the driveway across the street then turns to look in my direction. My heart stops. Instantly, I recognize the boy as Al James's son. He's really tall... taller than I ever realized before. He has the same strut as Weird Al. It looks like he's carrying something... perhaps a bag of some sort. No, maybe it's a stick. As I gawk with my nose pressed against the window pane, I realize that it's a gun. Jesus! Staring, I realize it's not a real one. It appears to be a bb gun I think, but a gun just the same.

"Like father like son," I snarl.

Quickly, I place Jay into his carrier, snap him in securely then I grab my purse and we get the hell out of Dodge.

Driving back to Augusta, I 'study', as my Daddy always says, the past couple of weeks. How did I survive? I have no idea, yet somehow I did. I look in the rearview mirror. Jay's sound asleep, making sweet little baby sighs. I know in my heart that God saved Jay and me for a reason. We both are destined to do something significant with our lives. I feel it in my gut and know this to be true. But what do I do now? What's next for me now?

It starts to rain lightly. I can't figure out how to turn on the wipers. A second later, the rain starts to fall in big fat drops so hard that I can barely see in front of me. Okay Karl, where are the freaking wiper controls? Finally, I find the correct knob and turn the windshield wipers on. As I watch the road and the rain, I contemplate the mess my life has become. I miss Jason so much I cry every day. My friends are in Atlanta and my husband is in Florida. Perhaps I should go back to work. Just maybe going back to work will help keep my mind occupied and off the past.

When I was hired as a flight attendant for Southeast Airlines five years ago, I had never aspired to be a stewardess. It was actually Ryan's idea that I go to the open call that was being advertised on the radio. I recall balking at the idea. I had no desire to leave Ryan or to fly across oceans. But Ryan was pumped over the idea. He said I would love it and that absence makes the heart grow fonder. Being young and impressionable, I warmed up to the idea and eventually gave in. I told Ryan I'd give it a shot.

Ryan had accompanied me to the interview. He waltzed in looking handsome and debonair, as if he was there to apply as well. He wore a gray pinstriped suit with a white shirt. He was freshly shaven and smelled good enough to eat. Ryan had the flair and the personality to charm the panties off a Nun. As I filled out the application, I watched him rub noses with an elegantly dressed Caucasian woman. I had no idea who she was, but it was obvious that she was totally taken in by Ryan. I remember everything about her. She had big green eyes and long fiery red hair. Her hair was very straight, in a cute style that framed her face. Her hair must have extended damn near to her tail bone. She was very slim, waif-like, even though she had worn a cream colored pantsuit. Everyone knows light colors are supposed to make you appear heavier. But this was not the case. I hated her instantly. She held a clip board and an ink pen, so at least she gave the appearance of officially working.

I tried my best to concentrate on the task at hand but the task foremost in my mind was the thought of losing my husband to this seemingly very put-together older and classy woman. She appeared to be at least ten years my senior. I eyed the two while pretending to complete the application. Since he entered the door, Ryan hadn't left her side. I can still see and hear her as she threw her head back and giggled loud enough for everyone in the building to turn and stare. I had wondered what was so damn funny!

The number of applicants that day must have exceeded two hundred. However, I made it to the next level which meant I was entitled to a one-on-one interview with the lead recruiter. I was nervous. I looked over at Ryan for reassurance but he was totally engrossed with the green-eyed redhead. He didn't look my way.

The recruiter that interviewed me that day was strikingly beautiful as well. However she was very nice and I relaxed right away. The interview lasted only fifteen minutes or so. She told me I should hear something in a few weeks. I walked out of the interview room and was surprised to see that Ryan was actually waiting for me. I scanned the area for the redhead. Easily I spotted all six feet of her not too far away. I remember it like it was yesterday.

"How'd it go?" Ryan had asked excitedly.

"Okay, I guess," I said non-expressively.

"I was talking to one of the marketing ladies, the one over there." He points to the redhead.

"Yes, I saw," I snidely replied.

"She says that SEA is offering open calls for flight attendants all around the globe. But that they're doing most of the hiring here in Atlanta. They plan to open a hub here."

"She must have said a lot more than that." I am jealous and he can tell. "You two were talking forever."

"She was just being friendly, Pam. And I was simply singing your praises, darling."

"Yeah right! Sure you were."

Slick ass motherfucker.

Thinking back on it now... I suppose had it not been for Ryan's sucking up to the tall redhead, I may not have gotten the job. Who knows?

It's only been three months since I went on leave from SEA. I worked as long as I was allowed to... which was through my seventh month of pregnancy. Momma's going to say it's much too soon to get back to work. I can count on that.

I look in the rearview mirror again. Jay's eyes are open but he hasn't made a sound. His head is turned to the side and he's watching the rain drops thump against the windowpane. He's staring intently as if he, too, is contemplating the future.

I try to break his stare. "Hi baby! How's mommy's boy?"

The rain is slacking up a little and the sun starts to shine through the parted clouds. It reminds me of one of those religious pictures of Jesus. You know, the ones where the light is shining through gray skies and Jesus is looking up towards the heavens.

"Jay. Jay," I repeat, trying again to get him to look towards me.

"Mommy's going to have to start back to work soon, Jay."

Finally Jay looks my way and smiles. My heart expands at the sight of his smile. I feel all warm and content inside.

"I'll miss you terribly, baby. But mommy needs the distraction. And most importantly, we need the money."

With Ryan acting so strange these days, I really should start looking out for myself. I haven't saved a dime since we were married. There should be some profit from the sale of the house. And, since I won't have a mortgage to pay, perhaps I can save a little bit of money. I have a son now. I have to start acting more responsible. But then again, shit, so does Ryan. The decision is made. I am going back to work.

When Never Comes Again

Chapter Seventeen

I've been back at work for only two weeks yet it feels like I've been back so much longer. It didn't take much to get the ball rolling. After the trip to Atlanta, I called my manager at SEA. She faxed me all the necessary paperwork that I needed to complete. I got that done in no time then faxed it back to her. Just as I thought, Momma didn't like the idea of me returning to work so soon. However, she did agree to take care of Jay while I was away working. Ryan's comments about my return to work were typical. In one breath he says we could really use the money, and in the next breath he says Jay needs me more. Duh.

There was a time when I thoroughly enjoyed my job. I loved the traveling and I loved meeting new people. Now, however, every time I sit on the airplane's jumpseat, I'm practically on the verge of tears. My life is so very different now. It's extremely hard to adjust. My nightmares continue even on my overnights.

It doesn't matter how exhausted I may be or how beautiful and exciting the city I sleep in happens to be... I still wake up in the middle of the night in a cold sweat, not knowing where I am and always screaming out Jason's name.

Maybe I really do need professional help. All my friends keep insisting that I do. I'm just not ready to go there. I have prayer. I pray all the time. Every day, ten times a day. I have always had a strong belief in God. But now, since Jason's death, I feel that I have a personal relationship with God. I believe that I have a purpose on this earth even though it's not exactly clear to me what that purpose is right now. Jay and I, we were both spared for some reason. I know in my heart that Jay's destined for great things. And maybe I am too... destined for great things that is. I feel that I have an obligation to inform the world that there is a God and that He can make miracles happen. He made a miracle for me. The Bible says to walk by faith and not by sight. I'm trying to have faith and I'm doing my best to stand by it. Sometimes, it just ain't easy.

I usually write as a means of releasing my feelings. I speak to God, to Jesus, to Jason, and even to Weird Al through my writings. Oftentimes the words I write are not very nice. But there's no one else on this planet I can talk to that can truly understand what I'm going through. I have my girls, my crew. But even they, no matter how hard they would try... can relate to what I'm feeling.

I'm afraid to bring up Jason's name to my family because the mention of his name may cause them more pain. They never talk about Jason. No one does. Not Momma, not Lois, no one. But then, neither do I. I never talk about that day. I have a nagging feeling in the pit of my stomach that my family blames me for Jason's death. But why wouldn't they? I blame myself don't I? I tried once to talk to Ryan about how I feel, but he had cut me off.

"Pam, it's over, forget about it." He said.

"It just isn't that simple, Ryan. Oh how I wish it were. The pain seems to grow rather than subside. I can't shake it."

Ryan didn't understand. No one did. So I turn all my energies to Jay. I live for Jay and for Jay only. That's probably one of the reasons why my marriage is going to shit.

Ryan is coming to see the baby and me less and less frequently. I rationalize that it's because of my work schedule, yet I highly suspect that all is not right in the world. All I talk about is the baby. I know, too, that I'm not the only one hurting and grieving. Ryan is hurting, too. But is it my fault that we're not together? Maybe it is. I am the one that didn't want to go to Miami with Ryan in the first place.

Lately, I've tried to reach out to Ryan by calling and talking about exciting things like places I've seen or by recommending places we should travel to together. When that doesn't work, I even try talking dirty to him. It's been a long time since we made love. I've been physically able to have sex for quite some time. At my six weeks checkup, the doctor said I was good-to-go. But with Ryan not showing up very often, I've resorted to satisfying myself when the urge hits me. My hands have become skilled and I almost prefer them at this point. Me, myself and I have become pretty close... a real freaking love triangle. I do have to be mommy, daddy and Pamela don't I? I pray masturbation isn't a sin as it's implied to be. If it is... I'm going straight to hell for sure.

Enough is enough. I've invited Ryan on my overnights. I'm the one that does all the calling. And he's seems more distant than ever. I want to see my husband. If he won't come to me then I'll go to him.

While preparing to make my surprise visit to Miami, Momma asks if I'm sure I want to go without first informing Ryan.

"Of course I do, Momma. Why wouldn't I? We need to talk. He hasn't called me or his son in six days. What's wrong with this picture? I don't know, but I'm sure as heck about to find out!"

"As long as you sho' darling. I don't want you to be the one in for the surprise!"

"I hear you, Momma. But what will be, will be. All I know is that I can't keep going on like this. I need to know what's going on in Ryan's head. I need to know."

The flight to Miami was uneventful. Just the way I like a flight to be. When I arrive in Miami, I pick up a rental car then quickly browse the map located conveniently in the glove compartment. I have an address but that's it. I've never been to Ryan's place here nor have I ever been invited. He claims to be staying in this apartment with a roommate. All I know about this roommate is that he is male and his name is Bob.

I arrive at the apartment. I smooth my hair, take a deep breath then tentatively knock on the door. A very surprised and speechless man opens the door. I assume this is Bob. Obviously, Ryan has at least showed the man a picture of me because immediately he recognizes exactly who I am. He's very uneasy.

"Hi," he finally says.

"Hello. I've come to see Ryan. Would you tell him his wife is here, please?"

He stutters and balks as he makes up an excuse for Ryan not being home.

"Would it be okay if I wait here for him?" I ask innocently.

Jerk.

Bob's eyes become as big as saucers. Hesitating just a tad too long... he finally recovers, and then addresses my question.

"Sure," he says as he throws his hands into the air. "Why not?"

As I enter the apartment, I take in my surroundings. Typical bachelors' pad, I surmise. The furniture looks fairly decent and appears comfortable. Several Playboy magazines are lying on the coffee table in front of an old beige couch. There's a big burgundy Lazy-Boy recliner next to it. A wet bar sits in the left corner of the room with bottles of wine resting in a wine rack on the counter.

I take a seat on the lumpy couch.

"I guess Ryan will be in shortly. Make yourself at home."

Bob excuses himself. He has papers to read, he says.

Liar.

An hour passes but still no Ryan. I try not to jump to any conclusions, but I'm nobody's fool. I thank Bob for his hospitality and leave frustrated. Walking back to my car, reaching into my purse for the car keys, I hear a car pulling out of the parking lot. I look up and see someone that looks an awful lot like Ryan. The car, a cobalt blue Camaro or Trans Am, speeds out of the complex onto the main road. Perhaps my eyes are playing tricks on me, but my gut tells me different. I stand there next to the rental car for a minute or two just to see if the car shows up again. Finally, I unlock the door, start the car and head to my hotel. I can't wait to get the hell out of Miami. Morning can't come fast enough so I can fly back to Augusta.

The flight went quickly. Before I know it, I'm home.

"Pam? Pam that you?" Momma asks coming out of the kitchen wiping her hands on her apron.

"Hey, Momma." I kiss her cheek. "How's Jay?"

"Jay's fine. Lois has him. Why you back so soon?"

"Don't want to talk about it." I say flopping onto the couch.

"Just know you were right as usual."

The telephone rings. I pick it up.

"Hello."

Ryan's voice is on the other end.

"Hi, Pam. Sorry I missed you last night. I had to work a double shift."

He's lying. I know it. I feel it.

"I tried calling you at work." I say, heat in my tone. "I was told you were off last night."

"I worked at a different center last night. Pam, I'm flying into Augusta later this evening. I need to talk to you."

"Oh. So now you need to talk to me? I haven't heard from you in a week, Ryan. You don't even call to see how your son is doing."

"Pam, I know. I know. Things have been crazy. But we really do need to talk."

"Okay. Whatever. I'm here."

What the hell? What is this about? I've tried over and over to see this man. And one visit to Miami prompts him to finally come see his wife and baby?

Ryan arrives at Momma's door looking as handsome and debonair as ever.

Being charming as always, he kisses Momma on the cheek then says "Hi, Momma." Avoiding eye contact with me, Ryan speaks to Jay who's nestled in my arms. "Hey, my little man."

Ryan lifts Jay from my arms and embraces him tightly. Jay's light brown eyes, which sometimes appear green, stare at Ryan with wonderment. He grabs Ryan's nose.

"Momma, can you take Jay while Ryan and I go for a walk?"

Momma gets my drift.

"Sure. No problem. Come on, big boy." Momma takes Jay from Ryan's arms, yet her eyes are focused on Ryan. "Come here to ya Grandma Jay. Let your Momma and Daddy have some time together. It's been a while."

It wouldn't have been Momma had she not gotten her jab in at Ryan.

Good, serves his ass right.

I grab my coat. We walk down to the stream. Once there, Ryan wastes no time. He gets straight to the reason for his visit.

"Pam, I had an affair." This he blurts outs as if to say he had the flu.

"It's over now. I promise. I made a mistake. A huge mistake." His shoulders sag. "I've found us a house in Miami Gardens. I want you and Jay to come to Florida. I love you, Pam. I haven't acted like it lately, but I do."

I stare at him. I had already pretty much figured out that he was cheating. Why else would he stay clear of me? But now the part about the house comes as a surprise. There's more to this. There's got to be. I stare at Ryan and wait.

"I need to tell you one more thing, Pam."

I knew it... Ryan's nervous as hell. What else is he about to confess? Can it get any worse?

Ryan continues in a barely audible tone of voice.

"The girl I had the affair with claims she's pregnant with my child."

What? I must have misunderstood. This can't be. An affair is bad enough, but a baby?

Please God, don't let this be true.

"Pam, I don't believe the baby's mine. But she says it is." Ryan rocks back and forth on the balls of his feet as he twists his hands. "I'm not in love with her or anything either. Shit, I just had to tell you before you heard it from someone else."

I've just been slapped in the face. I actually thought I knew what he came to tell me. But I am not prepared for this. How dare he tell me that he's gotten a house and ask me to move to Florida... and then in the same breath, tells me some little bitch is pregnant with his bastard child? Jesus. What did I do to deserve this? Jay's barely three months old. Ryan must have been cheating since Jay's birth. How else could this girl realize she's pregnant now?

"How pregnant is she?" I have to know.

"Come on Pam, what difference does that make?"

"How fucking pregnant is she, Ryan? How far along?" I say through clinched teeth.

Never looking up at me he says, "Two months... I don't know, maybe nine weeks."

Good grief! Was I to blame for this, too? Did I force my husband into the arms of another woman because my head is so fucked up from pain and guilt?

Yes. Of course, Pam. You know it's your fault.

"I can't deal with this right now, Ryan. I just can't."

I begin to walk away and I keep walking. My God! Jay's going to have a sister eleven months younger than he. I am pissed! No, I'm hurt. How dare he put this shit on me after all I've had to deal with! What am I going to do now? What to do? What to do?

I ask myself again and again as my eyes swell up with tears.

I walk into the house, slamming the door behind me.

"What is wrong with you, child?" Momma asks, clearly startled.

"Nothing!" I shout, taking it out on Momma.

"Don't seem like nothing to me. And lower your voice. The baby's sleeping."

Ryan walks in behind me. Momma takes one look at his face and decides she should keep her peace. But instinctively she knows he's fucked up somehow.

I head straight for my mother's room... slamming the door behind me. Falling onto the bed, the tears flow easily. I can't imagine throwing my marriage away by simply handing it to another woman on a silver platter. My first intuition tells me not to let Ryan go... to at least try to make our marriage work. But how do I put something back together that has fallen to shreds? I'm not sure that I have the energy to try to reestablish a connection with Ryan.

I hear Jay crying and Momma ordering Ryan to go see after his child. Jay needs a father. Quickly, I make a decision. I'll wait for the holiday season to end, then Jay and I will move to Miami. Everything will work out. It has to. I've lost too much already.

When Never Comes Again

Chapter Eighteen

Today, like every other day in Miami, is hot as hell and extremely humid. I'm usually up each morning by five-thirty to feed Jay. Ryan leaves the house around seven. It's eight-thirty and Jay's sleeping soundly in his crib. I contemplate returning to bed, but instead, I make a pot of coffee and dread the day ahead.

Since moving to Miami I've had to deal with harassing phone calls. Sometimes they happen two or three times a day. A lot of times they come in the evenings when Ryan isn't here. But there's always that early morning call between seven-thirty and nine-thirty, guaranteed. I know it's the pregnant nineteen-year-old that claims Ryan's the father. I just know it's her.

I pour a cup of java and open the blinds to the patio door that leads to the small backyard. The grass needs to be cut.

There are also weeds in the small flower bed that surrounds the hibiscus plant.

Ryan is slipping on his chores.

Right on cue, the telephone rings. Okay, let's get this over with.

Today is the day I get this bitch to speak. I can't take this anymore. Enough is enough.

"Hello."

Only silence on the other end.

"Hello." I say again. "I know you're there. Please say something. This calling and hanging up routine has gotten old."

Still silence.

"I tell you what... let's handle this like adults. That's a novel idea, isn't it? Let's meet for lunch. There's no reason that we cannot discuss this like civilized women."

Dead air.

"Come on.... Say something." I hate myself for pleading. "Please say something, and stop this ridiculous childish behavior."

"Okay."

"Well..." Finally a response, a meek response but at least she can actually talk. *Do I hear an accent?*

"...Great." I say. "You tell me where and when."

Spitting it out quickly, as if while having the nerve, she says... "Tomorrow. McDonald's, on the corner of Flagler and North Miami Avenue. Twelve thirty."

McDonald's? Wow, she's really revealing her level of maturity.

"Fine, how will I know you?"

"I'll know you," she states crisply. "I've seen you a thousand times."

Click! All I hear is dial-tone.

At noon the next day, I drop Jay off at my neighbor's house. After hopping on the turnpike, it doesn't take long to reach Flagler. I pull the car into McDonald's parking lot. Intrepidly, I walk inside.

Looking around, I see two mothers with two toddlers each and a male employee sweeping up straw covers and French fries from the floor. The mothers in sight look a bit old for Ryan's taste. I see no one else.

"Excuse me, over here," a soft voice speaks behind me.

Turning around quickly, a Hispanic girl motions with her finger for me to come to her. This woman looks nothing like I expected her to. She is even younger than I imagined. Her long jet black wavy hair is tied behind her head in a pony tail. Her dark brown eyes seem kind and gentle. Her aura is pleasant not menacing.

I stretch a hand toward her. She wipes her hand on a napkin then shyly shakes my hand. Sitting down, I place my bag in my lap.

"Would you like to order?" She asks, barely looking at me. "I was starving and couldn't wait."

Her English is perfect. There's no hint of an accent now. I'm shocked by her politeness and manners. "No, no thanks. By the way, my name is Pamela. What's yours?"

"Theresa. Theresa Ricardez."

"I don't know where to start, Theresa. I mean, this situation is awkward to say the least."

She takes a bite from her Big Mac then looks me straight in the eye. This is my opportunity to get right to the point. I do not mince words.

"You claim that you're carrying my husband's baby."

"I am carrying Ryan's child and I didn't know Ryan was married when we starting seeing each other. He told me after I fell in love with him."

"So you think you are in love with my husband?"

Straightening her shoulders she answers with conviction. "I know I'm in love with Ryan. We plan to get married."

It's my turn to sit up straight. Her statement catches me off guard.

"Oh really?" My voice elevates. "That would be a neat trick. Just how do you think that can happen? Does Ryan plan to practice polygamy?"

"Practice what?"

"Never mind." I say.

KISS — keep it simple stupid Pamela... that's what this conversation calls for.

Speaking slowly for emphasis, I say to her, "I'm not going anywhere, Theresa. That's why I moved to Miami, to keep my family together. And together we are, and together we will always be."

"Oh yeah? I don't think so."

The accent is surfacing. It sounds like a mixture of Spanish and hood. Theresa continues, the nails (or should I say claws) are out now.

"For your information, Pamela... Ryan lived with me in that house before you came to Miami. That house is our place. It was only guilt that made him bring you here!"

The bitch has got spunk, I'll give her that.

"Well, who's living there now? Tell me that." I feel my blood pressure rising but I continue in an eerily calm manner. "I am, little girl, that's who. Not you! And guilt or no guilt, Ryan did bring me here. It's our baby and it is me that's living in that house with Ryan. Not you."

Theresa gets up, inadvertently pushing the table closer to me with her large round belly.

"Okay. That's the way it stands for now, but you'll see. It won't last." She says adamantly.

I stand, too.

"Yes, we will. We will see."

Chapter Nineteen

I hate fuckin' Miami. I have no freakin' friends here. I have no freakin' family here. Plus, Ryan's behavior toward me hasn't changed much. I have a hard time sleeping and when I do sleep I continue to suffer from nightmares. I've tried different prescription drugs to alleviate my pain and to help me cope. I've taken pills to sleep and pills to wake up. But lately, the pills only seem to increase my anxiety.

Contessa was here on business a month ago. It was great to see her. She treated me to a grand lunch at the Fontainebleau Hotel on Miami Beach. That was the one and only time I've been out to a decent place since my arrival.

Tess, Tik, Ge and I still do our weekly conference call. They've been extremely worried about me. I should be an award winning actress... each week I convince them that I'm okay. However, seeing Tess in person, I had a much harder time convincing her that I was alright.

"Pam, you look like shit!" Tess says disgustedly.

"And hello to you too, bitch!" I laugh.

"Where's Jay? I was hoping to see him."

"He's with my neighbor. I need some girl time. No baby, no bullshit. Just some real talk."

"Well okay. I can handle it. I'm done with business for the day so let's order some food, have some drinks and get fucked-up!"

"Sounds like a plan," I agreed.

I opened up to Tess about my meeting with little Miss Ricardez, something I didn't do with Tik and Gerhia. Tik would be ready to come down and kick her ass. And poor Ge, she would have cried all night, feeling sorry for me.

Tess and I stayed at that restaurant until it closed. It was great seeing her. Tess was so very intelligent but really street smart, too. In the end, Tess simply provided sound advice.

"Stay with your husband and deal with this shit if that's what you want. If it isn't, then leave the son-of-a-bitch! All your girls got your back!"

My friends are the very best but Jay is really my only saving grace. Without him, I would die. Thank God that Jay's a healthy, beautiful, growing baby boy. We go to the beach almost every day. Miami's only asset is the ocean. What an awesome and soothing sight. When I gaze at the ocean, admiring the glow, and watching the shimmers of the sunlight dancing on the waves, I imagine Ryan and me strolling, holding hands, and exchanging passionate kisses.

Jay loves the water same as I do. His skin has a beautiful golden brown color and his curly, dark brown hair now has a hint of gold as well from sun exposure.

The sun and the ocean are the only things that I like about this city. The sound of the waves crashing upon the shore and the sight of the seagulls soaring relaxes me. The glaring sun beaming down upon me burning my skin makes me feel alive.

I find the people in Miami to be very prejudice. The Whites seem to hate everyone except for their own and the Latinos hate everyone, including their own. The true Blacks, as far as I can tell, seem far and few between. Or, maybe, it's just that I can't decipher real Black people from the Latinos. God knows they can't figure out what Jay and I are. I am so sick and tired of saying "No comprendo," that I don't know what to do. I suppose there are no "true", one hundred percent black people here in Miami.

I try to maintain my sanity by continuing to express my fears and secrets on paper. Because everything going on in my life is so difficult, I have so many thoughts and ideas in my head on how to help not only myself, but hopefully how to help others as well. I have a dream of starting a nonprofit organization in honor of Jason. I've begun drafting the business plan and have decided on a name for the foundation. It will be called FVCV, Families of Violent Crime Victims. Somehow, a victim's family members must learn to survive. When Jason was murdered, I received no help, no advice, not nothing from no one. The city of Atlanta seemed to have swept the entire tragedy under a rug, pretty much just like my family has. I pray every night that I find a way to make this dream reality. It would be wonderful to start this nonprofit organization out-reach program to help families that have lost loved ones to violent crimes. However, I realize that before I can help others like me, I must figure out how to help myself. And right now, I'm just not strong enough. Right now, my world is rocky and my marriage is hanging by a thread. If I make it to the next day, I'm happy.

My other dream is to write a book. I want to take all this pain and all the feelings that are bottled up inside of me and share it with other women in hopes that someone can benefit from my struggle. I write all the time. Basically, I write down all the things I'm either too afraid or too ashamed to say out loud. Perhaps, if I take these thoughts that I've written and share them, I could enlighten other women that there is life after the death of a loved one or a marriage.

It's only a pipe dream, of course. All of it is. Who the hell am I fooling? I'll never find the time to write a book or much less achieve the skills to write a book. I have to empower myself before I can write a book on empowering others or before I can start a foundation for that matter. I can't even get my own husband to listen to me. What the hell makes me think I can get strangers to hear me?

Today, is rougher than most. It's been exactly one year since Jason died.

I call Momma to check on her. I know today must be really hard for her as well. We both put on a good face for each other... neither of us admitting the pain that we feel. Momma opts to focus on me, never once mentioning Jason.

"How are things going down there, Pam?"

"Well, I'm still here."

"Yes, child I know that. But that's not answering my question. You and Ryan getting along okay?"

"Depends on what you mean by okay. Ryan and I exist in the same house. Most of the time he's preoccupied and the rest of the time I'm just too tired to care."

"Well, that don't sound good."

"No, I suppose it doesn't. Momma?"

"Yes, Baby?"

"Momma, I think Ryan was present when his bastard child was born. I don't have proof. It's just a feeling I have. He's gone most of the time. And when he is here, he's not here. Physically yes, but not in mind or spirit."

"How you know when the baby was born? What she have?"

"Jay has a baby sister. Ain't that a bitch! Oops, sorry Momma. I didn't mean to curse. It slipped out."

"I'll let you slide this time. Go on."

"I know when she was born because I heard Ryan on the phone telling his mother. Momma, he sounded so proud. He was gushing about how beautiful she is. He was there. I know it. He was not there for me, yet he was there for her."

"Pamela, there's too much secrecy between you and your husband. A marriage can't operate that way. You need to confront Ryan, get it off your heart. You gonna explode trying to hold all these things in. Talk to the man, Pam. Talk to him."

"Easier said than done, Momma. Easier said than done."

Ryan walks into the kitchen while I'm feeding Jay his dinner. Jay reaches for Ryan but Ryan turns, opens the refrigerator and takes a beer out.

I swallow hard. There's a lump in my throat.

"Ryan, we need to talk."

Sighing, Ryan spits his words. "Not now, Pam. Please, not now."

"If not now Ryan, when? You get up, go to work. You come home, watch television, then get up off that couch, take a shower and you leave again. You come back after I'm asleep. If we don't talk now Ryan, when will we talk? When?"

I pick Jay up, wipe his hands and mouth then take him into his room. Carefully I put him in his playpen, kissing his forehead. "Play with your toys. Mommy will be right back."

Ryan has his car keys in his hand.

"Pamela, I can't deal with this shit right now!" Ryan states.

"Put the damn keys down!"

"What?"

"You heard me! Put the goddamn keys down! We need to talk now! Ryan, I just can't wonder anymore. Do you love me? I mean really love me? Why don't you make love to me? I love you, Ryan."

I hate myself for sounding so pathetic, yet I continue.

"I'm in love with you! I want this marriage to work. But when I say work... I mean that I want both of us to be happy. I believe that a marriage is more than just two people living together bound by a legal document. It's more than sharing financial responsibilities and raising children. Marriage should be fulfilling and ..."

"Pam, please!"

Ryan never liked confrontations. But I'm in his face anyway.

"No, damn it! Let me finish. I've got to get this out!"

I place my hand over my heart. It feels as if it's crumbling. Yet I continue.

"There should be laughter, kissing, petting, cuddling and lovemaking in a relationship. The latter should be often and plentiful. But, intercourse... sex... is only one way to express love. Ryan, the distance between us started a long time ago and we have not bridged that gap. You never talk to me about your feelings, our future or our dreams. Ryan, your feelings are just as relevant and important as mine. You are who you are. I'm not trying to change you into what I want you to be. The man I fell in love with was okay by me. But you are very different now. I suppose I am different, too."

I pause only a second while looking deep into Ryan's eyes.

"Yes, you've told lies... so many lies that I don't know what to believe anymore. But do you think I'm stupid? Do you actually think that I don't know what's going on? I'm a smart woman, Ryan. I know you're still seeing Theresa. I know you were there when your illegitimate baby was born. I know it! You were there for her but not for me! I deserve better Ryan. I was willing to love your bastard child. I was willing to accept the cards that fate had dealt me. I was ready to love that little girl because she is a part of you, a part of Jay. But you didn't have faith in me. You wouldn't believe that someone could actually love you that much! That someone could love you so unconditionally. Instead you put effort into deceiving me. Ryan, you couldn't speak the truth if you tried. It's easier for you to lie and deceive! You told me it was over between you and that girl! You told me that the baby she carried wasn't yours. You are a liar, Ryan Hogan! You lied about it all!"

"Pam."

"Pam. Pam. Pam. What? What! Is that all you can say is Pam? Okay. That's my name. What else you got to say? What else Ryan? Are you ready to speak the truth? Are you?"

"I'm sorry. I'm so sorry, Pam."

"Yeah, you're sorry alright! A damn sorry excuse for a man. A sorry excuse for a husband!"

Spent, I sit on the arm of the chair.

"Ryan, God knows I tried to be understanding. I know that I've been very self-absorbed since Jason's murder. I know that it seems as if the only one I care for is Jay. I know you've missed the loving side of me. I know that you have your needs and that you need to be loved physically. But I tried to be strong, Ryan. I tried to show you that no matter what the circumstance, I would love you... I would be there for you. But through all of that, you lost sight of what we had. You lost sight of our love... of us! Jay needs a father, Ryan. A full time father and not just someone that's around when he feels like it! But it seems that you've made your choice. And that choice does not include me and Jay."

"I'm sorry, Pam." Ryan repeats.

"Yes. We've already established that fact. You are sorry! Sorry, is not what I was hoping for Ryan. Sorry was not what I wanted from you. But like I said, I'm a smart girl. I can read between the lines. It's okay. At least it's out in the open now. Leave! Go ahead! Leave. Just know that this time, Ryan, it is over between us. Really over."

I get up and walk deliberately away from the man I once thought I would love forever. I watch Jay chewing on his rattle. A flood of tears begin to stream down my face as I hear the sound of the front door closing.

It's been less than a week since I had the show-down with Ryan. Daddy arrived from Augusta via airplane just this morning. On the way from the airport we stop to rent a U-Haul. Daddy's driving the truck back to Augusta. Even as we load the U-haul, I realize that I still love Ryan Hogan's 'dirty ass draws'. But at the same time I know what I have to do. And I'm doing it. It'll take us thirteen hours to drive to Augusta. But once again I have the same feeling I felt before. I'm anxious to leave this place and ready to be home again. It is definitely over between Ryan and me. I have to move on. Ryan will have to be the one that files for the divorce. I can't afford to pay for it and it doesn't matter to me whose name is labeled plaintiff or defendant on a piece of paper. The only important thing is that soon I will be free.

Slowly, I follow Daddy out of the driveway, maneuvering carefully so as not to shake loose the luggage strapped on top of the car. I glance at Jay in the backseat asleep. Already my heart feels lighter. On Jay's first birthday, we flee Miami and the sunshine state.

Chapter Twenty

Nearly nine months has passed since I left Ryan and I never missed a beat. I stayed with my parents while I searched for an apartment and within two weeks time I had my own place. I'm holding three-day Osaka trips right now, which is great. I still work nine days a month but my schedule is worth a lot more time. I can certainly use the fatter paycheck. Ryan's awful about giving up money for Jay.

The one bad thing about flying international is that I can't afford to make international calls... which means that I can't check on Jay like I want to. This also means... that I have to exercise patience and patience is something I don't have. When Jay's with Momma, I don't worry so much. Momma will certainly find a way to get a hold of me if need be. But Jay's in South Georgia right now visiting with his paternal grandparents and they aren't as resourceful as Momma.

Just finishing two trips back-to-back, I can't wait to speak with my baby. Jay's not talking yet, but whenever he hears my voice over the phone he squeals. As soon as I get off the plane in Atlanta, I pick up the pay phone and dial my former mother-in-law's telephone number. As soon as she answers the phone, I can tell something's amiss. She tries to keep her composure but before the end of her sentence, she's nearly hysterical. She tells me that Ryan came to see Jay and that he took him.

"What do you mean, 'took Jay?'" I ask, trying to remain calm.

"He came... here Pam... and took him to Florida."

"What did Ryan say? Why did he take him to Florida?"

"Just that... he... he wanted to visit with his son. That he hadn't seen him and that he would bring Jay back once you returned from Japan. I'm so sorry, Pam. But there was nothing I could do to stop him!"

"Okay... okay. I'll call Ryan to see what is going on. Everything's fine. I'll call you back after I get back to Augusta. Calm down before you give yourself a stroke. Okay? Bye."

Hurriedly, I dial Ryan's number.

"Hello, may I speak to Ryan?"

"Who's calling please?" a woman's voice asks.

"His wife!" I shout with plenty of attitude. I hear faint voices in the background. Then Ryan answers.

"Hello."

"Ryan, why did you take Jay from your mother? Florida was not part of the plan. Your mom is practically hysterical. Shame on you for upsetting her."

"I wanted to see him. Momma wouldn't accept that."

"You saw him in Savannah."

"I wanted to spend some quality time with him. He's my kid, too, you know."

"Yes, I'm well aware of that."

"Stop tripping, Pam. I'll bring Jay back to you on Monday morning."

"What time Monday morning?"

"When I get there."

Slam! The MF hangs up on me. I try to call back but the son-of-a-bitch doesn't answer the telephone. I try several more times. Ryan doesn't answer. What a bastard! How dare he? I consider catching a plane to Florida right now. But I'm so jet-lagged I can hardly stand. Day after tomorrow, I tell myself, trying to gain my composure. Day after tomorrow... that's as long as I'll have to wait to see my son. Yes, I'll give the bastard until then.

Two and a half hours later, I'm home. I flip the light switch on as I enter. Home never seems like home when Jay's away. I ignore the nagging pain in my heart as I climb the stairs. I throw myself across the bed and give in to my tiredness. I dream of Jason and Jay.

When Never Comes Again

Chapter Twenty-One

It's Monday morning and I anxiously anticipate the return of my son. I wake up early with a familiar feeling in the pit of my stomach. It's an eerie feeling that I try to ignore, but I can't. At ten minutes to eleven, the doorbell rings. I rush to answer the door expecting to see Ryan and my baby. Instead, it's the Sheriff. I stand there with my mouth hanging open.

"Pamela Ryan?" the officer begins as he hands me legal papers.

"Yes." My words sound cracked and feeble.

"You are hereby served." With that he does an about-face and walks away. I follow him for a few steps, in disbelief. I watch the car pull away and still somehow I expect to see Jay. Maybe he's hiding somewhere, playing with me as he so often does. Or perhaps the cop will return... having made a mistake.

After coming to the realization of what's really happening... clutching the papers, I hurry inside and pick up the telephone. Scanning the papers briefly, my deepest fear is confirmed... Ryan is filing for custody of Jay! I dial Ryan's number. No one answers. My hands are shaking and my pulse is racing. I dial my mother's number next. By now I'm a hysterical mess. I'm crying and yelling into the telephone.

"Momma..." I take a deep breath and begin again. "Momma, I... Momma. Momma I was just served with papers by the sheriff. Ryan's got Jay. Oh God! He's filing for custody Momma." I sink to the floor, tears rolling down my face and onto the summons that's crumbled next to my heart.

"Momma, he's got my baby. Jay's my life... why? Why would he do something like this? Oh God, why is this happening?"

"Get a grip on yourself child. Come on now. Shhh... Shush Pam. Calm down. Tell me agin' what happened. You not makin' no sense." She's a rock as always.

I repeat what I said before. Only this time I do it slowly and deliberately.

"It's gon' be alright Pam. You just calm down, child. The first thing we're going to do is hire a lawyer. I'll be right over. You hear me? Its gon' be alright. Momma be there in a second!"

I'm so angry I'm shaking. Why is Ryan doing this? He knows damn well he doesn't want custody of Jay. He's just trying to hurt me. Why? I don't know, but he's succeeding. My heart hurts as it did a year and a half ago. I didn't think anything could cause me that degree of pain again. Heaven help me please. Bending over, I hold my mouth. I'm going to throw up. My head is pounding and I have the urge to hit something, break something, fuck something up! A primal instinct takes over. I start throwing things. I tear at my clothes. I break dishes. I grab a knife and put it to my wrist. I place pressure on it until I see it bleeds. Suddenly, I stop. I can't do this. My baby needs me. Throwing the knife down, I curl into a fetal position and sob. Twenty minutes later this is how Momma finds me.

"Pam! Pam! Come on baby girl, talk to me."

A noise comes out of me that mimic a wounded animal. It's a

low deep unnatural grunt. However, I am not physically hurt. I am dumbfounded, thunderstruck. I have been sucker-punched. Ryan has duped me and taken away my reason for living. Momma does her best to soothe and comfort me. She rubs my back and holds me, until at last, the animal sound subsides. She helps me up the stairs and into my bed, where I fall into a deep sleep for the rest of the day.

I wake up alone the next morning. It's quiet. No signs of Momma moving about. She must have left last evening. Good. I'm glad she did.

Jumping out of the bed, I head downstairs. The first thing I do is grab a bottle of Hennessey from the liquor cabinet. I open the bottle, throw it back, taking a huge gulp. I hug the bottle as if my life depends on it. Thank goodness I didn't break it in my rampage yesterday. I drink until the pain in my heart becomes a dull ache. One would think that I would be at least a little tipsy.

I am not. I feel nothing. I shower, dress and telephone Momma. She reports that we have a meeting this afternoon at one o'clock with attorney, Allan Gibson.

The lawyer Momma consulted is an old acquaintance of Lois. She and he dated years before. Momma says he's a good guy. Someone we can talk to. Someone we can trust. We arrive at his office promptly at one.

"Mrs. Hogan." He begins with a pleasant smile. "I'm Allan Gibson. I went to school with Lois. As a matter of fact your father cut my hair when I was a little boy."

Allan Gibson is a tall, dark, and no way near handsome middle-aged man. His eyes are too close together and he's a bit overweight. His lips are thin like a white man's lips. But his voice sounds sincere. He's dressed in a white shirt, gray pinstriped suit and has on... what looks like very expensive shoes. Crocodile. I can tell a lot about a man by his shoes. Expensive shoes are a plus in my book. If a man cares about his appearance from his head to his toes, he's usually a caring man.

I feel at ease with Allan, about as at ease as I can feel right now. I explain my situation in full detail. He listens intently then reiterates what he heard. He then explains my rights as a parent. The man seems to know what he's talking about. Nevertheless, I don't like what he saying. He tells me that because there is no written agreement between Ryan and me as to who has physical custody of Jay, whichever parent that is in possession of the child, has control. As usual, Ryan has all the balls in his court. What else is new?

"So what do I do?" I plead.

"My legal advice at this point is that you should talk to your husband. Try to come to a mutual agreement prior to the court date."

"I can't even reach Ryan right now. All I know is what I've told you. He could be out of the country for all I know!"

"Keep trying, Mrs. Hogan. Keep trying to contact him and when you do... come to an agreement. You say Ryan doesn't really want custody and that this is some kind of payback because he hasn't seen the child lately. Appeal to his fatherly side and reach an agreement."

"And what if we don't reach an agreement?"

"Then this will have to be settled in court," says Allan frankly.

He stands, our signal that there's no more business to be done here.

"I don't have a license to practice in Florida. You need to seek counsel there. But be warned, this case could be a costly and time consuming situation."

Chapter Twenty-Two

It's the following day. Momma and I are flying to Miami. On the flight, I reflect on the changes I have gone through in my life. Jay is my everything... my world, my life... my reason for existing. What would I do if Ryan kept him away from me forever? How would I go on? How could I go on? I struggle to retain self control when everything in me is screaming totally out of control. I want to ask the flight attendant to bring me a drink but I don't. I have to drive when I arrive in Miami and I need to keep my wits about me. Bottom-line... no drink for Pam.

Upon our arrival at the airport, a strong feeling of déjà vu sweeps over me. The feeling is so strong, that it's like a slap in the face. Miami International Airport exudes a smell that is both pungent and sweet and almost suffocating. You notice it the second that you step out of the plane and onto the jet-way. It's everywhere. I supposed some would call it pleasant, an island-like scent. However to me, the smell is overwhelming and sickening. A flood of memories bombards my mind. Terrible memories... memories of Ryan and his adulterous affair. Memories of commuting from this airport to

Detroit during the most painful time of my life. Memories of all the terrible pain I've incurred comes back with a force so powerful that I have to steady myself... my feet become nailed in place for fear of falling over.

"Pam!" Momma yells to yank me out of my reverie.

I manage to get a grip and refuse to be deterred from the task at hand. "Y-yeah." I stammer. "I'm fine. Let's go!"

As a preferred Avis customer I don't have to wait in line. I pick up my reservation and we catch the shuttle to the rental car lot. Miami's sky is cloudless. It sparkles like a flawless gem. The problem is I have come to hate beautiful days. Beautiful days are simply camouflage in order to catch you unprepared for the horrible and painful things that life will cast your way.

Ignoring the gorgeous weather, we exit the bus and head straight to the designated parking space. It's a cute car, a convertible mustang.

"Momma, you want the top down?" I ask already knowing the answer.

"Child, did you bump your head during that flight?"

Gotta love Momma. She's predictable but she could always make me smile.

I burned a little rubber as I left the lot, just to add insult to injury. I laughed out loud looking at Momma's expression as I drove recklessly to the Police Department in Hollywood. I have to get my jollies where I can.

The police at Hollywood's Number 4 precinct tell us the exact thing the lawyer in Augusta said... that there is absolutely nothing legally that can be done. And even worse... come to find out, Ryan does not live in Hollywood anymore. When I locate the apartment with the address I have for him, I am told that Ryan has moved. The move occurred over a month ago. I wonder if Ryan lives with his new girlfriend. I wonder if he even lives in Hollywood. I wonder if he still lives in the state of Florida. Or has he indeed fled the country with my child?

I have to get a grip. I am losing it again. Of course, Ryan still lives in Florida. He has to. The papers that were served to me had come out of Broward County. I am going to have to do some investigating on my own.

I go to Ryan's job. At least I go to the last place I know of as his place of employment. Bingo! I'm on to something. I spot Ryan's vehicle. It's three o'clock in the afternoon. He should be getting off soon. Momma and I wait for him to come out of the building. Momma's getting antsy... two hours have passed. Finally, Ryan emerges from the building at ten after five. I don't make a move until he reaches his car. I start the rental car then pull directly behind Ryan's car. I jump out the car and I'm in his face before he can blink an eye.

"You sneaky son-of-a-bitch!" I yell pointing my finger in his face. "Who the fuck do you think you are keeping my son away from me? I ought to scratch your goddamn eyes out!"

Momma's yelling at me from the passenger window. She's telling me to get control of myself and to not make a scene.

Oops too late. I plan to not only make a scene... I am going to knock the shit out of this lying motherfucker! How dare he take my baby and keep him away from me!

"Where's my son, Ryan? Where is he?" I scream.

"Pam, all the cursing and screaming in the world will not make me give you Jay back."

Did this motherfucker just say what I think I heard him say?

"I bet if I get somebody to fuck your ass up, you'll tell me where my baby is!"

"Pam, stop tripping."

"Oh, motherfucker you ain't seen me trip yet!" Saying that... I lunge for his neck. Momma jumps out the car.

"Come on, Pam. Stop it! Acting like this ain't gonna get you Jay back. Come on now, child. Stop this!"

I let go of Ryan's neck. He is a fucking bastard, but I know he won't hit me. I get into the car and pull off like a bat out of hell. I am steaming, not just at Ryan... but at myself as well because I have lost control and accomplished absolutely nothing. This is not the way to reach an agreement. I have to be smart. I need to be conniving like Ryan. But most of all, I have to find my baby.

Momma and I check into a room at the Sheraton Airport Hotel. I receive an airline employee discount at certain airport area hotels. I'm a lot farther out than I want to be but at this point I also have to be as economical as possible. I have a feeling that this custody thing is only the beginning of the expenses I will incur before I get my son back.

Momma's hungry, so we order room service. We are both physically and mentally exhausted. After dinner, Momma takes a shower then goes to bed. I, on the other hand must start to plot a plan of action.

First thing I do is telephone an old acquaintance that I met when I lived here in this God forsaken place... Mark Williams. I suppose Mark was a nice enough guy. Certainly not my type or anything like that, but in this situation he might prove useful. I'm not at all sure that I can reach him. The telephone number I have is an old one. At this point I have nothing to lose and I am desperate. I look over at Momma in the other bed. She's out cold and snoring softly. Poor dear, she's too old for this kind of shit!

I grab the phone, hoping I can talk on the balcony. Thankfully, the cord reaches the glass doors. I close the sliding door gently behind me as I step outside. I dial the number that's on the worn piece of paper that I've carried around in my wallet for over a year. The phone rings but only to discover that the number's been disconnected. Damn! There's a pager number as well. I try it. This number seems to be working. It allows me to leave a numeric call back number. I walk back inside as quietly as I can then I pull a pack of cigarettes out of my purse. Lord knows I'm trying to quit, but I need a cigarette right now. I slip back onto the balcony. I light the Kool Mild then take a long slow drag. And then I wait.

Fifteen minutes pass. The phone finally rings. I grab it quickly. I don't want to wake up Momma.

"Hello?" I whisper.

"Hello? Who's this?" Mark's voice booms back at me.

"Mark, this is Pam, Pamela Hogan. Remember me? We met a while ago..."

He replies before I can finish my sentence.

"Pam! What the hell, girl? How you doing, baby? Where you at? You back in town?"

Mark appears stunned to hear that it is me. Stunned, yet completely delighted. I explain to Mark what is happening and relay all that I know about Ryan's whereabouts. He tells me to stay put until he calls back. I'm relieved that Mark is on the case.

Mark Williams is a seedy type of fellow with connections on the street. At one time, he was a drug dealer. I have no idea what he's into these days. I met Mark when Jay was only six months old and we were living in the rented house in Miami Gardens. I hated that house just like I hated Miami. The first time I walked into that house, I found a pair of worn pantyhose in the closet. Later I figured out that the hosiery belonged to Ryan's teenaged lover. Finding old pantyhose should have told me that I was not the first woman to be there with Ryan. But I had turned a blind eye. I had wanted my marriage to work. I was so stupid.

I clearly recall when Mark first strutted into the house in Miami Gardens. Mark acted as if he had died and gone to heaven. Ryan introduced us, but he never stated Mark's surname. At the time, I didn't care to know. Mark seemed surprised to meet me and even more surprised when Ryan introduced me as his wife.

As far as I knew, Ryan had only done drugs occasionally... perhaps smoking a joint while socializing with the guys. However at the time, maybe because of his situation with Theresa and her being pregnant with his child and all... who knows... maybe Ryan was doing more than I thought. In addition to his situation with Theresa, I suppose my nightmares and continuous sobbing over my brother's death didn't help any either.

I need to stop. I'm still making excuses for Ryan.

After the very first time Mark and I met, Ryan no longer had to call him and ask that he come over. Mark would simply drop in. As a matter of fact, he dropped by damn near each week. And when he made his guest appearances, he always had a little something for Ryan. Mark was completely infatuated with me upon sight. Every time he showed up at our place, he'd announce himself by saying "Mr. Williams is here... sweet thing have no fear."

Ryan of course was too blind (or too stupid) to see that this man wanted me in the worst way. All the while Mark was cozying up to me and keeping me supplied with my own stash.

Mark and I never had a sexual relationship, much to Mark's chagrin. Mark offered to take me places that I had no business even thinking about going. Most often I refused to be alone with Mark in any capacity, let alone go anywhere with him. However, there were a couple of times when I didn't resist because I was either too depressed or too pissed off with Ryan to refuse. There was a brief period of time when I tried every drug imaginable... prescription and street. I was so desperate to stop thinking about my problems and to forget everything that happened in Atlanta. But nothing worked. Drugs didn't take control of me. I was lucky. No, correction, I was blessed. Nothing could make me forget Jason or stop the nightmares. No matter how high I attempted to get... Jay was always foremost on my mind.

Nothing caused me to neglect my son... not in any way. Jay was never without my love or attention. Thank God I was smart enough to leave the drugs and Mark Williams alone. Mark was forever trying to get between my legs. There was zero payback from my acquaintance with Mark and the risks were simply too high. Neither drugs nor Mark was the answer.

Ryan never knew Mark offered me drugs. He didn't seem to realize that I was trying to extract myself from reality and our miserable situation through drug use. But perhaps I'm the fool. Maybe Ryan did know. Maybe he just didn't give a fuck.

One thing is for sure... I can't let Momma know about Mark. She would sense his crudeness and sexual attraction to me. She would never approve. Besides, she doesn't need to know. The less my mother knows the better. I don't want to incriminate her in any way. Mark will find Ryan. I am sure of it. A rat can always smell another rat. Besides, Mark never really liked Ryan anyhow. He used to tell me all the time... "If a man has a wife that looks half as good as you do, that man is a fool if he doesn't take care of her. I'd take care of you, baby. Just give me the chance. I'd take real good care of you."

In his dreams.

Men like Mark and Ryan only care about a woman's appearance. A good looking woman on their arm is considered a feather in their cap. Mark had said that he knew that I was not being taken care of. He'd said if I had been protected and taken care of the way that I should have been... then there was no way the two of us would have ever met.

He's right. Ryan should not have introduced us. Mark had always assumed that Ryan caused my pain. I never bothered to confirm or deny his assumption. There's a reason for everything. Now I know the reason I met Mark Williams.

Sleep evades me as usual. Tossing and turning, anxiously I wait to hear from Mark. I close my eyes and begin to pray that I will soon see my son, touch my son, smell my son. Eventually, I manage to fall asleep.

The next morning, the phone awakens me. I grab it, knocking over the glass of water on the night table. Shit.

"Hello."

"Hey, Pam."

"Mark?"

"Yeah baby, wake up."

"What you got for me?"

I wipe the water up with the hand towel I left at the foot of the bed last night. I let Mark's reference to me as 'baby' slide. I need him.

"I got everything, baby. Didn't I always tell ya I got everything you need."

"Yeah, Mark, sure. So you got an address? Where's Ryan staying?"

"I can do better 'n that baby. Ask me where your kid is right now. Ask."

"You must be shitting me! Don't play with me about this.

Where Mark? Where?" I ask as I try to keep my excitement down to a minimum. I don't want to wake Momma.

"He's at Ryan's bitch's house. And I don't mean that Latino bitch that had his baby. What was her name? Terrie was it? Nahhh, it wasn't Terrie. Theresa. That was it... that was her name."

Mark burps loudly yet doesn't miss a beat as he continues to enlighten me on Ryan's love life.

"Ryan's got a new girl now. Carolyn Breakstone. This girl

lives with her mother and sister. The mother keeps your baby most of the time, you know... when Ry's working and shit. The mother and daughter both look pretty damn good, too. The Momma's quite a looker. She fine as hell to be an old dame. I wonder if Ryan's kicking it with the momma and the daughter. You know our boy Ry... player player, all day player. Maybe he's fucking both of 'em. I wouldn't put it past pretty boy Ryan." Mark states admiringly.

"Mark, spare me, please. Where's my son? What's the address?"

I write down the information, and then repeat it just to ensure no mistakes. Once I know I have it down exactly right, I thank Mark profusely and promise that he will hear from me again. I am anxious to check it out. I hang up the phone just as Momma comes out the bathroom.

"I know where Jay is Momma," I say, voice quivering.

"Then let's go child. What we waitin' for?" she asks.

Momma is a smart lady. She doesn't ask how I found Jay's location. She's smart enough not to want to know.

We follow the directions that I've written down on the paper. It takes about thirty-five minutes to reach the Fort Lauderdale address. When we arrive, I drive slowly past the house. I turn around then pause two doors down from it. I had been in such a hurry to get here that I did not stop to think about exactly what I would do once I arrive. I sit in the car contemplating.

"Why you stallin', Pam?" Momma asks. "Go get my grandbaby."

"I'm waiting to see if there's any activity going on here. Let's wait a few more minutes and then I'll go and knock on the door."

We wait ten more minutes. Nothing happens. No one comes in or out. I place the car in drive and pull into the driveway. The house is a two story contemporary style dwelling. It's large and very expensive looking. It is made of stucco and has a fancy red tile roof that's common in Florida. There is a tall black metal fence around the yard. I can see that there is a pool in the back. Whoever lives in this house has a little cash. No this is south Florida — they have a lot of cash. The house is not a new one, but it has been well maintained. This is the upscale side of town. The neighbors will not look kindly on anyone raising hell and interrupting their fairy tale lives.

I open the car door and step out. I instruct Momma to stay in the car. As I walk to the front door, I can see the curtains part and a woman looking out the window. I ring the door bell.

A middle aged light skin woman with long curly hair opens the door.

"Yes, may I help you?"

"I'm here to pick up my son." I say as calmly as I can.

"I beg your pardon?"

"My son. Jay Hogan. I'm his mother and I'm here to get him. Don't bother denying that he's here. I know that he is."

"You must have the wrong house. Sorry," she lies then tries to close the door in my face.

I place my hand between the screen and the door.

"No. I have the correct house. May I have my son?"

I'm trying my best not to be nasty. However, I can tell from her attitude that the nice approach is not going to work with this woman.

"I have no idea what you're talking about." She tries again to close the door in my face. This time she actually smashes my fingers. But she succeeds in closing the door.

I scream out in pain. But I'm not deterred. I'm just ferociously pissed!

"Listen lady!" My teeth are grinding together. "You better bring me my son before I break this fucking door down!"

I begin to beat on the door with both fists. By this time, my mother is out of the car. She hears the entire conversation. She decides she will give it her best shot.

"My daughter only wants her baby." Momma says nicely and stately-like to the closed door. "We don't want no trouble," Momma adds for good measure in her most professional voice.

The woman appears again at the door. She cracks it open slowly and speaks through the small opening.

"I said I do not know what you're talking about. Now, leave!"

This nasty bitch! Now I'm really losing it!

"Listen lady, I want my baby and I want him now!" I scream.

She's relentless as well.

"If you don't get off my property, I'm going to call the police!"

"Call the goddamn police. Call the fucking Army and the National Guard, too, if you want. Either way I'm not leaving here without my son!"

Momma starts to panic. Just the mention of the police get's her bent all out of shape. She grabs my arm and attempts to lead me to the car.

"Come on, Pam. We don't know anybody down here in Florida! If they lock us up, there'll be no one to call. No one! Come on. You're not on your own turf, baby. Let's go!"

"Momma, I'm not leaving without Jay!"

Before the words were out my mouth, I hear brakes screeching as a car pulls in front of the house. Ryan jumps out.

I continue yelling, pointing my finger towards the house.

"I thought you said I had the wrong goddamn house, you lying bitch!"

"Pam, get the hell out of here!" Ryan yells.

Jay is crying now. I hear him from outside the house. God, how I long to see my baby. Ryan rushes past me and goes into the house. When he comes back to the door, the woman is standing behind him with my son in her arms. If I could spit venom, I would.

And they'd both be long dead.

"Ryan" I plead, "Give me back my baby."

Ryan steps outside and looks at me with disgust.

"No! You'll have your say in court. Say what you have to say to the judge!"

"Ryan, I need my baby. He's all I have. Please. Just let me hold him."

I fall down on my knees, tears streaming down my cheeks. I grab Ryan's hand. I place it on my heart.

"Please, Ryan. I'm begging you. I'm on my knees. Please. Just let me feel those little arms around my neck. Let me kiss his sweet face. Please, for the love of God. Please."

Breaking down completely, I feel my heart shattering in fragments so small that I know it will never be whole again. Momma is crying, too. She leans over, puts her arms around me and whispers into my ear.

"Come on baby. Don't beg no more. Your pleas are falling on deaf ears."

But I can't give in. I have no pride. Jay's all I have.

"Ryan, please. Please!" I beg. "Just let me see him. Pleaeeeese Ryan! I won't even touch him, if that's what you want. I promise, but please just let me see my baby! Let me see his face for God's sake! Please!"

As I look up at Ryan, for a fraction of a nanosecond I think he's about to give in. I can swear that I see a flicker of mercy in his eyes. This brief glint gives me hope... just for a second... that I will actually get to see my son. But instead the expression in Ryan's eyes changes quickly. He looks at me in abhorrence then he turns and walks away. But before he enters the house, he lunges one last dagger into my heart.

"Here," he says as he tosses a business card onto the ground. "Contact my lawyer. Don't bring your ass back here again." He goes inside the house.

"Ryan!" I scream. "Ryan! Please!"

Momma picks up the card then puts her arms around me, trying to lift me off my knees.

"Come on child. That's enough now. Let's go. Everything will be okay. It will. I promise. I know you don't believe me now. But it's going to be alright Pam. I swear, it will."

"No, Momma, things will never be okay. Never!"

Rising from my knees, my heart is so heavy I can barely stand. I stumble but somehow control my balance. I manage to walk away. I don't crawl, even though that's what I feel like doing, crawling. And crawling is what Ryan would love to see me do.

Trying to catch my breath I say, "Momma-ma... Momma... how can I live without Jay? How can I go on without my baby? Without my lifeline?"

Through teary eyes she answers.

"You won't have to baby. Trust me, you won't have to."

We manage somehow to make it back to the hotel room. I have no idea how I drove back. I cry all night. My mother, strong woman that she is, keeps her head on straight and knows just what to do. First thing Momma does after ordering take-out for dinner, is look for a lawyer in the Yellow Pages. That's a hell of a way to hire counsel, but it's the only way she knows how. I'm just grateful I have my momma here with me. Lord knows what I'd do without her.

The next morning, we meet with the fancy high-priced Fort Lauderdale attorney that Momma found in the Yellow Pages. My mental state is definitely questionable at this point. I drive to the law office in a fog. As I park the car, I admire the beautiful craftsmanship of this magnificent structure. I know I can't afford to do this. But I get out the car and enter the building anyway... all other options depleted. I decide to perpetrate a fraud and somehow convince this guy that I have the money to honor whatever fee he decides to charge.

Continuing to look around as I exit the elevator on the twelfth floor, Momma appears to have her doubts as well.

"Pam, what you think?" she asks softly.

"I think you must have selected the most expensive lawyer in the Yellow Pages. That's what I think. What made you select this firm anyway?"

"I liked the name. Vanderbilt and Associates. I always did like that woman clothes. What's her name? Ah you know. Gloria, that's it. You know, Gloria Vanderbilt. I like her jeans. It was the only familiar name in the entire dang book."

I smile at Momma. She has a reason for everything she does or doesn't do.

"I like her jeans, too, Momma."

We turn the corner headed for Suite 1218. It's a corner office. Figures. My palms start to sweat. I don't like lawyers. Not particularly anyway. I feel as if I'm heading for the gas chamber. I see the fancy glass doors at the end.

Dead man walking.

We give our names to the young big breasted blonde perched comfortably behind a huge mahogany reception desk. Her physicality falls into the category of most under twenty white females in Miami. While checking out her beautifully manicured fingers she picks up the phone and announces our arrival. The receptionist looks like a ditz and she appears extremely bored. She's probably the law partner's daughter or niece... and she really has no need for cash but is working only because her parents insist she experiences a taste of the real world. She directs us to a huge conference room.

"Mr. Vanderbilt will be with you momentarily. Please have a seat. May I get you a drink? Water or a soda?"

"Thank you. No. We're fine," I say.

Momma elbows me. "Actually, I'll take a diet Coke, if you have one."

"Sure, no problem. Be right back."

Momma looks and says, "I'm thirsty. It's included in the price anyway... probably."

Five minutes later, a fairly nice-looking middle-aged white man walks into the room. After he hands Momma an ice cold diet Coke, he introduces himself as Jonathan Vanderbilt, Esquire.

"Call me Jon," he says amicably.

After I provide a brief recap of my circumstance and reveal all the pertinent information I have regarding Ryan's place of residence, employment and so on... he agrees to represent me. Jon assures me that he will do everything possible to get my son back. He states that he plans to contact Ryan's attorney this afternoon and will get back to me as quickly as possible with an update. I shake his hand then Momma and I take our leave.

Unfortunately, we also leave Florida without my baby.

When Never Comes Again

Chapter Twenty-Three

Three weeks later and I still do not have my child in my possession. I viewed the past weeks through a drunken stupor. Obviously, I'm not handling Jay's abduction very well at all. I keep telling myself I'm okay because I'm not falling down and throwing up drunk, but I am a numb and not giving a damn about anything kind of drunk. The agony of it all is unbearable. I have never felt such pain before... not even when Jason died. It's as if someone has my heart in their hand and my heart's being twisted like a pretzel. Tears swell up in my eyes and roll down my face. They flow without shame. I only pray that with time my heart will heal.

My family is worried sick about my health as well as my mental stability. But I'm not crazy... not yet anyway. What I am right now is hurt and I'm handling this shitty situation the only way I know how. I miss my baby so much, I want to die.

Jon has advised me not to 'harass' Ryan. He says it'll make me look bad in front of the judge. Therefore, I spend my time drinking and simply trying to make it through the day. I'm on leave of absence from SEA. I informed my supervisor of the situation and surprisingly, he was sympathetic. He said to take all the time I needed. My job would be there when I was ready to return to it. Good thing he understood what I am going through. I can't imagine having to go to work right now.

My cousin Melissa comes over every day to check on me. Ever since Jason's death, I've alienated myself from almost everyone that loves me. Contessa, Gerhia and Tikki have stopped trying to contact me. Instead, they call Momma to find out how I'm doing and to get news on Jay. I think my family has me under a suicide watch. But I'm not going to harm myself. I'm going to fight. I'm going to get my baby back.

Of course, Jay isn't old enough to call me on his own and Ryan seems adamant about not allowing me to talk to him let alone allowing me to see my son. Boy... Ryan's being such a bastard. I would have never, not in my wildest imagination... not even in a million years... thought that Ryan was capable of such underhandedness and cruelty. I guess I didn't know him as well as I thought I did.

The first time I laid eyes on Ryan Bertram Hogan I just about came in my pants. I was standing at the teller window in the Georgia Railroad & Trust Bank located in downtown Augusta, Georgia. The bank was on Broad Street... the pulse of the city. I turned from the teller window and there he was... all six feet of him. Talk about fine! This man had long bow legs and an afro that had to be two feet in diameter. With his smooth brown skin and captivating green eyes, I was totally mesmerized. He had the face of a Roman god. I was smitten from the start. I was checking him out and vice versa. I procrastinated as I exited the bank... trying not to stare but failing miserably. Ryan had watched me as I exited the bank and somehow he managed to catch up with me two blocks away at the crosswalk. It was love at first sight.

I was totally floored by this man. I was seventeen years old. I had lied to my parents telling them Ryan was only twenty-two when he was actually twenty-seven, ten years older than me.

Ryan had swept me off my feet. He was a smooth talking New Yorker and I was just a young, little, Georgia, country girl. Before I knew it, I had dropped my high school sweetheart like a hot biscuit... bam and bye-bye... he was gone. I no longer had time for little boys. I wanted a man. Ryan became my world.

Ryan courted me throughout my first semester at Spelman College. Ryan continued to live in Augusta but he rode his motorcycle to Atlanta on weekends to visit me. We were married four months after our first date at the beginning of my second semester at Spelman.

We moved into a small apartment in southwest Atlanta. Ryan, being older, had a lot more experience in life than me. He had served in the Army, entering when he was eighteen. He had been married and was divorced at twenty. He introduced me to a life style that was foreign to me. Nevertheless, I caught on quickly. We partied all the time. We were one of Atlanta's beautiful couples, going out every night. We were on everybody's A-list. Always the first to be invited to parties and always amongst the last to leave.

Ryan Hogan was a jack-of-all-trades, master-of-none. It was not that Ryan couldn't master things, he just didn't. He was too busy trying to do everything. He was always after the quick dollar. Ryan was the type of guy that was everybody's friend. At least, that is what he thought. He loved meeting people. He loved those that were influential, and those that had money. He was a well versed talker and had no problem making acquaintance with the in-crowd.

Little did Ryan know — behind his back most of his so-called friends were trying to screw him... and me, for that matter. We both fell into the kind of life that I had once only imagined... riding in fast expensive cars, and drinking champagne on a beer budget.

I should have known that it was a superficial life style, filled with superficial people. But I was just a teenager. I didn't know any better then.

Regardless of all the partying and phony people, I have to admit that Ryan Hogan brought two wonderful things into my life and I will be forever grateful. The first is our son Jay and the second is Wiley Moore.

Wiley Moore was a wonderful friend to me. He was kind, generous and loads of fun. Wiley made me laugh. He brought me endless joy. He was the most generous friend I had ever had.

Wiley was the first self-proclaimed, out of the closet, homosexual I had ever known. Wiley hailed from New York, New York like Ryan. It seems the two became friends instantly. Besides the gay part certainly, other than being native New Yorkers, Wiley was totally unlike Ryan in all other aspects.

When Ryan and Wile (I called him that), first met, I had no idea what to think of him. Here was this mysterious, flamboyant character like no one I had ever met in my lifetime. Instantly, I was sure Wile wanted my husband. Boy was I wrong. Wiley didn't want Ryan. Deep down, Wiley was just a simple guy that enjoyed meeting people. And when Wiley met me, we became inseparable. He fell in love with me.

Wiley would ask me so many questions. "What is it like to be a woman? Where'd you get that sweater? Have you ever considered modeling? Can you do this move? Can I go to Augusta with you to see where you grew up?" I would never know which angle he'd come from.

Wiley wanted to know me. He wanted to know everything about me. I suppose this young country bumpkin from Georgia intrigued him. Wiley had a curiosity about me that could never be satisfied.

I recall this time when I was still in college, not working, and Ryan was in-between jobs. Our electricity had been turned off the day before my twentieth birthday. Ryan never told me, but I saw Wiley passing Ryan money and I heard him say, "We can't be without lights during our girl's day, now can we?"

There were times when I wondered if Wiley really wanted to be me. Perhaps I was the female he would have been had he'd been a female. Wiley treated me like he worshiped the ground I walked on. We loved each other dearly. There was nothing we would not do for each other.

Wiley was quite the gentleman... even if he did have a few feminine attributes and mannerisms. As we entered restaurants or when I got in the car, Wiley would always open doors for me. He would pull my chair out for me to sit down. Yes, he was debonair and charming. Wile never dressed in drag, never wore makeup or did anything like that. Wiley was comfortable with who he was. He was one of a kind and I loved him.

Wile could also cook his ass off. I loved my Wiley's cooking. He could whip up the most glorious scrumptious meals, both plain and fancy. My most favorite meal that Wile cooked was his delicious standing crown rib roast. The presentation was fabulous and the taste would make you want to slap your momma... it was that good. I always felt like Marie Antoinette or someone when Wile prepared his special meals. God, I miss him so much!

Wiley was dark, well built with a fine-ass physique. He was also very tall. He stood well over six feet five inches... yet he was as graceful as a prima ballerina. He had a heart the size of Texas. His big dark beautiful eyes could melt your heart. His complexion was the color of dark chocolate with skin just as smooth.

Wiley's tongue though, oh... Wiley's tongue was sharp as a blade. He would crack me up talking about his lovers. He would tell me all the sordid details. Once, he explained to me what a 'Picasso' was. Of course, I thought he was referring to a painting or to the artist.

"No, no baby girl," Wile laughed. "It's art alright but there's no paint and easel involved."

He would place one hand on his hip and the other would be waving flagrantly about as he weaved his tale.

"Girl, let me tell you. This man had a dick the size of a loaf of French bread and it tasted just as good. Yum." Wiley would then fall onto the floor laughing. "Anyway, honey child, when he put that big old thing inside me, I created art all over it. It was a damn masterpiece."

I looked at him totally perplexed.

"Pam, you can be so naïve sometime," he said, completely exasperated with me.

"That big, fat thing was so far up... I shitted girl! I 'Picasso-ed' that big sweet thing! Get it?"

I'm completely shocked.

"Ughhhhhh, Wiley! That's totally gross, Wile. You are lying. Please tell me that's not the truth."

"Of course not, girl! I told you that you were naïve."

Yes, Wiley had the power to shock me. He was a real free spirit. He lived life for the pleasure one could get out of it. I admired that about him. Wiley and I were kindred spirits.

Wiley moved back home to New York in 1981. We stayed in touch via Ma Bell. We called each other twice a week. He never confided in me that he had contracted AIDS. I don't know why he didn't. I wondered if he imagined that I would disown him or something. He should have known better than that. I discovered he had AIDS only when he became very ill. I flew to New York to see my Wile when Jay was eight months old. We were worried about each other, actually. He wanted to see for himself that I was okay... after everything that happened with Jason. I wanted to see him before it was too late. By the time I arrived in New York, Wiley was completely blind. He never got to see the pictures I had brought along of Jay. He never got to see me, for that matter. Wiley died not long after my visit. I was unable to attend his funeral because by that time I was out of my head with missing Jay. I was too selfish to think of anyone but myself. So, add Wile's death to Jay's kidnapping and I just knew the combination would be the straw that broke this camel's back.

As I think back on my relationship with Ryan, all in all, I suppose we had a pretty good marriage. For seven years it survived. Sure, we had our ups and downs, but what marriage doesn't? Who would have ever guessed that a tragedy would be the one thing to tear us apart? Sometimes tragedy brings people closer together. Then again, who knows? Maybe we would have split anyway. Ryan hadn't been the perfect husband but I hadn't been the perfect wife either. When I first became pregnant, in my mind I thought that maybe having a baby would change us. I had hoped that somehow we would become stable, serious adults and parents.

I was dim-witted enough to think this after all my disgust for women that get pregnant with hopes of trapping a man. But I guess my case was different. I already had the man.

There was never any doubt in my mind that Ryan and I loved

each other deeply. Yet, somehow, even from the beginning, I never really felt that we would be together forever. Our time together was never serious, it was always fun, traveling, getting high... hanging out and trying to keep up with the Joneses. Besides, our relationship started with a lie. I lied to my parents about Ryan's age because I knew he was too old for me. Then I lied to myself about my own feelings toward Ryan, I felt empathy at one time... which I confused with love. My gut told me Ryan was weak. I knew his history with women. Ryan had been married before and he had a son he didn't even know.

I don't know. I suppose I could have been a better wife. Perhaps I could have made him better by setting a better example myself. But instead, I had not always been the wife I should have been. I should have been stronger.

Payback's a bitch. In the end, I was willing to fight for my marriage. I even fooled myself into thinking our marriage could work... even in the midst of Ryan's affair. After everything, I had tried.

Yes... tragedy changed Ryan and me alright. Ryan's changed into someone I don't even recognize. He's being a complete asshole. I don't even recognize myself anymore. I'm at the lowest point in my life... quickly becoming the pathetic alcoholic that will never forgive him.

Chapter Twenty-Four

We left for Florida the evening prior to the hearing. This time I'm traveling with both my mother and my Auntie Grace. Grace is Momma's youngest sister. Auntie Grace is a law student and extremely intelligent. She insisted on accompanying Momma and me. I can use the support. No argument here.

When we arrive in Fort Lauderdale, it's raining cats and dogs... but this soothes me. The rain is a good sign. It's sunny weather and deceivingly beautiful, easygoing days that make me nervous. The bad shit always happens on the most gorgeous days.

We check into our hotel and head to the fifth floor. As we open the door to the room, that familiar Florida smell invades my senses. The smell is an overwhelming combination of salty sea water, chlorine and musk. Even still, the room is pretty nice for a Holiday Inn. I booked two rooms... one for me and Momma, and an adjoining room for Auntie Grace. Momma said she didn't want to have to wait in line for the bathroom because when she had to go she had to go.

We settle in and change into our nightgowns. It's been a long day... yet I'm pacing like a tiger. I can actually feel the carpet in the hotel room wearing beneath my feet.

Auntie Grace suggests I take a Valium and then she snaps. "Pam! Pamela Hogan! Please sit down. You're going to drive me crazy with that pacing!"

I stop pacing long enough to reach into the ice bucket and grab a few cubes of ice, then dropping them in the plastic cup. I walk into the bathroom and get water from the sink. Auntie Grace is digging into her toiletry bag searching for her valiums. She has the constitution of a horse and takes them on a regular basis... before and after class.

She hands me a couple. I toss both of the small yellow pills in my mouth and take a big gulp of water to wash them down.

"Pam," Auntie Grace shouts. "I didn't give you both to take at the same time!"

"Oh well, too late, now. You should have been more specific, your honor."

"Don't get cute with me young-un. I bet your ass stop pacing now. But if you fall asleep standing up, I won't be dragging you into the bed. Will you please lay down now? Please?" she pleads.

"Okay. Okay." I get into bed.

Auntie Grace blows me a kiss as she leaves the adjoining door open behind her. I look over at Momma. She's sound asleep. I'm so glad she and Auntie are here with me. I close my eyes as soon as my head hits the pillow. Good thing, too, because morning comes quickly.

It seems to have taken forever for my day in court to arrive. It's been six weeks. Six excruciating weeks. Six weeks without my precious son. I've waited six weeks for this day. And on this day, I pray that God gives me a reprieve for acting like a weak, stupid, irresponsible bitch the past few weeks.

The Broward County courthouse is a southern antebellum style building. The hallways echo as Momma, Auntie Grace and I walk towards the courtroom. I am afraid. I am afraid that on this day, I could lose my son forever. The Breakstone's', Ryan's lover's family, seem to be very well-off. I have no clue as to the type of political connections that they may have. They could have bought off the judge on this case or even my own attorney, for all I know. My imagination is steadily conjuring up the worst scenarios.

As the three of us search for the appropriate courtroom, I spot Carolyn's mother, Ms. Lola Breakstone, standing in the corridor. There stands the Broom Helga, the wicked witch of the South... the very witch that lied about having my son in her house.

Suddenly the air becomes thick, musty and stale. I feel as if I have to fight for every single breath that I attempt to draw into my lungs. Once I see Ms. Breakstone in the hallway, I know that we're headed in the right direction. It's do or die time.

"That's Ryan's girlfriend's mother, standing over there. We're on the right path." I inform Auntie.

"Where?" asks Auntie Grace.

"Up ahead." I say then point towards Broom Helga.

Aunt Grace focuses in on her and begins to check her out. Ms. Breakstone is wearing a tight little yellow dress with white bunnies all over it. Who the hell did she think she was? Mother Goose? I still wonder if Ryan's fucking her. She's always been the one to be around and with her nose all up in my shit... never the daughter that Ryan is supposed to be dating. Yes, always the mother. And it was the mother who threatened me and Momma. Why the hell is she here? She probably thinks she can testify against me or something. I wish I could snatch that little tight ass dress right off her then shove it down her thin pretentious throat!

I dressed very conservative this morning. I'm wearing an off-white, almost cream colored Jones of New York tailored suit. I have pearls in my ears and a single strand around my neck. My low heel off-white pumps are Enzo Angiolini. I'm not wearing a stitch of makeup with the exception of a pale sheer lip gloss. I was way too nervous this morning to put on any more than this.

Tenaciously we approach the courtroom... the thud of our footsteps seem to echo even louder throughout the corridor. I stare Ms. Breakstone up and down and if looks could kill... this bitch would definitely be dead. I'm about to pass her and enter the courtroom, when audaciously Lola Breakstone speaks to me.

"You know, you ought to be grateful that Jay has a father that loves him so much."

What the fuck did she want to say that for? I am about to jump this bitch and kick her ass. I lunge towards her. Auntie Grace grabs my arm in just the nick of time. I am on the verge of showing this bitch my Sugar Ray Leonard version of a right upper cut. The rumble in the jungle is just about to take place in a Florida courthouse. I am so mad I can spit nails.

"Lady, let me tell you one mother-fucking thing." I hiss. "When Ryan Hogan breaks your fucking daughter's heart... and he surely will... or when he tries to take your daughter's baby away from her... then you can talk to me about being grateful for the kind of man that he is! In the meantime, you can kiss my natural black ass!" I spat on the floor near her feet. She's lucky I didn't spit in her face. She knows not to fuck with me.

As I break free of my Aunt's hold, Ryan walks out of the courtroom.

Calmly, he looks at me and says, "Pam, can I see you a minute?"

I look at him as if he's lost his ever-loving mind. Can't he feel the tension in the air right now?

"For what?" I'm practically screaming.

"It's about Jay."

"What about Jay? You ready to give me my baby back?"

"Pam, I need to speak with you alone. Please?"

Momma looks at me as if to say, don't trust him. Auntie Grace still thinks I may throw a punch. I look at them both appreciatively. "It's alright. Give me a minute."

Ryan and I walk to the end of the corridor. We sit on a bench. Ryan acts as if he doesn't know how to begin. We've been here before.

"What is it Ryan?" I ask impatiently.

"I think this whole custody thing has gone too far. I think we should resolve this, you and me... not some judge."

"Oh, no shit. Is that what you think? Fine time for you to start thinking this way. Why couldn't we have resolved this weeks ago. I tried. But no-oo-o. I have not seen my child in six weeks. You wouldn't even take my phone calls. In six weeks, Ryan. In six weeks you wouldn't even call me back! Six goddamn weeks, Ryan!" I'm furious... and hurt... and I'm tired.

"I know, I know. But listen, I want to end this now. I propose that we share custody of Jay." Ryan states.

I am about to interrupt but Ryan holds up his hand.

"Wait a minute Pam, please let me finish." Ryan continues. "We will have joint custody but you will have physical custody. I want to see Jay for one week every month. I'll come to Georgia to get him each month. But there will be times when you would have to fly to Florida to pick him up. I'll also pay you one hundred and fifteen dollars a month child support."

"One hundred and fifteen dollars? A month? What is that? That won't even pay daycare for a goddamn week!" I am incredulous. "What about a roof over Jay's head, food in his mouth, clothes on his back? Does any of that mean anything to you?"

"It's all I can afford right now on a twenty-three percent pay-cut, Pam."

I place my hands over my face then run them through my hair... a nervous habit of late. I look into Ryan's eyes and ask, "You're going to pick Jay up and bring him back every month?"

Right back, he stares straight into my eyes.

"Yes... when I can. Like I said, sometimes you will have to pick him up... depending on my work schedule."

"How can I trust you?"

"It'll all be on paper. All the terms. Legal. I will stick to my end of the deal."

"Some damn deal! You come out smelling like a fucking rose as usual."

"Take it or leave it, Pam! If you want to take your chances with the judge that's up to you."

The motherfucker is threatening me now. So I can't waste much time thinking it over. I know I have to take this deal. I'm not going to take the chance of losing my baby. I long to see Jay and to hold him in my arms... I want this so bad I can taste it. Ryan knows this. He knows it's an offer I will not and cannot refuse. This son-of-a-bitch!

"Alright," I say softly. "When do I get my baby?"

"As soon as we tell the judge we've reached a mutual agreement... it'll all be over. You get Jay as soon as I can bring him to you."

"You swear?" I ask.

"I swear."

Ryan reaches for my hand. Uncertainly, I shake his hand. We had not touched in any way, shape or form in so long that I expected to feel a jolt of some kind... repulsion, love... something. But I felt absolutely nothing for the man that still held the title of my husband

and father of my child.

We walk back to the courtroom, silently, except for the sounds of our footsteps reverberating throughout the hall. When my mother sees us approaching she meets me and asks if everything's okay.

"Everything's fine, Momma" I say, lying through clenched teeth. "Everything's fine."

A bailiff calls out "Hogan versus Hogan!" It's time to face the judge.

I walk lightly into the room. I feel as if I'm floating... as if I'm in a trance with Mommy and Auntie Grace by my side. I take in the scenery as I enter. The courtroom is poorly lighted and the dark paneling on the walls doesn't help any. My eyes are squinting as I make my way to the front of the room. I take my place next to my lawyer. The bailiff orders everyone to stand, and then he announces the Honorable Judge Weinsencoff.

The judge is a large, white haired man with a permanent scowl on his face. Weinsencoff? What heritage is that? German? Or maybe it's Jewish? German and Jewish perhaps?

He calls us to order with a knock of his gavel and the proceedings begin. Ryan's lawyer speaks first. He asks the judge if counsel may approach the bench. The judge takes his time to answer. He sips water from his crystal glass then he nods and grunts permission. My lawyer asks me if I'm sure that I want to accept Ryan's terms. Am I sure that I don't want to negotiate a better deal? I shake my head vehemently. I'm sure. I agree to everything Ryan wants. I can't chance losing Jay.

The lawyers speak to the Judge for another minute... the judge is listening intently and taking notes. Next, the judge declares the terms of our agreement then grants joint custody of Jay. The proceedings are over in less than twenty minutes. Good. Great. All I want is my child.

Afterwards, Ryan and I arrange to meet at my hotel. I update Momma and Auntie Grace on the way there. They are still reeling from the quick course of action. Basically, I'm a nervous wreck. I want to believe that I am finally getting my child back, yet I'm afraid to believe it. So much has happened. So many bad things, so many unthinkable things. I wish it was raining, I'd feel more optimistic about Ryan keeping his end of the agreement.

I wait at the hotel. And just as I had this morning, I'm pacing the floor wondering if the ordeal is truly over. I want my baby so badly that I would actually kill for him at this moment. And... God forgive me... if for some reason Ryan tries to back out of his end of the deal, I know that I really would kill him. I know this without doubt. I will kill Ryan if he reneges.

I say absolutely nothing as I wait for Jay to arrive. I only pace and I pace and I pace. We are already packed and ready to go. It is only a matter of Ryan showing up with my child. I look down at my watch for the thousandth time.

Ryan finally arrives with Jay after what seems like an eternity. He calls my cell phone and I race to the lobby and to the parking lot. I can barely wait for Ryan to get out of his car. He does and he turns to release Jay from his car seat. When I finally get Jay into my arms, I hold him so close I almost squash the poor child's ribs. He smiles and makes goo-goo sounds, obviously just as happy to see me as I am to see him.

"Ma-Ma," Jay utters.

I cry. Tears flow uncontrollably down my cheeks. I never want to let him go. Jay is my life. I love him with every inch of my being. I swear out loud to Jay, to the world and to the Lord Almighty above... "We will never, ever, be separated again!"

Chapter Twenty-Five

Every single day is a struggle. Almost a year has passed since the custody hearing… but I still can't shake the nightmares or the grief. I have nightmares about losing Jay. I have nightmares about going to jail because I murdered Ryan, or I murdered Lola or sometimes I dream I murdered them both. Crazy dreams that cause me to wake up in a cold sweat, unable to go back to sleep again. And when I do go back to sleep the dream picks up right where it left off. Sometimes my dreams continue from one night to the next. What the fuck is wrong with me? Jason's death is hard enough to deal with… but I can't even bring myself to talk about Jason's death with my parents or siblings. I want to let it all go, cry on Momma's shoulder or talk to Lois about what happened that day. But I can't. I just can't bring myself to do it. I'm afraid of their reaction. Afraid they will blame me as I blame myself. Jay is my only saving grace. He is the one and only thing that makes any sense in this fucked up crazy ass world.

I think of Jason each day, hoping and praying that the ache in my heart would subside somehow. But yet it's still there. The pain is like the nasty sticky gum that gets stuck to the bottom of your shoe. You scrape and scrape, trying to get it off, but no matter what, there's always some left... bugging the hell out of you because you know it's there. You feel it each time you step. It just won't go away.

I know that if fate had taken a different turn, it would have been me or Jay, or maybe us both, that would have died that day. Jason was my savior. He gave his life for me and for my son. I will forever feel the heartache. I will forever be indebted to him. I will forever live my life with the awareness that I am here because my brother gave his life. Jason protected me to the end... his end. Somehow, someway, I will make the world aware of his gift. I know in my heart that Jay is destined for greatness. There is no way God would have spared us for anything less. Jay will know his uncle through the stories I tell, through the pictures I share, through the love that I will always feel in my heart. One day at a time. One foot in front of the other, that's how we'll make it. It'll take time... but we will make it.

Jay and I are still living in Augusta but I have plans to move back to Atlanta. I swore when Jason died that I would never live in Atlanta again... but commuting from Augusta to Detroit by way of Atlanta is too hard. So I'm moving back. Just goes to show... you never know. Never say never.

There are a few things left to get in order. We move in three months. One thing that I'm waiting for, the main thing really, is for the divorce to become final. When I move back to Atlanta I don't want to be married to Ryan. I want to start over fresh... no baggage.

Ryan has seen Jay every month since the hearing. So far, he's living up to his end of the deal and returning my son on schedule. There's always the fear that he'll do something stupid. I never thought that seeing something in writing would mean so much to me.

It's Friday afternoon and I'm thrilled to be finished flying for the month. There's plenty to do. The crew, Contessa, Tikki and Gerhia, is driving down from Atlanta this weekend. They've been complaining that they never see or talk to me anymore. Thank God we're all close again. For a while, I wouldn't let them in.

Contessa said she has a surprise for me. I never did like surprises. But I think I can guess what this one is. Tessa's been talking about getting her PhD for some time now. I bet she's enrolled for fall semester at Emory University. She's so damn smart. She's already an executive with Coca-Cola making plenty of money. But the girl's ambitious. Tikki calls her avaricious. But that's like preaching to the choir.

Tikki has her own real estate business and she works as hard as anyone I know including Tessa. Everywhere she goes she's passing out business cards, telling potential clients to call her day or night. Tik is hooking me up with the place in Atlanta. The townhouse vacancy is dependent upon the current tenants actually closing on their new house which is being built. Tikki keeps telling me that I have nothing to worry about. She says the house is coming along great. Everything is on schedule.

Gerhia is a housewife with two kids. She's also an artist. She paints part-time, earning spending change for those designer extras she loves so much. She's the quiet one in the bunch. I'm always telling her to speak her mind... don't be nobody's pushover.

I look forward to seeing them, today. I need to go to the market and get some fresh fruits and vegetables. I mustn't forget the champagne either, although Tessa will bring at least five bottles with her, guaranteed.

I look down at Jay playing with his building blocks on the kitchen floor. He's such an intelligent child. He's walking and talking now. Well, I suppose you can call it talk. He still is and always will be the light of my life. As if he knows I'm thinking about him, he looks up and smiles at me. His smile can light a city block! He is so handsome.

"Hi there, my little kissing bandit." I pick him up. He places his chubby little arms around my neck.

"Momma-ma. Wuv you. Wuv you, Mom-ma." he says in a language all his own then plants a big fat wet kiss on my cheek.

"I love you too, my little darling." Jay squirms, signaling he wants down so he can get back to his blocks. I place him back on the floor. He looks up and grins at me again. My heart melts. Lord knows, I am so grateful to have him back. He is my world. My life. My everything.

"Ready for lunch, Jay? Ready to eat-eat?"

"Ready to eat-eat," he sings. "Ready to eat-eat."

The door bell rings.

"Who is that Jay? Who's that ringing our doorbell?"

"Who's dat?" Jay tries to repeats.

I wipe my hands and navigate around Jay. I look through the peep hole. It's the postman. I open the door.

"How you do, ma'am? Certified letter for Pamela Hogan."

"Hi, I'm Pamela Hogan."

"Sign here, please."

I sign, take the mail and close the door behind me. I place the mail on the counter.

"Let's get my boy his lunch." I put Jay in the high chair and place his plate of macaroni and cheese with green beans in front of him.

"Blow it, honey. Blow it," I say.

I pick up the certified letter. Ask and ye shall receive. This has to be what I've been waiting for. I tear open the envelope. Yes, it's my final divorce papers. I start to cry. I don't know why I'm crying, yet I am. In my heart I know there is no future for Ryan and me. The divorce papers are only a wakeup call for me to get on with my life.

"Hey-ey!" Tikki says, as I meet them outside my door.

"Hello."

"What's the matter?" Contessa always could feel my moods better than anyone.

"Nothing's wrong." I put on a smile and pull them both into my arms, kissing them both on each cheek. "I'm so happy to see you guys. Where's Gerhia?"

Tikki pulls her diva shades down and looks over them and directly into my eyes. "Liar. Something's wrong." Thank goodness she lets it go and changes the subject. "Ge's babysitter had a last minute emergency so she couldn't make it. Ge didn't call you?"

"Nope, at least I don't think so. I was out running some errands earlier and I haven't checked my messages. Come on you two. I want to hear Tessa's surprise, and I want to know how the real estate business is treating you," I say convincingly... staring right back at Tik.

"Look what I have" says Tessa. Tik and I turn. Somehow Tessa's cradling four bottles of champagne against her chest and one's dangling from her hand.

"Oh my goodness, Moet White Star. We are celebrating aren't we?" I ask.

"You damn skippy we are!" answers Tessa.

"Alright then, let's get this party started!" I grab Tessa's Louis Vuitton satchel and we head inside.

Cracker crumbs are lying flagrantly all over the patio table and the buzzing of electrocuted mosquitoes fills the night air. Two empty bottles of Moet are thrown in the corner of the deck next to the outdoor fan.

"You want some more?" Tik asks me as she fills Contessa's glass.

"Please," I reply. "I haven't had this much to drink in a long time."

"Well, you need a break. And besides we're not only celebrating my pursuit of my Doctorate, we're celebrating your divorce. To hell with Ryan Hogan! There are bigger and better things out there for you, Pam. Just wait and see."

"Here here," Tik slurs. "You're beautiful, you're fun and... and... you have us for friends. Shit... girl you got it going on!"

We laugh. It feels good to have them around.

"Yes, you are so right. I have no idea why I was so down about getting the papers yesterday. I've been waiting for my freedom. And now I have it. So here's to freedom!" I lift my glass.

"To freedom." We clank glasses spilling champagne.

"Alright there now. Don't be wasting this shit. It ain't Andre's." Tessa scolds.

Tik sticks out her tongue at Tess then gives her the finger. Now she turns to me and says, "Seriously Pam, you are better off without him. You deserve, and Jay deserves, so much more. With all the stuff you've been through, and all he's put you through, you can still talk to him like he's a human being? Hell, you're more woman than I could ever be."

"I agree with Tik. I don't know how you survived," affirms Tessa.

"I survived because I have a great support system! I love you guys!"

"We love you, too," they say in unison.

Tik takes a swig of champagne and says, "Okay. I wasn't going to say anything, but since you both have news, I'll share a bit of news myself."

"Do tell." I say.

"Well, remember the guy I told you both about, Timothy? Well, Tim asked me to marry him last weekend."

"What?" Tessa screams.

"And you were able to hold this in?" I ask. "What's the deal?"

"Well, I'm just not sure if I love him enough?"

"What do you mean enough?" Tessa asks.

"What if it doesn't work? Tim is a great guy. But they all seem like great guys in the beginning. And we've only been dating four months. I'm just not sure."

Tessa wastes no time handing out advice. "Well, if you ain't sure... don't do it. If you were sure, there'd be no question."

Tikki says sadly, "I guess you're right."

"Okay." I say. "The question must be asked. How's the sex?"

"The sex?" Tik asks innocently.

Contessa looks at me. "Yes, the sex, Tik. You know... when a man and a woman..."

"Yes Tessa, I know what sex is."

"And?"

"And... we've never had sex."

Tessa spit out her champagne. "What?"

"We've never had sex." Tik says smugly. "Tim believes that sex is for after marriage."

"Does he now?" Tessa winks at me.

"What the hell does that mean? What the hell are you winking for? Some people do actually believe that sex should take place after marriage."

"I know. I know."Tessa professes. "But why should you wait? Tik, you're not a virgin. Is Tim a virgin?"

"No. No. No."

"So who you trying to convince that waiting is the right thing to do? Us or yourself?" Tessa asks.

Tik looks at me for help.

"Leave her alone, Tessa. She's a grown woman. She knows what she's doing? Don't you, Tik?" I ask, trying to support my girl.

"Of course I do!" Tik says.

She then places her face into her hands as if she's hiding or playing peek-a-boo. From behind her hand she continues to talk.

"Shit. Who am I fooling? No. No, I don't know what I'm doing. There's something about him, you guys. I mean he's debonair, cute, has a good job... but he's never even tried to finger fuck me! That's not having sex... not really."

I almost dropped my glass.

"Tik, you little whore! If the man is celibate, he's celibate. If he starts playing around, let alone finger-fucking, he probably can't handle it."

"Yeah." Tessa agrees. "You know they can't start something and not finish it. It's not physically possible for them. Men, once they get hard, they gotta get em' some."

Tik sighs. "I hope that's all it is. But I tell you what. I like to try on new shoes before I buy them. You got to make sure they fit."

"I hear you, girl." Tessa and I say in unison.

Tik has had enough focus on her relationship. She turns to me and asks, "So Pam, speaking of sex, when was the last time you had some?"

I exhale. "Don't start in on me now. I don't have a boyfriend."

Contessa can't wait to get her two cents in.

"And what the fuck is up with that, Pam? You're fine, you're smart, and you have a good job. Why aren't you getting some?"

"Because I don't want to have sex just to have sex." I say.

Tikki gives me the evil eye. "Now look who's trying to fool who. Girl, you've always loved sex. You a freak-a-leek!"

"Well, there comes a time in a girl's life when you just don't want the bullshit that comes along with having sex."

"I hear you Pam. But it's not healthy to keep all that stress bottled up. You have to release it. You'll feel better." Tik says.

"You're one to talk, Miss Celibate Boyfriend." I say rolling my eyes.

"Just because my boyfriend doesn't want to have sex until we're married does not mean that I do not release my stress. That's why they make toys."

"Toys?" Contessa asks.

"Yes, Tessa, toys. Sex toys. Vibrators and such." Tik continues to give us the low down.

"I have one called the Butternut. It's a dream. I discovered it about three months ago. An acquaintance at work gave me the scoop on it. It is battery operated. It has a rotating head, three speeds and it's waterproof! It slides in so smooth it's like butter... hence the name... and it's guaranteed to make you bust a nut. There's a three-pronged finger like attachment that works the clit while... you know... the rest is doing its thing. I'm telling you, you've got to try it! Mr. Butternut is the best thing since sliced bread. I swear."

I can't stop laughing. "So Tik..." I ask, "...has Mr. Celibate met Mr. Butternut?"

"Hell to the naw! Why would I do that? So Tim can call me from work every day, twice a day, to ask if Mr. Butternut has come out to play? No... hell no, I don't think so. Shit... Mr. Butternut is saving my relationship and keeping me stress free!"

I finally gain my composure and say, "Tik, Mr. Butternut sounds like a perfect companion. Good thing I never knew about this before. As good as Mr. Butternut sounds, if I had it in my life I may have never gotten married in the first place."

Contessa stands and refills our glasses with champagne.

"Ladies, this calls for another toast." she slurs, swinging the bottle dangerously close to my head.

"To Mr. Butternut... may he always have batteries and forever bust a nut."

Tik and I stand too.

"To Mr. Butternut!"

We all touch glasses then fall out laughing.

It's been two weeks since I received the final divorce papers. It's my turn to pick up Jay from Miami so I wait anxiously in Miami's Airport for Ryan and Jay to show. I still hate this place. So many bad feelings emerge when I'm here. I glance at my watch. Come on Ryan. The flight back to Atlanta leaves in forty-five minutes. Around the corner, here comes Ryan, Jay and Carolyn. I didn't expect to see her.

Ryan looks like the cat that swallowed the canary when he says, "Hi Pam." Carolyn follows suit.

"Hello Pamela." Carolyn says in that squeaky little Minnie Mouse voice of hers.

"Hello Ryan. Carolyn." I say perfunctorily as I nod my head.

Then to Jay I speak affectionately.

"Hello my darling boy! How are you? Give Mommy a kiss!" Jay jumps gleefully into my arms. "Did you get bigger? Huh? Did you?" Jay grins and hugs me tightly.

"Pam," Ryan starts nervously. "I wanted to tell you in person and not on the phone." He clears his throat and takes Carolyn's hand.

"Tell me what? What is it? Spit it out. Our flight leaves in less than thirty minutes. They're boarding already." I put Jay down and look at Ryan curiously.

Ryan speaks.

"Carolyn and I were married on Saturday. Jay's going to be a big brother in about six months."

"Well, well. I suppose I should say congratulations." Then turning to Carolyn, I add, "And good luck. Believe me girl, you're gonna need it."

With that, I pick up Jay, snatch Jay's bag out of Ryan's hand, then turn, heading for the gate to board my plane.

When Never Comes Again

Chapter Twenty-Six

Patiently I wait for the party at the other end to pick up the phone. Finally she does. "Hi. Melissa, let's go out tonight. I want to hit the club!"

"Say what? Is this my cousin Pam? Or is this someone that sounds like her? It can't be Pamela Hogan. She never goes out. She's a hermit, a recluse."

"Ha, ha! Yes, Mel, it is I!" I'm ready to par-tee! Momma's got Jay for the night, it's Friday and I want to close the club down!"

"Oh yeah! That's what I'm talking about! I'll pick you up at nine o'clock sharp. Be ready and be fly!"

"No problem. See you then!"

Augusta's night life is nothing like Atlanta. There are a few places to go, but none of them great, if you ask me. But I've not been out in forever and after hearing about Ryan's marriage plans, I decide I need to have a life, too.

We decide on Club 909. We grab a seat at the bar. Mel knows every bartender in the city. I turn toward the door and in walks the man of my dreams. He's so fine, built just the way I like. He is sharp too, suit, white shirt and tie. I love a man in a white shirt and tie. It's just downright sexy! This guy seems out of place in Augusta. Where the hell did he come from?

"Mel." I nudge her. "Mel, who the hell is that?" nodding my head toward the entrance.

"Who? David?"

"In the suit and tie."

"Yes, that's my cousin, David Casey."

"That's David Casey? The guy that married Barbosia Atkins?"

"That's him."

"Shit."

"What's wrong?"

"Wouldn't you know that the only fine guy in the entire club would be Barbosia Atkins's husband?"

Melissa falls out her bar stool laughing. "Want to meet him? He is my cousin after all."

"No no. I don't want to. "

"David! David, over here!" Mel's still laughing at me.

David Casey swaggers over.

"Hello there."

"David Casey meet Pamela Hogan, Pam meet David Casey."

"Hel... hello David." *I'm stammering... shit!*

"Please, call me Davie. If you'd like. Nice to meet you, Pamela Hogan. I've heard a lot about you."

This guy is trouble. He's flirting with me.

"Have you now?" I ask. "And call me Pam... please." I'm flirting back.

He turns, hugs Melissa and kisses her cheek.

"How you doing, cous? I haven't seen you in a long time."

"Yes, it's been a while."

"Ladies, there's an empty table over there. Care to join me and my friend Craig Thomas. Craig should be here momentarily. Let me buy you a drink. Please?"

Melissa wastes no time responding. "Sure Davie." Melissa says as she winks at me.

After ten, the club got crowded quickly. Melissa, Craig, David and I laughed the entire evening. David had a great sense of humor. Craig and Mel went to dance, leaving me alone with David.

"So Pam, how do you like being a Flight Attendant?"

"How'd you know I am a Flight Attendant?"

"I know a lot of things about you?"

"Do you now? Like what?"

"Well, let me see... like you have a brother named Gabriel that attended Paine College and one named Karl that's a manager at Taylor Crates. Like your father cuts hair and has a shop on the Hill. Like you went to Eastside and you were a cheerleader. Like you are married and have a little boy. Should I go on?"

"Wow. You're pretty well informed, except for the fact that I'm no longer married.

David smiles at this comment.

I continue.

"I'm at a disadvantage here, however I do know a few things about you."

"Okay, give it to me."

"You are married to Barbosia Atkins and you work for the U.S. Postal Service."

"Want to dance?"

The Disc Jockey is playing Prince's *"When Doves Cry"*, one of my favorite songs.

"Yes. I'd love to."

I'm mesmerized by this guy. He's classy, funny and sexy. He moves on the dance floor as if he owns it. In my mind, I'm holding up a cross sign with my fingers. This guy is taboo. He is totally off limits. Not only is he married but he's married to my childhood enemy!

When Prince ends and a slow jam begins to play. Without asking, David takes me into his arms and without complaining I stay there. He looks me directly in the eye and smiles, saying nothing but pulling me closer. I feel very at home in this man's arms. We move together like parts of a well oiled machine. He feels too good. Song please hurry up and end. This man is so off limits.

Once seated at the table, Mel and Craig are yapping away. David leans over and whispers into my ear. "I really enjoyed that. I truly hope I see you again."

The hairs on my neck stand up and I tingle between my legs. Yet determined to stand my ground, I whisper back, "Never, not in this life."

He doesn't respond to my reply. He only stares at me intensely with a smirk on his face as if to say 'we will see'.

David Casey turns the other way, motions for the waitress then orders another round of drinks.

Chapter Twenty-Seven

The time to move to Atlanta comes before I know it. The condo Tik was working on for us didn't pan out. However, I did find a nice apartment in the suburb of Norcross. Norcross is on the opposite side of town from my former Atlanta residence. I didn't want to be anywhere near southwest Atlanta.

Our place is one of four town homes in a single building. The place is ideal for Jay and me. It has three bedrooms, one of which I use for Jay's playroom. The quadra-plex is located right next to Gerhia's subdivision, which is extremely convenient for me, since Gerhia takes care of Jay when I'm away working.

"Come on Jay, honey! Did you find Scrappy Bear yet?"

"Yes, Mommy," Jay comes tearing down the stairs with his favorite stuffed bear in tow. He raises his hand to show me and smiles. "I got him, Mommy. See?"

"Yes, I see that! Okay you, let's get going. Auntie Ge is waiting for us and Mommy's got a flight to catch!

I manage to make it to the airport with five minutes to spare before boarding my commuter flight to Detroit. This month I have two Frankfurt trips and one Osaka. The trips are only 3 days long, but, I'm working them back to back so that I can have the rest of this month off. I really want to get my holiday shopping done early this year. Jay wants everything he sees on television and then some.

When boarding the plane, I eye this fine, big chocolate brother sitting in first class. He's eyeing me, too. He looks like a football player, definitely an athlete. I nod my head as I pass his seat. He nods back.

I'm catching some Zs when I feel something touch my hand. I wake to see Mr. Fine Ass from first class standing in the aisle next to my seat.

"I didn't mean to wake you. I was just leaving this note on your tray table."

I wipe my mouth to make sure there's no drool seeping from the corners and smooth my hair.

"Why are you leaving a note on my tray table?" I say trying to sound intriguing.

"Because I saw you when you boarded and I liked what I saw. Are you married?"

"No. Are you?"

"No, I'm not but I want to be."

"That sounds like a personal problem to me."

"Oh, does it now? You got something against marriage?"

"Hey... been there, done that. But if it makes your boat float... I say go for it."

"You sound cynical."

"Please don't judge me. You don't even know me."

"But I want to."

"Yes, you do. I remember. That's why you were leaving the note, right?"

"Yes."

A flight attendant squeezes past my admirer, taking much more time than required. He realizes this and blushes.

I look him in the eye and ask, "You sure this note is not meant for her?" pointing at the flight attendant that just passed.

Wow, he has the most sensuous eyes. They are light brown, almost hazel and when he looks at me it seems he's looking straight into my soul. He has a mustache and goatee with just a hint of gray which I find very sexy.

"No, the note's for you. I'm positive."

"And what exactly is in this note?"

"Why don't you read it and see?"

I open the piece of airline stationary. I admire the handwriting... not bad for a man. I read the note silently.

Hi, my name is Royal Dutton. I saw you as you entered the plane and from that moment I knew I had to know you. Will you have dinner with me? If you grant me the honor, please join me in first class or you can call me at 313.434.7898. Anytime. I'll be waiting.

Royal Dutton, hey?

I fold the note paper neatly, place it in my pocket then look up sheepishly at the wonderful male specimen. I extend my hand.

"Hi Royal, my name is Pamela Hogan. It's a pleasure to meet you."

Royal grins from ear to ear revealing the most extraordinary perfect teeth. Oh yeah, the brother is paid. Those veneers cost a pretty penny.

He takes my hand in his, raises it to his lips then places a gentle kiss on the end of my fingers. I'm creaming in my pants, his gestures are so erotic.

"I'm thrilled to meet you, Pamela." His voice is heavy with passion. "Will you do me the honor of having dinner with me?"

"I will. But you'll have to wait a few days. I work for Southeast. I'm on my way to Detroit to report for a four day trip to Frankfurt."

"What if I fly to Frankfurt, too? Will you have dinner with me?"

I'm shocked. "You're going to fly to Germany just to have dinner with me?"

"Yes, if there's a seat in first or business class."

"Oh... so you don't do coach?"

"Not if I can help it."

Attitude. I sort of like that.

"Okay then, sure. I'll have dinner with you. I may fall asleep on you though."

"I'll do my best to keep you entertained." He says. "But if you do fall asleep, I'll enjoy watching you drool."

Mainz is a small German town about an hour from Frankfurt airport. On the bus ride into Mainz, I admire the sights. Mainz, Germany is a gorgeous place with its fountains and historic cathedrals. The bus stops in front of the Mainz Hilton and the crew exits. We sign in but we must wait for our rooms to be cleaned. I turn away from the front desk, looking for a spot to rest my weary body when I see Royal across the lobby. He walks toward me.

"My my... you are the resourceful one aren't you?"

"You did say yes to dinner?"

"I did."

"So, I know you're tired after flying all night. I figured, why don't we make it easy and just have dinner here? There is a beautiful and secluded restaurant right here on the premises. That way neither of us has to leave the hotel... unless of course we want to."

"Okay."

Okay is all I can say. I'm exhausted. All I want to do is take a nap.

"Why don't we have an early dinner? That way you can get to bed at a decent time." Royal suggests.

So is he reading my mind now, too?

"Okay."

Don't be an idiot Pam, say something besides okay.

"That sounds good Royal. I'll meet you here in the lobby at five-thirty."

The concierge is passing out keys.

"Hogan!" He shouts and looks across the lobby.

"My room is ready." I say then yawn. "See you later."

Still looking fresh after traveling all night, Royal smiles and says in his cocky way, "Yes you will."

The hotel restaurant is gorgeous and fancy. We sit down for dinner and I order a glass of Riesling. Royal selected a German beer, Eisbock. Eisbock beer is about fourteen percent ethanol by volume. I know this because I experienced Eisbock before... several Eisbocks, actually. I became so intoxicated at the time that I had to take a cab back to the hotel, walking wasn't an option. Lesson learned... never again. No Eisbock beer for me, Royal can knock his self out. I need to stay alert for this date.

The conversation flows easy between us. I learn about Royal and his family. Royal is an assistant football coach for the Detroit Lions. He played ball in college, at UCLA, and even played professionally with the Chicago Bears for a little while. But he banged up his knee and had to quit. He says it was sheer luck that landed him the position as assistant defensive coach with the Detroit

Lions. He loves what he does and hopes to be a head coach one day. His parents are retired and living in Florida. He has two sisters and an estranged half brother.

I tell him all about Jay. How old he is, what he loves to do. I run down the list of Jay's favorite toys. Royal listens intently... then says that he looks forward to meeting the "little man." I also tell him a little bit about the drama that's occurred in my life, but I supply no details. I'm not that comfortable talking about Jason's death and my divorce from Ryan yet. It just doesn't seem appropriate for a first date anyway. Just thinking about all that awful crap makes me nervous. I begin to fidget with the collar of my white blouse, wondering if I should have dressed appropriately. I went for comfort tonight and kept my outfit simple. An old pair of Levi jeans accompanied by a white cotton blouse by INC.

Royal must have read my mind.

"You look lovely, Pam. Really lovely!"

"Thanks, Royal. So do you."

Royal does indeed look great in a silk blue shirt and dark slacks. He is certainly out dressing me at the moment, but who knew I'd be on a date my first night in Mainz? My plans had been to sleep all evening.

Dinner is delicious. I love the way Germans prepare sausages and potatoes. And the schnitzel is simply to die for. Royal ordered the sausage... me the peppercorn chicken schnitzel. We eat out of each other's plates and feed each other in a sensual way throughout the meal. It was a big meal with every local trimming you can imagine... sauerkraut, garlic home-fried potatoes, white asparagus, which happens to be in season right now. I totally understand why so many Germans are huge. We cleaned our plates, which is un-lady-like to do, according to some, especially on the first date. However, I was famished and Royal encouraged me to eat up.

"Would you like dessert?" Royal asks.

"No, oh no, thank you, I'm stuffed. I couldn't eat another bite if I tried. But please, you go ahead, have dessert if you want."

Royal looks at me intensely. "Really?" he asks sounding like a kid receiving permission to order the largest banana spilt sundae on the menu.

"Yes, really. I'll just have one last glass of wine while you have dessert." I'm smiling uncontrollably. It's been a great evening. I shamelessly continue to tease the man.

"So, what would you like, Royal? What sounds good here?"

"What would I like?"

I lean back into the chair.

"Okay, do you plan to answer all my questions with a question?"

"Is that what I'm doing?"

We both laugh out loud.

Now, pretending to be serious, I place my right elbow on the table then I look at him with my left eyebrow raised while my face rest in my right hand.

It's Royal's turn now to lean to back into his chair. He lifts the napkin from his lap, wipes his mouth then flashes his sexy pearly whites.

"Okay, sorry, no more questions." He pauses then adds, "Please don't take offense at what I'm thinking... don't be offended by what I'm about to say."

Here we go.

"I'll try not to be," I say honestly.

Staring deep into my eyes... hell, deep into my soul, Royal says, "I want you, Pamela. I want you for dessert."

I'm not surprised. I felt it coming. Shit, it's been forever since I had sex. I'm ready for this and I plan to let him know that I'm ready.

"Mr. Dutton, would you prefer that order of sex with or without chocolate sauce?"

Royal spits out his beer in surprise, yet he doesn't miss a beat.

"Without, please. I want only to taste you, this night, our first night together."

I feel my spine tingle and my heart skip a beat. This man has sex appeal oozing from every pore. And he's definitely got me all hot and bothered.

"Alright, but you do realize that I've only had four hours of sleep in the past thirty-six hours, right?"

He grabs my hand and lifts it to his cheek. He closes his eyes as he moves my hand across his lips and to the other side of his face. With eyes wide open, Royal looks at me and in a deep voice filled with passion he says softly, "I'll be gentle. I promise."

Quickly, Royal throws a stack of bills onto the table and in no time at all, we're on the elevator headed to my room.

I swipe the key in the door lock as Royal's body leans close to mine.

Once inside my room, Royal kisses me deeply and my body certainly responds to this man. I'm ready. I feel myself get wet as my private part begins to ache with anticipation. God knows I need some dick. It's been a long time coming... no pun intended. I let out a short laugh.

Royal finally releases me. I almost fall. I'm swooning.

"What's funny?" Royal asks.

I walk towards the bed. "Nothing.," I say quickly as I remove my bag and place it onto the floor.

Royal comes behind me and kisses my neck. He turns me around to face him. I'm feeling things that I've never felt before. Or maybe I just forgot how the first time feels.

With dexterous fingers, slowly Royal unbuttons my blouse. Then he unzips my jeans. He pulls them down until they reach the floor. Automatically, I step out of them. He picks them up. Instead of throwing them somewhere, anywhere, he takes his time to fold them properly in the crease. Then he places them neatly onto the back of the chair. Patience is not my virtue. I pull at his pants and begin to unbuckle his belt. His manhood is rock hard. I run my hand over the hard mound. Instantly, his penis swells even larger from the contact with the palm of my hand. Chills run up and down my spine.

"Come here, Pam."

Royal sounds like he's got something stuck in his throat. He clears it once, then again.

He sits on the bed. His clothes are still on, which really pisses me off. But his wish seems to be my command. I straddle his legs. He rubs his hands slowly up my legs to my thighs. He stops just at the brink of my buttocks. I tremble with anticipation.

We kiss. It's a long wonderful kiss... the kind of kiss that happens between two people who are comfortable with each other. It's not the kind of awkward kiss that happens between strangers about to have sex.

Expertly and effortlessly, Royal flips me over onto the bed. Now he's straddling me. Slowly he slides my panties off. Next, he takes me in his arms. With nimble fingers, he unfastens my bra then places it on the night table.

"Do you have any oil or lotion?"

"What?" I ask, somewhat nervously.

"Oil or lotion, do you have any? I know you must have lotion?"

"Yeah, I have some baby oil."

"Perfect."

Now I'm getting worried. If he thinks that I'm going to get fucked in the ass tonight, he is oh so wrong.

"Where is it, darling? I'll go get it. I don't want you to move."

"In the bathroom. It's on the vanity." I speak the words easily, even though I'm still a little worried about his next move.

Royal returns quickly, baby oil in hand. He senses my hesitation.

"I need you to relax, Pamela." he orders, and continues, "I think a body massage will do the trick."

"A massage?" I ask softly.

Of course, what was I thinking? And why was I worried?

Royal pours some baby oil into one hand then rubs the oil between both his hands vigorously.

"Lay back baby, now turn over on your tummy. Just relax. You need to relax. You've had a long day."

"Don't you want to get out of those clothes?" I ask. "You wouldn't want to get those nice pants all greasy. Come here. I'll help you."

"That's the least of my concerns. I have plenty of clothes. But since you so graciously offered to help... yes, please remove my shirt for me."

Damn. Just the shirt.

Carefully I unbutton the sleeves. He already has oil in his hands so avoiding getting it on the shirt is a challenge. Royal appears amused. I take the front buttons apart, one by one. Then using my teeth, I undo the final shirt button. I then slide the right sleeve off, never once allowing the baby oil in his hand to touch the shirt. Then I remove the left sleeve and the silk blue shirt falls away fluttering from his body. Hmmm, muscles galore. Pecs the size of my thighs and a tummy flat as an ironing board. I think I'm in love.

Like a good girl, I leave his pants alone. I lay back onto the bed. When he touches my skin, it feels like fire touching me. It takes a few minutes for me to totally relax. I'm not used to anyone pampering me anymore.

Royal is an expert at this, a master black belt with real deep skills. His hands are strong and I feel my knotted muscles relaxing beneath his powerful touch.

I speak in whispered tones. "So did you say you were once a masseur?"

He laughs a deep, sexy, throaty laugh which excites me even more than I am already.

"No, I am not a masseuse. I'm a football coach remember?"

His goatee tickles my neck as he kisses my earlobe.

"Turn over."

He stares at my body, taking every inch in. His swag reminds me of a tiger focused on its prey, hungry and ready to attack.

"Sssshh ahhhh." He releases a small hiss like grunt. "You don't look like you've had a baby. Your breasts are firm and your tummy is real tight. You're beautiful."

He uses his tongue to outline my breasts, sliding it deliberately down and into my navel. From there, his tongue caresses the soft, curly pubic hairs that surround my 'special purpose'.

On reflex, my back arches and I moan loudly. My head thrashes from side to side. This man is driving me crazy!

He takes his large muscular hands, places one on each thigh then he pushes outward, spreading my legs wider but at the same time he is pulling himself closer to me. He lifts me into his arms.

"Open your eyes, Pam."

I look at him.

"May I kiss you here?" He rubs his finger across the lips of my vagina.

"Oh yes." Now my voice is deep and full of passion.

Royal smiles, never once taking his eyes away from mine. Gently he lays me back onto the bed. He leans down, kisses my forehead, my nose, each cheek and then he kisses me deeply in the mouth.

He steps off the bed.

I don't want this man away from me for even a second.

He removes his pants. Then finally off comes the underwear. I can't take my eyes off him. His manhood is long and hard. Hallelujah! It's the most beautiful cock I've ever seen. It's like a super-sized Reese's peanut butter cup rolled long ways with chocolate at the bottom and peanut butter at the tip. *Hmmm... yummy.*

He straddles me and lifts my legs again. His tongue touches the outer lips of my own special purpose and works its way to the inner lips. He moves his tongue in a circular motion. Playfully he caresses the most sensitive part of me. I scream out loud. This pleases him. He begins to suck that sensitive area until I'm thrashing with pleasure.

"Feel good, baby?"

"Oh God, yes."

"Ready for the rest of me?"

"Yes, I'm ready."

Quickly Royal puts on a condom. I admire him for being so responsible. He could have had me without it. I wanted him just that bad.

He continues to stare deep into my eyes as he enters me and the world stands still.

This man feels so damn good. He makes love to me slowly and deliberately. His kisses never cease as he goes deep inside and hits every mark. He pulls out slowly then goes even deeper with the next stroke. His hands never stop exploring. The man is a sex-machine. We make love for hours. He climaxes three times. How can he do this? He's insatiable. Each time he comes, he says he wants more. I oblige him. I've never been loved like this before. Never. I fall asleep easily in Royal's arms, completely spent from our night of unbelievable love making.

Room service tapping at the door wakes me. Instinctively I look at my Seiko. That can't be right.

Royal comes out of the bathroom in a hotel robe, opens the door, pays then tells the waiter that he's got it from here. Royal smiles at me as he rolls the table over near the bed.

"Good morning, sunshine."

"Good morning. What time is it?" I ask.

"It's only ten-thirty. I figured with the time difference, you wouldn't sleep too late. I believe I timed breakfast perfectly."

I smile, too. "Yes, I suppose you did."

He kisses me hungrily. I can feel my juices flowing again. This man certainly knows how to excite me.

"Pamela?"

"Yes."

"I had a wonderful time last night. I know it's crazy... but I wanted you the first moment I saw you. From the time you passed my seat on the plane yesterday, or day before yesterday... whichever day it was. I've never felt this way before."

"I had a wonderful time last night, too."

"How are you feeling today? Mr. Johnson is raw. How's your cooch?"

"Sore. Very sore."

"I'm sorry baby. I'll run you a bath after breakfast. That'll help."

Run me a bath? I've never had a man run me a bath before. It keeps getting better and better. I'm famished again and breakfast smells delicious. He's spoiling me. I'm bragging not complaining.

"What would you like to do today?" Royal asks as he downs the last of his orange juice. He refills our coffee cups.

"Nothing," I reply.

"Come on. We're in a foreign country. We have to do something."

"Royal, you forget. I'm often in a foreign country. I've been here a million times."

"Maybe. But never with me."

"True. But my flight leaves at O-dark-hundred in the morning. So I really want to get to bed early tonight."

He gets up out of his chair and sits next to me on the bed. "I can make sure you get to bed early baby." He takes may hand, looks into my eyes. "Pam, I want to spend every moment I can with you. Can we do that? Spend today together? It can be here in this room or in my room or maybe I can move forward with my surprise. It doesn't matter to me. Just as long as I'm with you."

"Surprise? What surprise?"

He laughs. "So that caught your attention, huh?"

"Yes, it did."

"It's not a surprise if I tell you, baby. First things first... do you want to spend today with me?"

"Yes," I say with no hesitation.

"Well, you pick. We can stay in and rest... or you can get dressed and find out what the surprise is."

"Royal, that's not fair!" I pretend to pout.

"Fair? Let's talk about being fair. I've fallen head-over-heels with a woman I barely know. I don't want you out of my sight and I never want you out of my life. You got me wanting to give you the world just so I can see your smile. Now, how fair is that?"

I place my napkin on the table and turn to Royal. I run my hand beneath his robe and over his chest. I kiss him, forcing my tongue deep into his mouth. My hand roams down his body. He grabs my hand.

"Now, if you do that, your choices will be revoked. We'll never make it out this room."

"What if I want this and my surprise?" I ask as I softly kiss his neck. "Can't I have both?"

He groans and we fall back onto the bed. "Girl, I see it now, you are going to have me wrapped around your perfectly manicured little finger."

We're waiting in the lobby. I'm dressed in brown Jones of New York slacks and a pink Liz Claiborne turtleneck sweater. My hair's in its usual ponytail.

I turn to see Roy as he steps out of the hotel's gift shop with a beautiful brown and pink scarf which he promptly places lovingly around my neck then kisses me on the cheek. Roy's wearing Ralph Lauren blue jeans and a brown Polo turtleneck sweater. He looks good. Really good.

"It can get chilly, you will need the scarf."

"Why thank you, Mr. Dutton. Where will I be going to need this?"

A limousine pulls up in front of the Hilton.

Royal points and says, "Soon you will see. Your chariot awaits my Lady."

The limo takes us to Mainz Harbor where a boat awaits. Royal's chartered the sixty foot yacht for the afternoon. As we step onto the boat the Captain tells us the weather's perfect today for a tour of the Rhine. Royal's like a kid. He's never toured the Rhine before. I admit I'm excited, too. I've never toured the Rhine on a private boat. We eat lunch onboard, cold lobster and fresh greens. We enjoy seeing the castles along the river. There was not enough time to dock and sight-see within the small towns along the river.

As promised, Royal ensured that we were back at the hotel in plenty of time to enjoy a light dinner before going to bed.

Lying in his arms, I wonder where we go from here.

As if reading my mind Royal asks, "Pam? When will I see you

again? You live in Atlanta, I'm in Detroit. How do we make this work? I want to make this work." He turns to me and takes my face in his hands. "I've fallen in love with you. I love you, Pamela Hogan."

I'm taken aback by his words. I just had a failed marriage. And even though I allowed myself to enjoy Royal these past couple of days, I want us to really get to know each other. I think I could be falling in love as well. Yet I will not let myself say the words. Not yet.

"We'll figure it out," I say, not at all really sure that we will.

"Okay. I'm into you baby and what you say is fine for now. Just know... I don't plan to let you go."

Chapter Twenty-Eight

Once again, I'm headed to Florida to pick up Jay. Royal has called my cell phone at least a hundred times since I left him in Detroit. I've picked up half that many. He's not allowing me the opportunity to miss him. We've only been away from each other a few hours. At the airport, he gave me every contact number in the world for him... his cell, his pager, his office, his Momma's home number, his boss' cell number. I mean really, is all that necessary?

As I sit on the 737 Airbus and gaze out the window, I think about my whirlwind romance with Royal in Mainz. I must admit I am intrigued. No one, I mean no one, has ever treated me as special as Royal. He's sweet, generous, good-looking and a superb lover. He acts as if he wants to give me the world. So, what am I afraid of? I'm afraid of failing again. Ryan and I started out hot and heavy, too. And how did that end up?

Pam, you can't live your life comparing every relationship to Ryan.

Ryan left a message on my machine stating that Lola Break-stone, Carolyn's mother, was bringing Jay to the airport. He said that he had an appointment he couldn't get out of. I haven't seen Lola since that day in the Fort Lauderdale courthouse. Seeing her again won't be fun.

When I arrive at FLL International Airport, Lola's waiting at the ticketing area just as planned. I look her way then hug my son... saying absolutely nothing to her. She doesn't say a word either.

Lola turns to Jay and asks him to give his Nana a kiss goodbye. I almost snatched him away but then I decide to be nice. I'll allow her more than she had been willing to give me when I had begged to see my son. Two wrongs don't make a right. Be a better person Pam to her than she was to you.

Jay gives Lola a loud smack on her cheek and says bye-bye in his little three–year-old voice.

Lola then says in her raspy voice, "Baby, Nana wishes she had enough money, you would never have to leave me."

I stare at this woman like she's lost her mind... the entire time I'm mumbling... *"Oh no she didn't say what I think she just said."*

Before I can stop myself I ask her, "What the hell is that supposed to mean?"

She looks at me as if she's the fucking Queen of the Sheba. I just want to slap that smug look right off her face. Instead, I don't wait for a reply. I grab Jay and turn in the direction of my gate. That witch really has some fucking nerve.

As I walk through the door, the telephone is ringing. I lay Jay on the couch then rush to pick up the kitchen phone. It's Royal.

"Hi baby. Just wanted to make sure you made it from Florida safe and sound. I tried calling your cell but your voicemail picked up."

Yes, I know. I turned the damn thing off because you wouldn't stop blowing it up.

"The battery died."

This is not good. I'm lying to the man already.

"How's Jay?" He asks.

"He's fine. Thanks. He fell asleep on the way home from the airport."

How can I be mean to such a caring considerate man? What is wrong with me? Why am I being such a bitch?

"That's good. Baby, I have to run now. We have a coaches meeting in a few minutes. Call you tonight."

"Okay. Bye."

"Bye, baby. I love you."

I place the phone down and I feel guilty for being so ugly. *What is the matter with me? Really?*

The phone rings again. Now, I'm really irritated. Why does he keep calling me every second?

"Hello!"

"Damn... don't blast my eardrum, bitch."

It's Tikki.

"Sorry. I thought you were someone else. What's happening, Tik?"

"I just closed on a million dollar house today, girl. That's what's happening."

She's excited and super crunk.

"Congratulations Tikki! I'm so happy for you. What are you going to do with all that commission?"

"Shop fool! What else?"

Instantly, I forget about Royal Dutton and Lola Breakstone. Tikki always could brighten my day.

Tik and I are at Saks Fifth Avenue looking at the fabulous fine jewelry on display.

"What's going on with you, Pam? Tikki asks. "You're way too quiet. Shit... here I am treating you to a shopping spree and you acting like you at the damn dentist. You keeping secrets from me, my friend?"

I continue to stare into the jewelry case... knowing I can't hold back anything from Tik. Finally, I raise my eyes to meet hers.

"I had the fuck of a lifetime."

"Stated so matter-of-factly. Well, well... it's about damn time. That's just what you needed, girl... some dick, some good dick. You were on the wagon much too long, darling. But what's the problem? Why are you so down in the mouth? Please, please don't tell me you're missing Ryan. Say it ain't so, Pam."

We walk over to the handbags area arm in arm, heads close together, like two people with a secret. Tik is eyeing a black Prada bag. I saw it, too. I attempt to pick it up and she slaps my hand.

"Talk to me Pam," she continues as if she saw the purse first.

"No, I'm not missing Ryan. That's not it. Honestly Tik, I don't know what's wrong with me." I tell her all about Royal... the note, the dinner, the boat tour and the sex.

"Hell, you don't want him? I'll take him. I mean Tim's a God-fearing man and all that... but shit. I still don't know what his dick looks like, let alone what it feels like. To hell with this celibacy shit!"

"Maybe it ain't all about the dick."

"Maybe what ain't all about dick?"

"Intimacy. Love."

"Who the hell's talking about love?"

"Royal."

"Royal?"

"Yes, Royal."

"Who the fuck is Royal?"

"Royal!"

Oh shit, I never once mentioned his name, even when I talked about the note.

"His name is Royal, Tik. Royal Dutton, to be exact. See, doesn't this tell you something? I talked all about our time together in Mainz yet I never once mentioned his name to you. Yet, I gave blow to blow details about the size, shape and color of his dick."

"I thought that was his name."

"You thought what was his name?"

"Dick."

"Come on Tik." I laugh. I can't help it.

"Hell, that's what I'm gonna call him, Dick. When or if I ever meet the man, I'll be like 'What's up, Dick?' I like the name Dick better anyway. Who names their child after a line of dishes? Royal Dutton, come on."

Tik burst out laughing so loud that the saleslady behind the handbag counter rolls her eyes at us to show her obvious disapproval of our public display.

"Tikki stop it. So, what if his name is Royal Dutton? In any case, he seems to be a wonderful man. He's a little smothering at times... but in general, he appears to be a dream come true."

"So why ain't you jumping up and down with glee?" Tik flashes a fake smile showing every tooth in her mouth.

I roll my eyes at her and say, "Now that's the fucking million dollar question."

"Okay. So now I know the deal. You had the fuck of your life. He's fine. He's kind. He's got money and style. But you're still not into the man for some unknown reason. Right? That's the situation?"

She doesn't wait for an answer. Tik continues.

"What do you say if we let it go for now and save the discussion for lunch, which by the way is on me, your fabulously wealthy and beautiful friend? For now let's just shop and figure out who gets the Prada."

She holds the bag up in the air, dangles it as if daring me to try and take it.

"There are no losers on this shopping spree. Why you ask? I'll tell you why... because whoever does not get the bag," Tikki pretends to do a drum roll. "... can buy a pair of matching Prada shoes. And since we're the same shoe size, we can borrow the bag or the shoes whenever we want... it's a win-win situation. Agreed?"

"Agreed," I say as I snatch the bag from her hands.

Chapter Twenty-Nine

It's raining outside. I hear claps of thunder in the distance. Royal turns over slowly to face me in bed. "What are you thinking about?" he asks. I face him and say, "Us." He gathers me into his arms and squeezes tightly. "What about us, my love?" I hesitate. Not knowing exactly how to say it. "Royal, what are we doing? You know I care about you deeply. But I think we're moving too fast." He lets go of me then sits up in the bed, adjusting the pillows behind his back. "What do you mean?" "Well, it's been almost five months since we met and we talk two, three, sometimes four times a day. We've seen each other every week since we met and you say you love me. But how can you love me, all of me and you've never even met Jay. I just don't think we should be so serious and you've never met my son."

"Baby, it's not like I don't want to meet the little man. Between my crazy schedule and you flying, it just hasn't happened that's all."

That kills me. He always refers to Jay as the little man, the little guy, your son. Rarely does he call him by his name. I want to scream.

"Well, if we are going to continue with this relationship, we're going to have to make it happen. Jay is everything to me. I don't like leaving him on my days off to stay here in Detroit with you just because it's convenient for you. He's only three years old and he needs his mother. When can you come to Atlanta?"

"Soon," he states unconvincingly. "I promise. It's just that the season is just starting up and it's a really busy time. It's hard for me to get away."

"Soon. That's the same answer you've given for months. Well, I'm telling you now Royal... I can't stay over next week. I won't stay over next week. I have to get home to my son. We're going to have to re-work this arrangement."

I snatch the covers back and start to leave the bed. To my surprise, Royal yanks me by my hair and before I know it, he's pinned me to the bed.

His face is contorted with anger.

"What are you saying? You trying to dump me, Pamela? Is that it? Is that what this is all about?"

"Royal let go! You're hurting me. Get off me!"

"Is it hurting? You don't want me no more?"

Royal tosses me off the bed like a rag doll.

Where the hell did this come from? This man is a stranger. Before I can help myself I begin to cry. My butt hurts and my elbow has a carpet burn.

"Royal! What the fuck is wrong with you?" I scream, still on the floor.

But Royal's the one that's mad.

"Get the fuck out!" He screams. "I do nothing but give you all I have to give and you treat me this way? Get out. You bitches are all the same. The more a man gives the more you want. Get the hell out! Go! Fuck it, I don't need you!"

I'm stunned. Who is this man? Who is this Dr. Jekyll - Mr. Hyde motherfucker? Jumping to my feet, I race to the closet for my bag. I call a cab from my cell phone while in the closet. Dressing as fast as I can, my head reels from shock and disgust. How could I have been so wrong about this man? How could he change so suddenly? Maybe it wasn't that sudden after all. Maybe something unstable and ominous was always within Royal. Better it shows itself now than later. I knew there was something insecure about him anyway, calling all the goddamn time, getting pissed off when I can't be reached... now the true Royal Dutton reveals himself.

One thing for sure... Royal, or any man for that matter, does not have to tell me twice to get out. I want to get the hell out of here before I see more of his wretched personality.

I grab my things from the master bath... toss them in my carrying case. I run down the stairs so fast I almost fall. Quickly, I roll my suitcase out the door and I wait by the curb in the pouring rain.

Two minutes later Royal's at the front door. I keep my eyes focused down the street in search of my yellow taxi.

"Pam? Pam. Come back, baby. Come inside. I'm sorry."

I ignore him.

"Pam, I didn't mean it. Come in out the rain. If you really want to go at least wait inside."

Now, I'm really furious. I turn to look at him. I wanted to slap his face!

"If I want to go? If I want to go! You kicked me out, remember." I'm boiling. "You know what? I was married for damn near ten years and never, not once, did he treat me with such disrespect, like a one-night whore or something. I didn't deserve that from you, Royal. I was simply trying to talk to you. Do I want to go? Oh hell yeah, I want to go!"

When Never Comes Again

Royal holds his head down in shame. Then he holds his hand out, beckoning for me to come inside but his pretty ass never leaves the house.

"Come on now, baby. I don't know what got into me. Damn. I said I was sorry."

"Fuck you, Royal! I don't want to come back in. You can't play me like that. I am not the one."

I turn around looking down the street wondering where the hell the fucking cab is. I check my watch for the twelfth time.

Then I turn to face Royal again. I spit the words at him.

"I don't want to ever, I mean ever, be in your presence again. I never want to talk to you again. And you know what else? You can kiss my ass! You hear me? Kiss my black ass! I am outta here, you crazy bastard!"

On cue, my taxi arrives. I throw my bag in the back seat, get in beside it and I don't look back. The tears come now, flowing down my cheeks fast and heavy. At least now I know why his mother named him Royal... he's a fucking royal pain in the ass.

Chapter Thirty

Seven Years Later...

"Honey, I'm so scared."

"Don't be. I'll be right by your side. I promise."

"What if something goes wrong?"

"It won't."

"How do you know?"

"Because I just know. We were destined to be together, remember? You were destined to be my wife and to have my baby. We were destined to be together."

I lean back into the seat trying to relax. Jay, now ten years old, squeezes my hand. He's afraid. He's never seen a woman in labor before. I let out a loud scream as my back feels like it's breaking in two.

Jay leans toward the front seat. I see tears trickling down his chubby cheeks. "It's breaking, it's breaking, Daddy David!"

"Your mom's going to be okay, Jay. I promise. I need you to be strong and take charge. It'll be over soon. You're going to have a baby sister soon."

I try to calm myself. I don't want Jay to panic. "Jay, it's okay. Mommy's okay. I need you to be a big boy. Just keep holding your mommy's hand."

David's right. Everything will work out. Nothing bad has happened since we got together. No one's tried to kill me. No one's tried to kill Jay. I would have never thought it would be. But here we are... together. We're a family. I thank God for bringing David back into my life, into our lives. I take a deep breath and think back on how it all came to be. We were simply destined to be together.

On a hot and humid Saturday in July, my cousin Melissa married her high school sweetheart. All of Augusta attended... it was the event of the season. Mel looked incredibly gorgeous. She wore an off-white gown and carried a bouquet of lilies and peach colored roses. I was her maid-of-honor. I wore a peach colored off the shoulder gown that was made seductively differently from the bridesmaids. It was a large wedding party. I did my best not to cry during the vows, but I failed miserably. I was so happy for Melissa.

The reception was held at the Landmark Hotel, a stately and historical building in downtown Augusta. I caught the wedding bouquet. Mel had definitely been aiming for me. I was somewhat embarrassed to catch the thing. I didn't want to catch it but it would have hit me in the head had I not. I don't believe in that tale about the catcher being the next to get married. I knew that I would never get married again.

Even Roxxy Lucas, our cousin who lives in Hawaii, had flown over for the big event. During the reception, I talked Roxxy into leaving Augusta early and to spending the night with me in Atlanta.

Before the wedding, I hadn't seen Roxxy since my overnight flight in Hawaii several years earlier. Her plan was to fly out of Atlanta anyway. So spending a night with me worked out perfectly.

When Roxxy arrived at my house, I was ecstatic to have the chance to spend some time with her. We talked and talked about any and everything. I told her I was playing the field. She told me that Julie, a mutual friend in Augusta, had set her up on a blind date.

"That sounds intriguing." I say.

"Yeah, I suppose so. But I'm not that excited. Think about it, Pam." Roxxy pauses to take a sip of her white wine. "What can really become of it? We live three thousand miles apart. I didn't want any part of this blind date stuff but Julie insisted."

"Well, Roxx, you never know, now do you? He could be the one. Who is this guy anyway?"

"Well, he's from Augusta. Julie says he's cute and quite the catch. His name is David. I promised her that I'd call him. But, I didn't promise I'd meet him."

I pick up the cordless phone and hand it to her. "Well missy, time's a wasting."

I decide to give her a little privacy, so I walk into the kitchen to wash our lunch dishes. Five minutes later, Roxxy's calling out my name.

"Pam? Pam, where'd you go?" Roxxy yells.

"I'm in the kitchen."

Roxxy hands the phone to me.

"What?" I ask.

Roxxy shrugs her shoulders and covers the telephone mouth piece.

"Telephone. He wants to speak to you."

"He who?" I ask.

"My blind date" she says.

I dry my hands on the dish towel and take the phone.

What in the world?

"Hello?" I say tentatively.

"Hello there, Pamela Hogan. This is David Casey. Remember me?"

I choke on my saliva! I pick up my wine glass and take a good swig.

"Yes. Of course. Hello." I probably sound like an idiot.

"How are you?" David asks.

"I'm fine." I say. I want to say more but don't know how to begin. Two years ago I had heard about Barbosia's car accident, but didn't want to mention that now. I wanted to say how sorry I was about her death and how I admired him for all the things I heard he had done attempting to rehabilitate her and make her well again.

Barbosia had been comatose for years and I heard that David had traveled the United States coast to coast, seeking the best medical attention available. He had left his job, or so the story goes, to devote one hundred percent of his time to his wife. I recall how I admired this man for his commitment. Sadly, Barbosia didn't make it. She died four years after her accident. Upon her death, David became the most eligible bachelor in Augusta. I had also heard that he had become a playboy. But of course, I didn't mention any of that. I really didn't know what to say. I never expected to talk to him again after the first time we met, seven or so years ago.

"How are you doing?" I ask, simply being polite and not knowing what to say.

"I'm good."

I just bet you are. I fidget with the phone.

"I'd heard that you were living in Atlanta again."

"Yeah. I've been back here for a while now."

"I'm in Stone Mountain."

"Oh, really. I didn't know."

"I moved here a year and a half ago."

"Do you still work for USPS?" I ask, trying to be conversational.

"Nope, I gave that up. I'm a man of leisure these days."

"Must be nice."

Smugly, he answers. "It is."

I can't think of anything else to say. He makes me nervous for some reason.

"Well, David, it was nice talking to you. I'd better let you get back to Roxxy."

David sighs then says, "Pam, no, please don't go. I'd really rather talk to you, not your cousin. She's probably really nice. But can we speak, instead?"

I want to talk to him, too. But he's Roxxy's date not mine.

"I don't know. Why do you want to talk to me?"

"Come on Pam. You know why. I immediately liked you on sight and I've been thinking of you ever since we met in the club in Augusta. I thought you felt something, too."

Yeah, I felt something alright.

"David, I don't know."

"You scared of me?"

He's goading me now and we both know it.

"Scared? Why would I be scared?"

"Because I just might be the man of your dreams. Your knight in shining armor."

"Well, Mr. Casey, all that glitters certainly ain't gold. I learned that a long time ago. Hold on a minute." I don't give him time to respond. I place the phone down.

Quickly, I tell Roxxy the whole story about how we met in the club years before. Roxxy finds the situation amusing and tells me to go for it. I ask if she's sure she's okay with this. She laughs and reminds me that she didn't really want to go out with him anyway. She pours us both more wine then she leaves the room.

I shake my head in disbelief. *What am I doing?*

"Hello. David, I'm back. Sorry about that."

"Is everything okay?" David asks.

"Honestly, I don't know. I feel weird about this."

"Why?" David asks.

"For one, you were supposed to be taking my cousin out but instead you're on the phone with me. And for two, I knew Barbosia."

"And?" he asks. "So what? We're both single adults, right? I can't change the past."

"True." No one can. No matter how badly we want to.

"Well, what if we start off slow? No pressure. Let's just get to know one another. How about lunch? No. A picnic. A picnic in the park? Come on, what harm could that do?"

I want to. I know I do, even if it is only out of curiosity.

"Alright. I give up." I give him my address.

"Great. I got it. I know the area. I'll see you tomorrow around one."

"Good-bye, David."

When I join Roxxy in the guest room, I realize that my pulse is racing. What am I doing? I explain to Roxxy my dilemma. David Casey has a reputation as a playboy. He's also the widower of Barbosia Atkins.

"So what?" Roxxy states with conviction. "Come on Pam. You know you like the guy. I just don't see the problem. Definitely don't worry about me. I live in Hawaii. Nothing would have become of that one blind date."

The next day, Roxxy leaves, heading back to Hawaii. David

Casey shows up at my house promptly at one o'clock, in a two-seater 1991 black Mercedes Benz convertible. Not too shabby for a man that doesn't even have a job.

He steps out the car looking like a male model for Calvin Klein casual wear. Again, my heart skips a beat just looking at him.

Jay pulls up on his bicycle captivated by the cool sports car. He looks at David and then at me. Normally, I don't allow dates over when Jay's around. But for some reason, I want the two to meet.

"Come here, Jay." I yell while beckoning him toward me. "There's someone I want you to meet."

David is great with Jay. Jay relaxes quickly and before I know it the two are playing catch in the front yard. Tik arrives. She's taking Jay to her house to spend the night.

Tik smiles at the scene. "Well, doesn't this look happy and all family-like?"

"Hey Tik. Thanks for picking up Jay and baby-sitting."

I look at David and Jay.

"Yeah, the two got along instantly... much to my surprise. You know how Jay is. He doesn't like anyone that likes me. He's very protective of his mommy."

Jay runs over to us. David is walking behind him.

"Hi Auntie Tikki!" Jay jumps into her arms, almost knocking her over. He's getting so big... much too big to be trying to jump up in anybody's arms. Jay's almost ten.

"Hello there, Jay! What you got there?" Tik points at the baseball glove.

"Catcher's mitt. I got it last year for Christmas. Me and Mr. Casey were playing catch." Jay smiles widely as he looks at David.

"Mr. Casey and I were playing." I say.

David extends his hand to Tik. "Hi. I'm David Casey."

"I'm Tikki, Pam's best and dearest friend." She says this

smugly, in a way that really says, 'Don't fuck with my girl, or I'll fuck with you.'

Tik adds sweetly. "It's so nice to meet you David Casey."

"Call me David, please."

"And you can call me Tik." Tik turns to me and winks. Obviously she approves. "Okay, Jay. Let's get out a here. We have a date, remember?"

"Jay, go wash your face and hands first, then grab your overnight bag. It's in your room."

"Ok, Momma." With that he races in the house.

Tik is still checking out David... scanning him from head to toe.

"So David... what are you and Pam doing today?"

"We're headed over to Stone Mountain Park. I've packed a picnic lunch."

Tik grins at me. "That sounds romantic."

David smiles at me, too. "I certainly hope so."

Jay shakes David's hand like a big boy then gives me a big tight hug. "See you tomorrow, Mommy!"

"See you, baby. Be good. Behave and mind your Auntie Tik!"

"That is and will never be a problem, will it, Jay?" Tik says looking sternly at Jay. Jay shakes his head from side to side.

Tik and Jay wave good-bye as they pull out the driveway.

I turn to David and say, "Come on inside. I need to grab my purse and lock up."

David walks around the family and living rooms looking at photographs as I pull the shades. Then he picks up a picture of me and Jay.

"You have a really nice kid, Pam." He yells toward the bedroom.

"Thanks David. Yes, he is a sweet boy. He's the light of my life, he's my everything."

Our relationship was beautiful from the beginning. From that day forward David and I became inseparable. He was determined to win Jay over. He even called a counseling service to get advice on dealing with a ten year old boy that lives with his single mother. At first, Jay was hesitant and perhaps a bit confused about the relationship. Jay told me he didn't like me making "goo goo" eyes at David. I had explained to him that I was in love. But I had also explained that there was plenty of love to go around. I told Jay that no matter how much I loved David, he would always be the number one man in my life. It took a little convincing but finally Jay allowed David into our lives and ultimately into his heart.

David proposed to me on my thirty-second birthday, three months after we started dating. The proposal was everything I dreamed of. He took me to the Sun Dial restaurant which sits seventy three stories above the city of Atlanta. We both enjoyed a wonderful surf n' turf meal. I had lobster and filet mignon. David had stuffed shrimp with a New York sirloin. We danced to the music of Nat King Cole. We drank Dom Perignon while watching the glittering lights of the Atlanta skyline.

Afterwards, we went to David's place and there we had dessert. David prepared a decadent mixture of hot fudge, fresh strawberries and French vanilla ice cream. I had whipped cream on top of mine. We ate dessert in his bedroom where a beautiful, sexy peach lingerie set awaited me. I changed quickly into my gift and when I returned to my dessert, a three carat diamond ring was nestled in the whip cream. I couldn't have missed it because a red ribbon which held a small square of paper was tied to the ring. I looked at David with wide eyes.

"Read it." He said simply, his eyes glistening in the glow of the fire that he had just started.

"Will you marry me?" I read out loud.

David approached me. He lifted my chin with his hand... his

deep dark eyes staring straight through my soul. He kissed me ever so softly on the lips and then he got down on bended knee.

"Pamela Vonetta Barnett Hogan, will you be my wife?"

"Yes!" I answer ecstatically. "Yes. Yes. Yes."

After David's proposal, the months seem to fly by. There was so much to do. I wanted a big wedding this time since Ryan and I had eloped. I wanted all the bells and whistles this time around.

As our relationship grew we discovered so many connections between us. Ironically, before either of us was born, we discovered that our parents had been close friends. David's Dad, who is deceased, had been a very close friend of my Dad's. Of course, our mothers had also known each... but they had lost contact after David's dad died some twenty years ago. David and I even had cousins in common — not that we are related or anything. Not only was Melissa David's cousin as well as mine... but Henry and Edward were both related to each of us. David even knew my brothers. He had met Gabriel in college at Paine and he knew Karl from when he had delivered mail to Karl's workplace. And of course there was the Barbosia connection.

During our engagement, I made peace with the fact that David had been married to Barbosia Atkins.

In a dream, one night, Barbosia came to me. I was shopping, in the dream, of course, admiring a gorgeous Dior dress, when suddenly, I heard Barbosia speaking loudly. She wasn't speaking to me directly but I heard her saying... in only the way she could... "I know Pam Barnett is dating my husband."

Then, in a blink it seems, there was Barbosia. She's standing directly in front of me, wearing a long, flowing, shear, white dress. She looks straight into my eyes and clearly says, "I only want the best for David. I've always thought that you were the best, Pamela."

We then embraced each other warmly and began to walk down

the street together. While walking, I turn my head to smile at her... but Barbosia is gone. Vanished just as quickly as she appeared. That's when I wake up.

The dream made me believe that it was okay to love David and not to have any peculiar feelings just because he was Barbosia's widower. It was okay. Barbosia had blessed the union.

Exactly one year after our picnic date, I became Mrs. David Casey, to the disappointment of lots of pining and envious women.

When Never Comes Again

Chapter Thirty-One

It was two o'clock in the morning when my water broke. David and I were laying in bed... our heartbeats in synch, his hands around my belly. That's when I felt the warm liquid begin to ooze from my vagina.

In no time we're in the car and David's driving like a bat out of hell. I'm in the backseat of the car with Jay who is extremely nervous. He's just about to squeeze my hand off when I should be the one doing the squeezing.

My prayers have finally been answered. Lord knows I have dug through plenty of dirt to get this rare nugget of gold. David certainly isn't perfect. And God knows I have my baggage. But somehow I made it through the pain. And even though there is never a day that passes that I do not think of Jason, I pray that I'm a stronger person because of my trials and tribulations.

I'll never forgive Weird Al for taking Jason away. But somehow, through the grace of God... I'm here right now, alive and well... with my son, with the man I love... who truly loves me. And, I'm about to have a baby under normal... I hope... circumstance.

David pulls to a screeching halt at Georgia Baptist Hospital emergency entrance, yanking me out of my reverie.

Everything goes like clockwork. Well, almost everything.

Dr. Roman Willis appears thirty minutes after our arrival. He's such a sweet man. He speaks soothingly to Jay, holds his the hand and tells him that he can watch television in the Staff's lounge until the baby is born. Jay looks scared.

"It's alright baby. Mommy will be fine." I say trying to convince him.

David, too, assures Jay that everything will be okay. Finally, Jay nervously takes the nurse's hand and follows her to the lounge.

Dr. Willis immediately begins to administer the epidural. David's knees buckles as he sees the length of the needle.

"Mr. Casey!" Dr. Willis shouts.

"I'm fine." David responds.

"Good."

I try to smile at David when a contraction hits hard. The baby is coming fast. The epidural hasn't even taken effect yet and it's time to head for delivery.

Although a bit wobbly, David is right there by my side at four-fifteen in the morning, as our beautiful four pound, fifteen ounce daughter, Brittani Davette Casey emerges into this world.

The staff allows Jay into the delivery room to see her, minutes just after she's cleaned up and placed into my arms. Jay's eyes are wide as saucers. I reach for him and after hesitating only a moment, he comes to stand next to me. He looks at his baby sister and says, "She is so small." He lifts her little fingers with his and watches her in awe.

David kisses Jay on the cheek then takes his hand. We all stare happily at the beautiful baby girl.

"David, I love you." My voice cracks as I look at my family. "I love all of you guys so much."

At this very moment, all is right with the world again. I cannot be more blessed than I am right now. And for the first time in a long time, my heart is full of love. At this moment, there is no room for pain or sorrow.

When Never Comes Again

Chapter Thirty-Two

After giving birth to Brittani, life as a flight attendant quickly stopped working for me. It no longer fits my lifestyle. I took a year off but that year passed in what seemed a blink of an eye. David keeps insisting that I quit but I keep hoping SEA offers a buy-out. I've been there too long to just walk out the door empty handed.

Right after his marriage proposal, David decided that he'd better go back to work. He was, after all, getting a ready-made family. David took a management position with General Electric. He's been there now for just over three years.

David hates leaving Brittani at Gingerbread House Daycare Center when I fly, and I hate he has to leave her there. I have anxiety attacks every time I leave home.

I've had two back-to-back flight scares. There was the engine fire... scary but not too scary. The fire was extinguished successfully, besides we still had the one engine. We landed safely and without formal emergency. The second incident on the airplane was frightening and made me catch a train home. The thought of what might have happened still gives me the shakes. I remember it like it was yesterday.

It was SEA flight number 380, non-stop service between Detroit and Tokyo. The flight encountered severe turbulence around twenty-five thousand feet. The pilots had been instructed to fly between two massive storm systems. Unbeknownst to air traffic control... there was a third storm system directly behind the other two. When the code six hit, it was totally unexpected. I was in the upper deck bathroom. The turbulence was so brutal that it threw me against the lavatory door. Somehow I managed to get out the lavatory and back into my jump seat and fastened in. After five minutes of relentless turbulence, the captain alerted us that now the cockpit window was cracked and that the aircraft had lost an engine. The majority of the crew took the news well, but one flight attendant panicked. She was such a mess that we had to sedate her. At the time I thought... one crew member down, eleven to go. The flight purser announced to the passengers that we were turning around and going to make an emergency landing in Detroit. First we had to dump gallons of fuel into the atmosphere. This allowed us ample time to prepare the cabin for landing. We were so busy there was no time for me to panic. We prepped the passengers, secured the cabin and took our jumpseats. I practiced the commands in my head on decent. Then I prayed. I prayed that we would land safely and that no one would get hurt.

My prayers were answered. We landed without anyone being injured. The passengers deplaned and then the crew. It was only after I was off the plane that the reality of what had happened hit me. The airplane looked as if it was riddled with bullet holes. I had no idea that turbulence could do that to an aircraft. My knees went weak and I almost fainted at the sight. The plane's nose cone was missing, the cockpit window cracked. I knew it was only by the grace of God that we had landed safely. Southeast's supervisors came and herded us to a secure location. They didn't want anyone talking to the media about the episode. The plane was quickly towed to the hanger. We were given the option to continue on another flight or to go home. We didn't have to work the flight, the crew manager said. It was a no-brainer for me. I just wanted to go home.

It took me four weeks to get back on an airplane. And even then I didn't want to. I knew in my gut that it was time to hang up my wings.

I begin a crusade to find another job, the kind that keeps my feet planted firmly on the ground. I have been a flight attendant for just about my entire adult life. I didn't complete my degree at Spelman College. When I got married to Ryan at eighteen, all of a sudden I became too grown to be in school. That's something I've always regretted, not finishing school.

I've always been smart and a quick learner. I decide to approach the subject with Contessa, since she's an executive director at Coca-Cola, hoping she can provide some ideas and advice.

"I know it's a long shot Tess, but I'm willing to start out anywhere, doing anything." I say as I watch Brittani playing outside with Jay.

"Pam we just don't have anything here. If we did you know I would hook you up. We're laying off in every damn department."

"I just want out of the sky, girl."

"I know, sweetheart, I want you out the air, too." Tessa says earnestly. Then she adds, "You know, I have an associate that works for Wang... Wang Industries. He sometimes hires contract workers. I'll give him a call and see if he's in the market for any resources at this time. I'll let you know."

"Thanks, Tess. I really appreciate it."

We changed the subject to personal matters.

"So how's that fabulous husband of yours?" Tessa inquires.

"He's great. I'm so happy it scares me." I reply.

"Stop it, Pam! You piss me off with that shit. You deserve every bit of happiness you get! You've been through more than anyone I know. Just enjoy it and stop thinking something bad is going to happen because you're happy!"

"I know. I know."

"How are the kids?"

"The kids are great, too. Brittani and Jay are in the backyard. I'm watching them now. Jay's relishing his role as big brother. He's pushing Brit on the swing."

"Well, tell them that their Auntie Tessa misses them and that I plan to come see them soon."

"I will and thanks Tessa. I really do appreciate you!"

"You better. Love you, too! Talk to you soon."

"Bye."

As I place the phone in its cradle, I realize how lucky I am to have a friend like Tessa. She and the rest of my crew have stood by me in good and bad times. God knows I love them dearly. Some people go a lifetime without a single true friend. I'm truly blessed to have three of them.

A couple of weeks later, Tessa calls all excited.

"Pam. I spoke with the associate I told you about, Gary Rexall. And guess what?"

She doesn't wait for my response.

"Gary says he has an opening at WI for a database admin. I told him you were perfect for the job."

"A database what? Tess, I don't know anything about databases."

She sighs as if completely exasperated.

"But you will before you go for the interview, Pam. It's not that difficult. I'll brief you on all you need to know to get the job. Once your foot is in the door, they'll provide on-the-job training. Believe me, you can do this. I know you can."

"From your lips to God's ears," I say warily. "So when is this interview?"

"Well, first we need to get your resume together. Then, we'll meet Gary for lunch. I'll introduce you. He'll let you know when to come in for the interview."

"Okay. Wow. I'm nervous. I haven't interviewed in years."

"Come on, Pamela! You got this. You talk in front of people all the time and you're good at it! Hell, you even put on that professional voice on your home answering machine." Tessa begins to mimic me, "Hello, you've reached the Casey family... no one is here to take your call..."

"Okay, enough. So I can speak professionally, big deal! That ability has absolutely nothing to do with database administration. What kind of database anyway?"

"Hell, I don't know. But I'll find out. Does that make you feel better? I'll find out and we'll get one of those books for dummies. Okay? You – will – be - fine!" She says each word slowly as if that's the only way I can comprehend.

"Go to hell, Tess!" I say smiling. "I get the point."

"Good. Gotta run. Talk to you later."

A database administrator, huh? What the heck do I know about database administration? Zilch.

I tell David about Tessa's phone call and the potential job at

Wang Industries.

"That sounds great, honey!" David's excited.

"Yeah, if you're a database guru." I say softly.

"What? Ahhhh. Come on, baby. You and I both know that you can do anything that you put your mind to."

David has been supportive of every endeavor I've ever embarked upon. He and the kids think I'm Superwoman.

"You really think I can do it, baby?" I ask seriously.

"Of course you can." David takes me in his arms and kisses me on the nose.

Tess gave me a crash course on Windows NT, bombarding me with all kinds of books to review. She did actually buy me "Windows NT for Dummies." But I'm not mad at her. That book was a godsend.

When I meet Gary Rexall, he seems to be a very nice guy. He's a tall, slender, Caucasian with black horn rimmed glasses and a receding hairline. He looks like he's forty-something and he smells of sweet onions.

After our very first meeting, I assumed that Gary had just finished a salad or something with onions. However, after getting the job and arriving at WI anxious to get started, Gary greets me at eight in the morning with the same odor. Fortunately, I will not be working for or with Gary.

Gary introduces me to Robert Lane. Robert, or Bobby as he is called, is a really big guy. Biggest guy I've ever seen in person. He's nearly seven feet tall and probably weighs over three hundred pounds. The amusing thing about Bobby is that he's a gentle giant. He's so soft spoken that I have to strain to hear him when he speaks. (After years of flying and hearing the start of aircraft engines... let's just say my hearing's not what it used to be.)   Bobby was really putting my hearing to the test.

Somehow, I manage to get through the on-the-job training with Bobby without constantly asking him to repeat what he's saying.

Before I know it, I've fallen in love with computer stuff and I become a real geek.   I am like a sponge... soaking up new knowledge. I even go so far as to enroll in technical school, so that I can obtain the technical credits I need to become a permanent employee at WI.

I'm on the right track, I just know it.   But never-the-less, I keep my position with Southeast Air.   I am able to take a leave of absence, which suits the situation perfectly.   In case things don't work out at Wang Industries, I can always return to SEA.   *God forbid.*

When Never Comes Again

Chapter Thirty-Three

It's Thursday morning. I walk into the office looking forward to the usual busy day. It's been nine months and things are going well for me here at WI. My day proceeds with the normal seemingly endless meetings with the overzealous objectives. I talk until my mouth is dry... giving presentation after presentation. I glance at the computer clock... the meeting's almost over. Soon, I can grab some lunch.

But instead of going to the cafeteria, I head now to the lobby to request access to the supply room downstairs... in the lower level of the building. I must get a new printer cartridge and some legal pads before my next meeting begins. Once that's done, I will grab a quick bite to eat.

I approach the lanky young security guard that always smiles when he see me. 'Lurch' obviously isn't working today. That's the nickname I gave the big, tall, freaky security guard. When he looks at me I get the creeps. I'm glad Lurch is not around. I inform the young guard that I need access to the supply room.

He smiles. "Sure. No problem. Beautiful day isn't it?" he

asks making small talk.

I return a smile. "Yes, it's gorgeous weather. I can't wait to get out of here and out there to enjoy it."

Once we enter the elevator, he pushes the button for Lower Lobby then leans against the elevator wall. I glance at "LL" as it lights up on the panel then my eyes roam to read the name on the young man's badge.

My heart skips a beat as my pulse quickens.

Is this possible?

I stare at the name on the badge as my throat dries up. I try to swallow, but all my saliva has disappeared. I let out a little squeak. I move to the corner of the elevator but there's no escape. I place my hand over my heart... it's trying to jump out of my chest.

"Are you okay?" asks the young Security Guard.

I try to speak but can't.

"Miss Casey, Miss Casey? You look like you just saw a ghost."

I try again and this time the words manage to come out my mouth.

"Do you have a younger sister?" I ask shakily.

"Yes"

Oh God. It's got to be him.

"Did you ever live on Woodgreen Way?"

"Yes, when I was little."

"Is your father Al James?"

"Yes. How do you...?"

The elevator stops. I run out nearly knocking over the poor woman about to get in.

I run into the ladies room. My palms are sweaty and I can't breathe. This cannot be happening. Of all the places in the world, all the businesses in Atlanta, how did I end up working in the very place that the son of Jason's murderer is employed? And to think that I've seen this young man for months. Not once had I ever even bothered to read his name badge. Al James, Junior, it read. There it was, big as day and in black and white. All I had to do was look at his badge.

The first day I laid eyes on him, I thought there was something very familiar about this guy. Even Larry made the same comment when we had lunch together here at WI just a few weeks ago. Now it all makes sense. His walk is identical to his father's walk. He has the same slow creepy walk as Weird Al.

Get a grip, Pam. Take a deep breath. This is not ten years ago. He is not his father. They are not the same people. There is nothing to be afraid of here.

Slowly, I get up from the floor and lean on the vanity. I turn on the water then stare at myself in the mirror.

Al James Junior, Weird Al's son. I had not seen him since he was a young boy. The last time I saw him he was walking down the street carrying a gun of some sort, looking as dangerous as his dad. But he was only a teenager then... around fifteen maybe.

I splash cold water on my face then cup my hands and drink some as well. I hope to God he's not out there waiting for me. I'm not ready to deal with this. The way I reacted tells me that I'm not at all comfortable being in his presence. Not now... now that I know who he is. I wipe my face and dry my hands. God I look a mess. I crack open the bathroom door to look out. Coast clear. No one is around. Thank goodness you can leave this area without security escort. Hopefully the elevator will take me nonstop to my floor.

I push the elevator up button then hold my breath as the doors open. It's empty. I get in and push the number nineteen on the panel. I continue to press the number, not releasing it, willing the elevator not to stop at the lobby.

Thankfully, the elevator does bypass the lobby. Once at my desk, I'm still shaking. I place my head down on my keyboard contemplating my next move. No matter how hard I try, I just can't focus. I might as well stop trying.

I pick up the phone and call my manager. I tell him that I'm not feeling well and need to go home. Without hesitation, he tells me to go home and to feel better. Hurriedly, I gather my purse. As I get into the elevator, I pray that I don't run into Al Junior. I watch the numbers light up one by one as I travel nineteen floors down to the lobby. Moving fast, I make it to the opposite side of the lobby, headed for the parking lot.

Reaching for the door that leads to the parking garage, Al Junior appears out of nowhere, startling me.

"Oh shit!"

"What happened in the elevator? Your posture changed, your face fell and you looked as if you were going to throw up. What's going on?"

"Nothing. Excuse me, I got to go."

His body blocks the exit.

"It didn't seem like nothing to me. Did I do something wrong? Why the questions about my family? Did you know my Dad?"

I really didn't want to go there. But obviously he's not budging so he's really leaving me no choice. Pissed that he has me in a corner, I say impatiently, "I used to live across the street from you when you were little... when you lived on Woodgreen Way."

He looks at me as if to say 'so what?' He's expecting more. I decide to give it to him.

I blurt out, "It was my brother that your father murdered!"

The poor kid looked as if someone had just shoved a knife through his heart. He stares at me in disbelief. I know immediately that he has no clue. He's truly stunned.

Before I can stop myself, I say, "Oh my God! I'm so sorry. I just assumed you knew. Oh God... I'm so sorry. I got to go. I got to go!"

"No wait. Wait!" He yells following me into the parking lot. He grabs my arm.

I whip around to face Weird Al Junior.

"Please, don't do that! Please, don't touch me!" I'm starting to panic now... thinking like father like son. I snatch my arm from his grip.

"Sorry."

"I have to go!" I say, my voice getting louder and louder.

He lowers his head briefly then looks at me again.

"Please tell me what happened. Please! Meet me tomorrow. I just want to know what happened. I need to know. Please?"

"I... I don't know." I begin to waver.

"Please?" He begs.

"Alright... okay... I'll meet you at lunchtime tomorrow. Twelve o'clock in the lobby."

With that I walk as fast as I can to my car without breaking out into a full run. When I get into the car I begin to cry as the ghosts from the past return and the old familiar feeling of guilt consumes my entire soul.

When I arrive home, I'm still a mess but at least somehow manage to arrive safely. It is mid-afternoon and I didn't bother to pick up Brittani. She can stay until six o'clock, seven if we pay a late fee. Jay's still at school and David will be at the office until around five. Good. I need some time to myself.

Throwing the keys on the foyer table, I proceed upstairs to the bedroom. I feel dirty. Immediately, I walk into the master bath to run a tub of water. As I undress, the episode plays over and over in my mind. As I lower my body into the tub, water splashes onto the floor. I pick up the remote from the tray on top the vanity. Soft, jazzy music fills the room. I lean my head back, wishing that I had poured myself a glass of wine before getting in the tub. But it's nowhere near cocktail hour, so it's probably best that I didn't. I do have to pick Brit up from school in a couple of hours.

Al James, Junior at Wang Industries. Of all the places in Atlanta, what are the chances of me working at the exact same place as Weird Al's son? A million to one maybe? I had better odds of winning the lottery.

I close my eyes and try to concentrate on the smooth sounds of Brian Culbertson on the piano. As I start to relax the phone interrupts Brian's piano playing. I grab a towel, step out of the tub and pick up the bedroom phone.

"Hello?"

"Pam."

It's David. He sounds really worried.

"Honey, are you okay? I tried to reach you at work. I left several voice mails. The last call I decided to zero out for your admin. She picked up and told me you left the office because you didn't feel well."

"You won't believe what happened today."

"What?"

"Long story short... I just found out that the security guard at WI is the son of the man that murdered Jason."

"What?"

"You heard me. The security guard at WI is Weird Al's son. seen this guy for months but never once knew his name. Today, he was escorting me down to the supply room and I just happen to read his name badge. David, I thought I was going to faint. I freaked out and nearly lost it. This man was like fifteen years old the last time I saw him. I ended up telling him that I was the sister of the man his father killed. David, he didn't know. He didn't know."

"What do you mean he didn't know? He didn't know you?"

"No. He didn't know that his father had murdered Jason. I

mean he had no idea! I felt like shit when I realized this!"

"How could he not know?" David asks.

"Well, he was just a kid when it happened. I assume his mother never told him what happened. I don't know. I couldn't focus on work. I was a nervous wreck! So I left. I was in the tub when you called... trying to relax. But it's hard. I just can't believe this!"

"Is Brittani still at school?"

"Yes. I needed some time alone. I didn't want to upset her."

"Okay, honey. Don't worry about Brit. I'll pick her up. Does Jay have practice after school today?"

"Nope, not today. He's going to Carlos's house after school. Carlos's Momma will drive him home after dinner."

I hear the line click. David has a call.

"Baby, sorry... but I've got to take this. We'll talk when I get home. Just try to relax. I'll pick up Brit and will figure out something for dinner. Love you! Got to go."

"Love you, too, honey. Thanks. See you when you get home. Bye."

"Bye."

I return to my bath, run the hot water then add a few more of Donna Karan's fragrant bath beads. But then I decide I'd like to have that glass of wine after all... now that I don't have to drive to pick up Brittani. Thank God for David! He's such a blessing.

With Chardonnay in hand, on impulse I pick up the phone to call my crew. Today's events justify an emergency teleconference. I need to tell them what's happened together, at the same time. I don't have the energy to do it in three separate conversations.

First I call Tik. Tik in turn calls Ge. Then Ge calls Tessa. That's how it works. All it takes is one simple statement. "I need my crew."

Once everyone is on the phone, I explain to them what has happened. I spare no details. There is no shame or pride between the four of us. We've been friends for over twenty-five years. We depend on one another. Ge, who is usually the last one to comment on any situation, surprisingly speaks first.

"Wow, Pam. Unbelievable. What are the odds? The odds of this happening? You must have been completely dumbfounded. Do you want me to come over? I'm here for you."

"No, Ge. I'm okay. Yes, I'm in a state of shock. I wasn't prepared to come face-to-face with Weird Al's son or any member of Weird Al's family, for that matter."

Tik piped in. "Obviously it was meant to be. We don't know why, but it was destined to happen. Your paths crossed for a reason."

"Are you really going to meet with him tomorrow, Pam?" Tessa asks... her voice full of concern.

I swallow hard, my eyes filling with tears.

"Yes. I am. I have no idea what I'll say... but yes, I am."

"Is he safe?" Ge asks, always the most cautious one of the crew.

"I think so. I mean, I've seen this guy off and on for months and even though there was always something vaguely familiar about him... I was never afraid of him."

"But that's before you knew his identity." Tik says.

"I know. But he's not going to do anything foolish at WI. If only you guys could have seen his face when I said 'it was my brother that your father killed'. I tell you, I would give anything to take those words back."

Tessa breathes heavily into the phone and says, "Don't start that shit, Pam. It's not your fault. How could you know that he was never told of his father's wrong-doing? You're always blaming yourself when there is no blame. You've got to stop that."

I sniffle then wipe my nose.

"I know. But this whole thing has agitated me and has awakened feelings that I hoped were buried forever."

Ge says, "You need some rest, girl."

"I do. When we hang up I plan to return to my bath that I started when I first got home. Also, I'm sipping on the one-hundred dollar bottle of Chardonnay that Tess gave me for my birthday. I figure now was as good a time as any to treat myself. And Tess, thanks, the wine is very good by the way."

Tess laughs. "Glad to hear it! You deserve it. Enjoy."

"Oh yeah..." I continue. "...it's wonderful. And... I used the luxurious bath beads that Ge gave me and I'm listening to the Brian Culbertson CD I stole from Tik's car."

"Hey, I wondered where my CD disappeared to. You could have at least asked for it, bitch!" Tik says in her typical offensive way.

"When was the last time you asked for something of mine?" I say pretending to be miffed.

"Okay. Okay. Keep the damn CD. As long as you're okay, I'm okay." Tik replies.

"And, as long as y'all okay, I'm okay." My voice cracks. "What would I ever do without you three?"

Confidently, Tessa responds, "Don't know. But aren't you lucky that you'll never have to find out?"

Ge joins in, "That's right. We are here for you. We're here for each other. Always."

"Always. Because that's what we do. That's how we roll," Tik confirms.

"I love you guys."

They respond in harmony.

"We love you, too!"

"Now get back to that expensive ass wine, your warm bath and that fine ass Brian Culberson!" Tikki orders.

"I'll do just that. I'll call you guys tomorrow. Bye now." There is a flurry of byes and clicks.

I sit on the bed for a while just thinking about how my friends and I have been there for each other. We've made it through births, deaths, marriages, divorces, break-ups and make-ups. I am so blessed to have them in my life.

I hit the remote again and the calming sound of Brian fills the house once more. *"Save the Best for Last"* plays. Is life saving the best for last for me? I replenish my glass with the Kistler Durell Vineyard Chardonnay. Slowly I sink into my tub filled with warm fragrant bubbles.

I remain in the bath until my fingers are wrinkled and the water turns icy. I almost drift off to sleep, when the buzz of the security system sounds, indicating that someone is about to intrude on my moment of solitude.

Quickly, I pull myself out of the tub, wrapping my well-worn terry cloth robe around my shriveled body. From the dresser drawer I grab something to sleep in.

"Momma-mieeee!" Brit yells running up the stairs, sounding like a stampede.

"Up here," I reply, as I pull the night shirt over my head.

Just as I sprawl across the bed feeling refreshed and renewed, Brit bursts into the room and jumps into my arms. Hugs and kisses abound.

"How's my baby?" I ask.

"I'm fine," Brit answers in her high pitched voice. "Mommy, where's Jay?" She adores her big brother.

"He's at Carlos's house honey. He'll be home soon."

"Mommy, are you alright?" Her little eyes are wide with concern as she glances at the wine bottle in the ice bucket.

"Baby, mommy is fine. I'm just a little tired. Don't worry. Go have dinner with Daddy. Did he get your favorite?"

"Oh, yes. He got spaghetti and meatballs!" she screams. "Yippee!"

With that, Brittani flies back down the stairs singing 'spaghetti spaghetti spaghetti' over and over.

David is in the kitchen making all sorts of noise as he usually does when he's in there. God knows he's worth his weight in gold but the kitchen is not his forte. But, thank goodness, he tries and he is excellent at ordering take out.

I've had too much wine to drink. I feel woozy and lose track of time. As I lie in bed, I feel a kiss on my cheek, then my nose, and then my forehead.

"Yes. Don't stop," I plead, never opening my eyes.

"You need your rest remember?" David whispers in my ear.

"Yes. But I need you more. Come here." I grab his shirt, pulling him down on top of me.

David kisses me deeply.

"You taste like chardonnay. Did you drink the whole bottle?"

"You taste like spaghetti sauce. And yes, I think I did."

"It wouldn't be fair to take advantage of you in this condition, now would it?"

I place my hands beneath his shirt and caress the curly hairs on his broad chest. Teasing, I gently squeeze each nipple.

"Okay now, you about to start something."

"One can hope."

"Brittani needs dinner."

"I know, I know, but I need you."

"You will have me baby. As soon as Brit is in bed sound asleep, you will have me."

He rubs my breasts cupping them in both hands and then kisses my navel.

"Daddy, Daddy!" Britani calls from downstairs. "The spaghetti is making bubbles!"

"Be down in a minute sweetie!" David yells then he plants another long passionate kiss on me.

"See... you Casey broads are so demanding! I'll be back soon. Rest up and be ready."

Chapter Thirty-Four

The next morning I arrive at work trying to pretend as if nothing has changed. I'm there early to avoid Al, Junior. Somehow, I manage to make it through the morning without a hitch – without freaking out.

But at lunchtime, I walk down to the lobby and Al James, Junior is waiting.

"Hey," he says then bites the nail on his middle finger.

"Hey back," I say. "Let's go down to the parking garage. I could use a cigarette."

He nods and follows me to the elevators. We take a seat at a small table which sits directly beneath the ventilation system. No one else is around.

He looks me in the eye and begins.

"I thought about what you said all night last night. You see... I knew something was wrong with me. I just never knew what. Why wouldn't my mother tell me what had happened? Why would she lie?"

I take a deep draw on my Benson and Hedges cigarette then blow the smoke out slowly. I try hard to steady my shaking hands.

"Well, first of all, there's nothing wrong with you. You are not your father. And second, if I was the mother of two young children and their father had snapped, I probably would not have told them either. I wouldn't have wanted them to grow up affected by the whole thing. At that age you may not have understood it anyway."

He stands up and places his hands in his pockets. He begins to pace, obviously agitated. He looks so much like Weird Al that I want to scream. I keep reminding myself that this is not Weird Al. This is simply a young man that has been shocked and who's trying to understand his life.

He sits back down. "I've always felt as if there was more. In my gut I knew it." He stands again. He lights a cigarette.

"I remember that day so well. It started out a fun day. My mother, sister and I went to Six Flags. When we got home, we couldn't get to our house. Police was everywhere. I remember my mother telling the officers that we lived on Woodgreen Way.

I remember the cop asking for identification. Then we were escorted to our house and questioned for hours. Mother told us that my father had been accidentally shot during an incident that happened with the police. She said that Dad was in the hospital. My sister kept asking about the shattered windows and the blood in the front walkway. Mother said it was all a mistake... an accident. She never gave more details than that. We went to stay at my Grandma's house that night."

He sat down again and continued. "We went to see my father in the hospital the next day but he didn't open his eyes. My Momma held his hand and cried the entire time. The police were back at our house that evening, searching, tearing our house apart. They found rifles and papers. They took all of it. I remember seeing all the yellow tape around the house across the street... your house. I asked my mother what had happened over there. She said she didn't know."

He starts to cry now. He's holding his head in his hands. His body starts to shake uncontrollably.

Before I even realized what I was doing, I was out of my chair.

"It's okay... it's okay." I lean over to place my arms around him.

"How can you touch me?" he asks, "Knowing what my father did? Knowing who I am?"

I don't stutter. I reply softly but deliberately.

"That's just it. I may not know exactly who you are but I do know who you are not. I know that you are not Al James. You are you. You didn't have any control over what your father did. You are not to blame. Please, try to think of what your mother was going through, what she had to deal with. She had no more control over your dad than you had. She's not responsible for Al James' actions either."

"You know." He wipes his nose and sits again. He looks earnestly at me. "I was glad when my father died. He was a mean son-of-a-bitch! He beat me, he beat my sister and he beat my mother. I knew he had that rifle. Shit... I considered using it on his ass many a times! But I never mustered up the nerve. I'm glad the damn police killed him. I'm glad."

As Al James Junior breaks down again, I pull up a chair and hold the son of the man that murdered my brother. I hold him tightly, rocking from side to side. Both of us are crying now. As we hold each other and cry I wonder what in the world does all this mean? Why would God bring us together? If someone had told me that I would be in this very place doing what I am doing, I would have laughed in their face. Never in a million years would I have seen this coming. The capacity of the heart to forgive and to love continues to astound me.

When we release each other, I see the pain in his eyes. It's going to take a long time for him to come to grips with this. Just as it has taken me.

"Are you going to be okay?" I ask as I release him.

Embarrassed, he wipes his face with his shirt sleeve.

"Yeah, I'm going to be fine. At least now I know the truth. I can live with the truth. It was the feeling that something in my life was missing that drove me almost mad. I knew in my gut that there was something missing, that there was something that I didn't know. Things just never added up. You know? I always had this feeling that there was something about me or about my life that I didn't know. So now I know." He shakes his head from side to side.

"What about you? Are you okay?" Al Jr. asks. Then he says, "I suppose that's a stupid question. How could you be?"

Now it's my turn to wipe away the tears. I look straight into his troubled eyes.

"I had to be alright. No one can turn back the hands of time. Besides, I had a son to take care of. I'm not going to lie or sugar coat it. I was fucked up for a long time. Hell, I'm still fucked up. But believe me, things do get better with time and life goes on. We learn to deal with things that happen in our lives. You'll learn to deal with this, too."

"I hope you're right. But like I said, at least now I know the whole story. Now I know why I felt that there was a big mystery and why what my mom said about that day never added up. Now I know. Now I know."

Al James, Jr. keeps repeating "now I know."

Chapter Thirty-Five

When Monday morning arrives, I expect to see Al Junior in the same place I always have, sitting behind the security desk. As I enter the lobby of Wang Industries, I try to keep my composure. But Al Junior isn't there. Instead a young lady looks up at me, smiling widely. I say good morning, pick up today's newspaper and proceed quickly to the elevators. It's a relief not to see him, even though I feel ashamed to feel that way.

The past weekend had been filled with sleepless nights and anxiousness about returning to work. David said that I cried and talked in my sleep each night, screaming Jason's name more than once. I couldn't seem to get Al James Junior or Jason out of my head. I moped around all weekend, neglecting David and the children. And now that I'm back in the office, I still have the he-be-gee-bees about seeing Al Junior again.

Two weeks past and still there's no Al James, Junior in sight. Even still, my nightmares about Jason and Weird Al continue and they are more intense than ever. I'm having a recurring nightmare that takes place in a cemetery. In the nightmare I'm visiting Jason's gravesite where I begin to read his headstone. As I read the words... 'Beloved Son, Brother and Father'... the wording changes to 'Husband, Father and Murderer'. Weird Al begins to rise from the grave. His face is deformed and skeletal with a single stretched eye. He has a dripping gerri curl. The monstrous character looks painstakingly like Michael Jackson in the Thriller video. Only difference being, MJ has two eyes. Cyclops Al also has a rifle. Yes, he's rising from the grave with a rifle. Just as he looks through the sight scope with the huge single eye, his face changes to Al Junior's face. Then that's when the shot occurs. I always wake up at this point completely covered in a cold sweat.

It's long past the time for me to do something about these nightmares. I simply can't handle them anymore.

I pick up the phone to call my job.

"Thank you for calling Wang Industries, Matthew Carlyle speaking."

"Hi, Matt. It's Pamela Casey. I'm not feeling well today and won't be coming in."

"Sorry to hear you're not feeling well Pam. Get better, okay? Give me a call on Monday if you're not better then."

"Sure will, Matt. Thanks! Have a good weekend. Bye now."

"Bye Pam. Take care."

David dropped the kids off this morning. He does that several days a week, in fact... each Monday, Wednesday and Friday. I do it on Tuesdays and Thursdays.

David knew I wasn't myself last night. David's been so supportive through this whole thing. He's wanted me to see a doctor...

well a psychiatrist, for years. He's had to put up with my screaming and crying during the middle of the night for a very long time. It's time to take action.

I dial information.

"What listing please?" asks the robotic person.

"Georgia. Atlanta," I say clearly into the phone.

I hate that everything is automated now. Why can't I get a telephone number from a living, breathing person?

"Dr. Allison Dicks," I speak slowly, sounding retarded.

"Sorry, I did not get that. Let's try again. What city and listing please?" repeats the automated voice.

I could scream.

Speaking loudly and slowly this time, I say "At-lan-ta! Dr. Al-lis-son Dicks!"

"Okay, I have it," states the machine. "Please hold for the number."

I grab the pen on the night table... frantically writing the number, trying not to miss it.

Tikki recommended this doctor. She laughed when she told me that one of her crazy associates had gone to see Dr. Dicks. Tik claimed that this Dr. Dicks had really helped her associate. She said the girl was only half as crazy now.

Tikki is such a hoot... that's one of the reasons I love her.

I quickly pick up the phone again and dial the number before I lose my nerve.

"Hello. Yes. I'd like to make an appointment to see Dr. Allison Dicks." I pop a Tylenol in my mouth.

"No, new patient. Yes, Cigna. Yes, I can hold." Jeez.

I start to hang up. But the receptionist returns too quickly.

"Yes, I'm here. Today? Wow, I didn't expect to get an appointment so soon. Oh, you just had a cancellation. Lucky me. No,

nothing, never mind. Huhhh... yeah... I... suppose I can do that. Yes, I have the address. Yes, see you at eleven. Thank you."
Shit... Can I do this?

Chapter Thirty-Six

I pull into the parking lot of the Buckhead address. I'm impressed with the building's façade. The old Victorian has been meticulously refurbished. The hip roof with molded window caps and wide cornices are quite indicative of a traditional Victorian design. The house seems to beckon me. One could never guess that this is the office of a shrink. A fortune teller or palm reader maybe but definitely not a doctor. I expected a cold, steel building of some sort. Not this.

I peek inside the angled bay window from the wrap-around porch to see a middle aged woman sitting behind a desk reading. She must have felt my presence because she looks up and smiles at me. I quickly turn away, embarrassed at being caught.

I push open the door. The strong scent of jasmine greets me. There is no receptionist but the door chimes certainly alerted anyone that's around. Inside is as surprising as the outside.

This place looks nothing like an office. Fresh flowers abound. The furniture appears cozy and inviting. A soft plum colored loveseat faces a stone fireplace. A side chair is upholstered in a pale lime green fabric with faint plum squares all over.

The pictures on the wall are Monet reproductions or so I assume. There's a round cocktail table with a glass top and a base made of dark teak wood. The table is triangle shaped. On top of the table are three round balls made of the same type wood as the base. The balls are placed inside a flat woodened square tray. The sofa table, beneath the largest of the three Monets, is designed just like the cocktail table. Again, there are objects made of teak on top and there's a jar of exquisite white flowers. Oleander blooms, maybe?

A tall, average-looking woman with glasses hanging from her neck interrupts my thoughts. It's the same lady from behind the desk.

"Hello. I'm Dr. Allison Dicks. But please call me Allison. You must be Pamela?"

She looks like someone's mother, or aunt. She appears very unassuming... she has kind eyes and a sweet demeanor.

"Hi. Yes. And please, call me Pam," I say while extending my hand.

Dr. Dicks shakes my hand vigorously as if she's had too much caffeine. I start to worry again.

"Come on in Pam," she says as she motions for me to follow. "It's very nice to meet you."

I follow her into the inner office with the bay window.

"Sit wherever you like." Dr. Dicks waves her hand.

I look around. The office is very spacious. There's a beautiful ornate desk with a flat panel screen on it in the far corner of the room. There are two chairs positioned adjacent to each other and a big comfy-looking couch on the opposite side. Nope, definitely not the couch... don't psychiatric patients always lie down on a couch? I decide to sit in the plum colored Queen Anne chair that has a modern circular design in beige. Dr. Dicks sits in the beige Victorian chair with tiny plum and lime green flowers.

Boy, this lady's got eclectic taste. I suppose she's reserving the couch for later.

"So, Pam... tell me about yourself."

Okay... I guess this is the part where I talk about my childhood and how I was abused by my mother as a child.

"What would you like to know?" I ask.

"Why are you here today? Let's start there. Do you mind if I take notes?" She picks up a note pad.

"No, I don't mind." I wonder how to begin. I decide to dive right in.

"My brother was killed ten years ago by my neighbor, in front of my eyes. I thought I was going to be shot. I was eight months pregnant with my son at the time. And two weeks ago I ran into his son. The son of my brother's killer." From there I continue to pour my heart out for the next forty-five minutes.

"Pam, why do you blame yourself for your brother's death?" She looks at me sternly.

"Because it was my house, my neighbor." I can't hold it... I begin to cry.

"Why are you crying, Pam?"

"I hurt. I hurt so much."

She passes me a Kleenex and leans forward.

"Pam, you are not responsible for Jason's death. Let me ask you something. What if Jason had hit the lottery jackpot while staying at your house? He bought the ticket while living with you so would you feel like you're responsible for his good fortune? Would you take the credit for his winning the lottery?"

I blow my nose hard. Her words hit home.

"No, I wouldn't."

Dr. Dicks continues to probe for the next five minutes or so. At the close of our session, she asks a favor.

"Pam, I want you to do something for me. I want you to ask your parents and ask your siblings if they blame you for Jason's death. Will you do that for me?"

"I'm not sure I can."

"You can do it, Pam. I already know you're strong. You can ask them, I know you can. And when you return let me know their response. Okay? Don't procrastinate, just ask them. But, one last question for today Pam. What do you want most out of life? What would make you happy?"

I have to really think about these questions. Then I realize I want the same thing I've wanted since the day Jason was murdered.

"I want to stop feeling guilty about Jason's death. I want some good to come from this awful tragedy. I'd like to be able... somehow... to help other people... people that have gone through a similar tragedy. I want to make a difference in the world, even if only to help a single human being. God kept me safe that day for a reason. I want to fulfill my destiny. And I believe my destiny is to help others. Be it through writing or a non-profit organization."

I blow my nose as Dr. Allison looks at me intently.

"Anything else?" she asks.

"Oh yeah, there is one thing. I'd also like to go to Maui on a really long vacation." I smile through my tears. "That would make me very happy."

"Okay then." Dr. Dicks responds delightedly. "I say, let's make it happen! I can't help a whole lot with the Hawaiian vacation but I can refer you to my travel agency."

She walks over to her desk drawer, pulls out a pamphlet.

"Here." She says and she hands the brochure to me.

I take the pamphlet which advertises "Bohemian Travel Agency." The name and number of the travel agent is imprinted on the front.

"Thanks."

"Now, for the part I feel that I can definitely help you with. I want to see you in two weeks. We would start next week, but I'm traveling to a conference in Las Vegas. It's my opinion that the sooner we get started the better. But delaying our session a week works out because you'll have some time to complete your homework."

Dr. Dicks smiles at me as she sits behind her desk then starts to type on her key board as she stares at the PC monitor.

"Let's see here..." she begins. "We'll start off with six fifty-five minute sessions, one each week. I'll assess your progress at the end of the six weeks and we'll take it from there. How does that sound? Will that work for you?"

"Yes. Yes, I believe so."

Dr. Dicks continues. "Same time, same day of the week alright for you, too?

"Yes, I think so." She's moving fast. "If not I'll call you."

"Don't worry Pam. Everything is going to be fine. I promise you it will." Dr. Allison Dicks takes off her glasses and smiles. Then without warning, she puts her arms around me and she whispers in my ear. "It will. I know everything's going to be okay."

"Thank you, Allison." I honestly believe her. Somehow, everything will be okay.

"Thank you." I say again.

That night, I tell David about my visit with Dr. Dicks, a.k.a. Allison. As always, he's supportive and encouraging. He asks me a million questions but that's only because he loves me so much and he worries. David feels good about Allison, too. Probably because I am comfortable enough to call her by her first name. He knows how I feel about shrinks.

After our conversation, I walk down the hall to kiss the children goodnight. I look at Brittani's angelic face and as always I become overwhelmed with love. I kiss her gently on the cheek then pull the sheet over her shoulders. A smile crosses her tiny face.

"Sweet dreams baby. I love you."

Opening the door to Jay's room, his television is on "The Fresh Prince of Bel Air." Will Smith is doing a silly dance. I tip toe across the room to turn it off.

As I lean over to kiss Jay on his forehead, suddenly he opens his eyes.

"Hi there," I say. "Go back to sleep."

"Hey Mommy. You okay?"

"Yes baby, Mommy's fine." Jay could always tell if something was on my mind. We had a strong connection to each other's spirit. "You okay?"

He wipes his sleepy eyes and say, "Yep, I'm okay, I love you. I was just dreaming about Uncle Jason."

"Uncle Jason?"

"Yeah. We were shooting pool and he was teaching me some really cool cue stick moves. I miss him. Do you think it's weird that I can miss someone I've never met? Do you ever think about Uncle Jason?"

I feel the tears begin to well-up in my eyes.

"I think about your Uncle Jason every day. And no, I don't think it's weird to miss someone you've never met. You may not have met him in person, but Uncle Jason knew you. And he loved you before you were born. I think dreaming about him is God's way of allowing you to get to know him. So no, it's not weird at all to miss him."

He seems content with my explanation.

"Okay. Night Mommy."

"Nite-nite Jay..." I plant a kiss on his lips. "...my little kissing bandit."

Afterwards I climb into bed next to my wonderful husband and fall asleep with the Bohemian Travel Agency pamphlet in my hand.

For the first time in a long time, I didn't dream at all.

When Never Comes Again

Chapter Thirty-Seven

Quickly glancing at my watch, I begin to tap my foot impatiently. *Why am I always the first one out of the house?*

"David, hurry up honey!" *Where the heck is everyone?* "Jay, can you please grab your sister and come on?"

My cell phone rings.

Digging into my purse, I finally find it. I flip the phone open quickly.

"This is Pam."

"You gone yet, child?"

It's Momma. God bless her soul.

"Hi Momma, no, we're just leaving now. I'm waiting..." I raise my voice hoping David and the kids hear me, "...for David and them chill'rin to come on!"

Momma chuckles. She rarely hears me speak Ebonics. It's good to hear her laugh.

"Well, I just wanted to say again 'have a great time'... but I know you will. Just let everything go Pamela. No work, no worries, no nothing. You hear? Just be free child, okay?"

I know what she's trying to say to me.

"I will, Momma. Oh yeah, I meant to call you back last night to let you know that your FedEx did arrive like you said. Thanks for the input. The book is coming along nicely... three-hundred and fifty pages and counting. Also, Tess called me this morning. Elle Franklin, she's an attorney friend of Tess, she's looking over the funding proposal for FVCV. It looks like the non-profit foundation may just become a reality."

"Oh Pam, that's wonderful! Pam, your Daddy and I just want you to know that we love you very much. And we're very proud of you and so glad to have you for our daughter. You mean the world to us. All our kids do. Please know that."

I know saying this is hard for Momma. I feel her love pour through the telephone line. I can read between her words. Momma's reaffirming that in no way, shape, or form does she blame me for Jason's death.

Three months ago, she and daddy absolutely thought the notion was ridiculous when I found the courage to ask if they somehow felt that I was responsible for Jason's death. I told them that I was so sorry and that I'd wanted to talk about Jason for years, but never knew how to approach the subject.

"I never wanted to upset you or Daddy," I said.

"Child, have you gone and lost your mind? It's no wonder you seeing that there doctor. We ain't blamed you! How the world you think we blame you?"

My siblings responded exactly the same way — each telling me in a jokingly manner that I must be nuts to even think such a thing. They all know about my sessions with Allison. And like me, they know I should have seen a shrink a long long time ago.

Larry said that he, too, had wanted to talk about Jason, to talk about that day. I think it was therapy for him to finally talk about it.

It's hard now to believe that we never had. I learned answers to questions that I had had for years.

We were all so afraid of hurting each other... no one ever really spoke of Jason. Everyone was especially careful not to talk about Jason with me. But for me, it seemed like they were trying to pretend that Jason never existed and that only pissed me off. Thank God we can all speak our minds now.

"Momma, you mean the world to us, too. I love you very much. Tell Dad I love him and give him a big kiss for me, okay?"

"All right-tee then," Momma says as she tries to veil a sniffle. "Don't let me keep you. Be safe and have a wonderful vacation."

"Bye Momma, talk to you soon."

Finally, David and the kids are in the car and we are all set to go.

"Okay, bye Momma. It'll be too late to call when we get to Hawaii. So, I'll call you first thing tomorrow morning. That's afternoon your time. Love you. Bye now."

David backs the car out of the driveway and onto the street. I turn to look at Brit and Jay happily settled into the backseat. I smile at them. Jay has turned into a fine young man. He's an incredibly respectful young man and a very loving big brother to Brit. They both look up at me from their respective hand-held games. Their smiles melt my heart. I blow them each a kiss. Jay winks at me. Brit pretends she's caught my kiss in her hand, and then she holds it near her heart.

I turn to face the front of the car, and let out a long sigh. How did I get so blessed? How did I end up with such great kids and such a great husband?

As if reading my mind, David seductively rubs my thigh.

"We're finally on our way, honey" says David. "Sit back and relax."

"You know I never relax."

"Never say never baby, remember? We never thought we would be married, but here we are."

I lean over and kiss David affectionately on the cheek. I inhale a deep breath then blow it out very slowly. I actually feel better than I've felt in a decade. It's been a long time coming. I prayed and hoped but never thought I'd actually get here. Not like this. Not this happy again.

The vivid, devastating nightmares about Jason's death are gone. Instead, most often, I dream of beautiful memories of years gone by. The heavy burden of guilt that I carried for so long is finally lifted. I'm finally free from its shackles.

There's no more heartache when it comes to Ryan. I've actually forgiven him and more importantly, I've forgiven myself for all the mistakes we made during our marriage or after. Ryan and I made peace with each other. There was no way I could move on with my life if I didn't forgive.

Ryan's marriage to Carolyn appears to still be intact. They've been together for a long time now. They've had three kids. I haven't spoken to Carolyn in years. Not since about five years ago when she called me looking for advice when she discovered that Ryan was cheating on her. Ironically, she was eight months pregnant at the time. What did she expect from me? All I could say to her was 'if he did it to me, what makes you think he wouldn't do the same to you?' Everyone knows history repeats itself. *Poor thing... But, better her than me.*

From what I can tell, Ryan really hasn't changed all that much over the years. He still wants to be everyone's friend. But mostly he wants to be friends with those that are influential in some way. I ain't mad at him. I stopped spending my energy hating on Ryan a long time ago.

Jay continues to visit Ryan regularly. I pray each time he leaves that he returns safely. I also ask the Lord every day that he grows up to be more like me than like Ryan. Not that I'm perfect or anywhere near... I just pray that when Jay get's older, he will be kind and good... and have the ability to be faithful. The latter is what has me worried. Strong genes can be a formidable foe. I'll keep praying strong for my son.

The deep hatred I once felt for Weird Al and his family has begun to dissipate. The whole ordeal of running into Al Junior turned out to be a blessing in disguise. I never imagined something as terrible as Jason's murder could happen and I certainly never thought something so bazaar would come again. But seeing Al Junior changed my life... again. I hope wherever Al Junior is, that he's okay. It was meant for him to find out about his father. It was meant for me to meet that young man. I really hope he found it in his heart to forgive his mother for not telling him that Weird Al committed murder. I hope he found peace.

Seeing Allison has given me the courage to deal with my grief. I have hope and it appears my life has come full-circle. All is right with my world... at least for the moment anyway. I'm in a phase in my life that I thought would never come to pass. I'm genuinely happy.

One never knows how life events will shape and mold us. We never know whose path we will cross and perhaps become intertwined with. Life can be funny that way. You can be sitting next to a stranger one day — just a regular Joe Blow or even some famous celebrity — then somewhere down the line... Joe Blow or that celebrity could be the very person that saves your life or perhaps, the very person that ruins your life.

Who knows, you may even end up married to your nemesis ex-husband. Life has a very odd sense of humor.

If I've learned anything, I've learned never to take anything or anyone for granted. We are all players in this game called life. Some are meant to be cheerleaders. Their sole purpose is to support others that play the game. Like Momma. Some play really hard while others hardly play at all. I'm determined to play hard.

Oddly, I recall this simple toy that I had as a child. It was a just a small cheap toy -- round and plastic with holes in the base of it. The toy contained tiny round silver pellets. The object of this game was to get all of the little pellets into a hole. In order to accomplish this, sometimes I would move the game very slowly and other times I would shake it really fast.

As I moved the game about trying to get the tiny pellets into the tiny hole, I would knock one pellet against the other, sometimes getting several pellets in the hole while at the same time, knocking others out of the hole. It took hitting the right pellets in just the right way to get all of them to fall into place. Trying to move one pellet without involving another was virtually impossible.

Winning that game was not easy and it took many failures before I got it right. Mostly I never got it right. But the fun of the game was the challenge of playing it. The drive which I possessed to stay in the game was just as important as winning the game. I'll always remember the feeling I had once all the pellets were in place. I'd actually won and it felt so good. I didn't even know how I had done it. It was always as if the pellets just magically fell into place somehow. I really loved that game. It helped me to understand the meaning and power of perseverance. It allowed me to believe in possibilities at a very young age.

At the end of the day, I suppose that's how life is. It's like that little toy. We shake, push and bump into each other, trying to get to where we think we should be. Sometimes we end up in the right place, sometimes we don't. Then at times, what we consider the right place isn't the right place at all. And everything that you thought you'd screwed up turns out to be the very thing that had to happen in our lives in order to get us to the end-state that God truly meant for us.

Leaning back and taking a deep breath, I close my eyes and give thanks for my many blessings. I look at David with all the love I feel for him and I take another deep slow breath. I'm close to tears... overflowing with my love for him and for my life.

"Baby, you okay?" David asks.

"Fine, baby. Never been better. Just in deep thought."

"About?"

"About what you just said. Honey, I think you are absolutely correct. Never is right now – never is this very moment."

David takes my hand in his and kisses it sweetly. He then puts pressure on the gas pedal and expertly navigates the car onto the interstate.

When Never Comes Again